Down at Dan's

M.A. Smyth

First Published in 2021 by Blossom Spring

Publishing Down At Dan's Copyright © 2021

M.A. Smyth

ISBN 978-1-8383864-7-4

E: admin@blossomspringpublishing.com

W: www.blossomspringpublishing.com

Front cover art by Natalie Smyth
Style and layout by Georgia Smyth

For my wonderful wife, truly inspirational

Chapter One

In search of shadows

Despite appearances, Dan O' Donoghue's wasn't the only pub in central London nursing a Christmas hangover that night, but it was the only Irish one. And as Irish pubs went, it was far and away the best, having an authenticity the others lacked. The owner, Dan, *was* actually Irish, as were half the staff. Whiskey with an 'e' was the predominate measure, as opposed to Scotch, and they knew exactly how to pour a pint of Guinness – supposing you had the time to hang around for one. It even had a peaty, Irish smell about it. How they managed that without an open fire, he'd no idea. But for Hugo, it was a fragrant, *and frequent*, reminder of home just a few minutes' walk from the flat he'd occupied for the last two years.

They'd just entered 'Dan's' in their usual manner, as though they owned the place and weren't about to be messed with. In saying that, staff there had a lot of time for them. They were generally respectful and occasionally very useful, particularly in 'coercing' certain people to behave themselves. Quickly scattering to find a table, they'd left Hugo the arduous task of getting to the bar. He'd have done the same to them, had he been any sharper.

Watching as his friends disappeared, he smiled as he recalled the craic with Pat, good friend and founding member of the 'Lads'(a title they were actually up all night thinking of), as they debated the power and influence of the modern music icon on their way to the pub, just minutes earlier.

"What do you mean you love Beyoncé? You can't

1

love Beyoncé," insisted Hugo.

"Who says I can't?" Asked Pat.

"You just... can't. She's a brand. A business. A marketing machine. Saying you love Beyoncé's like saying you love Google or Tesco. Anyway, she wouldn't even look at the likes of you. You'd be lucky if she let you clean the toilet or empty her bin," argued Hugo.

"God now, I'd do that," Pat said, eagerly.

"You're a sick man Pat, so you are. A very sick man," he called after him.

A cheeky thumbs up from Pat was the last Hugo saw of his friend before he turned to find himself engulfed in a sea of revellers that coalesced around him, like a slow, grinding field of pack ice. He looked from point to point as if triangulating an escape route, then up at the period style clock which hung, centre-stage above the optics on a finely carved wooden pediment. (A prominent feature of the pub, Dan insisted he 'rescued' the ornate Georgian edifice, totally legit, from a skip in Dublin's Henrietta Street. God was his witness... apparently.) He had to double-check the time. To his surprise, it wasn't even eight O'clock, yet already the lounge was packed to a standstill, the entire city it seemed, out on one final binge before Monday's return to work. Pointless trying to circumvent the crowd, he decided to shoulder his way to the counter, determined to reach it before midnight, or at least make it close enough to shout his order and hope for the best. Either that, he thought, or call it a day and 'off it' back to the adjacent, near-empty sports bar.

A familiar face at the weekend, few actually saw Hugo through the week, busy as he was, copy-writing and proof-reading, even fewer since he'd happily embraced online shopping – though he did miss the girl on the till in his local branch. Emma? He'd found himself looking forward to their regular 'checkout chats'. So much so, he'd begun to enjoy his twice weekly shop for essentials (soon contemplating thrice weekly for non-essentials). He wondered if she ever wondered what happened to him. If she *had* actually reserved a tiny space in her life, just for him. Not that that would have made a difference. The truth is, he'd already decided they were on the verge of starting something, so he backed off. It wouldn't be fair to her. He couldn't fit anything else in, empty enough as his life already was.

So, other than the occasional midweek appearance at Dan's, you could be forgiven for thinking he existed only at weekends. And if you never went to Dan's, well, you could be forgiven for thinking he didn't exist at all.

That was his CV. His life's course. The path he took when everything loosened and eventually unravelled. A bit dramatic perhaps, but then, it's not every day the woman you're set to marry 'offs it' to join her ex in Spain, leaving behind only her scent and the briefest of Facebook messages. And though he didn't yet know it, ultimately, the events of that day would see him too, gather what was left of his life and leave the small farming community he called home (being too visible, predictable and easy to provoke, left him little option). He needed refuge from his own notoriety and the prying eyes that tracked his every move across town. It was as if he were trudging the streets of some exotic, foreign capital under the hot, afternoon sun, looking for respite beneath the trees that lined the avenues and in the air-conditioned doorways that flanked them. Hopping from one shaded area to another, he'd become utterly defined by his environment, all time and energy now spent in search of shadows.

But instead of flying south to the Med, he would sail east to Liverpool before driving on to London and the small two-bedroom flat in Southwark his father bought several years earlier. A legacy of his switch from farming to property, it was hoped Hugo would have some role to play in the new family venture. He was smart, good with people, had a background in journalism and marketing, *and* he was soon to settle down, drop his 'lifestyle', up his game.

It was hoped.

But that alone wouldn't kickstart his life. Hope was no vehicle on which to hitch a ride from the past.

And yet, despite everything, he remained innately positive. Even the most catastrophic of events and disastrous relationships wouldn't change that. The chaotic, unseen forces of nature that delivered such trauma and heartache *would* one day deliver something special. He knew it. Sort of. Without actually knowing?

Into the light

Hugo's first reaction when he felt the sharp, painful knock to his ankle, was to hold his ground, almost to the point of pushing back. Turning his head slightly, he flashed a subtle yet defiant warning to the person behind, that he hadn't worked his way to within sight of the bar to just surrender his position. However, when it registered who was making such a rash attempt at squeezing past, he turned back quickly, this time fully around.

'God, I'm really sorry,' he said, as he shifted clumsily to one side. 'I didn't know you just wanted past. I thought you were...'

'Actually, it's me who should apologise,' she replied, amused with his comic efforts to make room for her, but aware her response didn't quite constitute an apology either. And why on Earth should it? She thought, as if he alone bore sole responsibility for her mood, which was now beyond exasperated.

Having left her flat just before eight, Daisy's first thought was home by ten or eleven? Two, maybe three hours max, she figured, on entering O' Donoghue's crowded lounge, in tow with friends and several things predominant. For one, she'd no desire whatsoever to venture out on a bitterly cold Saturday night. And she certainly had no designs on Ben, yet another potential partner deemed 'suitably appropriate' by best friend forever and constant social companion Katie. *Who,* incidentally, proclaimed her life would be at an end if she didn't at least give it a go! So, no pressure there then.

It didn't help either, trailing behind the multitude that beat her to the bar she just arrived at. She felt she strayed onto the heaving concourse of some huge football stadium, hordes of fans pushing forward as though forcing the turnstiles.

And finally, Mr Obstinate here to deal with. A man more rigid and less responsive than the pillars and posts she weaved amongst upon arrival. Could the night actually get any worse?

'No, no need to apologise,' he said, rubbing his ankle excessively. 'You're not a paramedic are you... just in case?'

'No I'm not, but I'm sure you'll survive.'

Hugo moved closer to allow someone out from the bar. 'I do feel a bit faint though.'

'Well, you look *more* than fine to me,' she replied, irritated now, and not least with the crowd which engulfed her once again.

'And you happen to look *more* than fine yourself,' he remarked, within distance to catch the scent of her perfume and steal a felonious look at her beautiful dark brown eyes.

Daisy sighed and shook her head, the last thing needed now, a complete stranger hitting on her in a bar she didn't even want to go to.

'I meant... you don't look like you're about to pass out or anything.'

'Ah right. Well, I'll take it as a compliment anyway.'

'You're easily pleased, aren't you?'

Hugo smiled. 'It's a fault of mine. Here,' he said, making room for her, 'be my guest.'

'No. I can manage just fine, thank you.'

'Yeah? Fair enough. Just it's a mad old place, you know, Friday nights and all that.'

'Friday? This is Saturday night.'

'I know. You should see it on Fridays,' he replied, grinning as Daisy frowned before a tiny smile forced an appearance and eventually spread across her face.

'So, what's on tonight then?'

'Getting to the bar for starters.'

Hugo laughed. 'Why didn't you say? Happens to be a speciality of mine that,' he boasted. 'In you come.'

She was about to decline his invitation yet again, but this time he was more forceful.

'Come on, I insist. Ladies first… always. Well, almost always,' she heard him say as he framed a safe passage – as if shoring the entrance to a mineshaft.

'Almost?' She challenged, manoeuvring in beside him.

'Yeah, almost. Apart from... you know, sinking ships and stuff.'

'Hmm, remind me never to take a cruise with you.'

'A cruise! Hang on now. Shouldn't we at least go for a drink first?'

'Not if it leads to a cruise.'

'Really. And why's that?'

'Holidaying on water? No thanks. Much prefer dry land.'

Hugo nodded. 'Can't see myself cruising either, to be fair. Unless I died abroad, and that was the only means of repatriation.'

'That's a bit morbid is it not?' Daisy asked, looking duly mortified.

Hugo was about to explain himself but stopped and smiled when he caught her vexatious little grin. 'By the way eh, sorry about earlier... when you tried to get past?'

'Oh yes,' she replied, remembering his comic double-take. 'Not good enough the first time was it. Or did you expect to see somebody *standing* behind you?'

Although Daisy could walk with the help of crutches, she felt more comfortable and considerably more mobile in a wheelchair. Having been practically house-bound for the last month (she wasn't counting, for obvious reasons, the numerous visits to hospital for surgery and physio), this was only her second time 'out' since her accident. Only it wasn't her accident. It was someone else's. Someone consumed with haste and disregard. Someone who left her for dead just yards from her house. It was as if some great intent were made to rob her of her mobility, her entire system for movement, smashed like a lightbulb in a sock. (She insisted she felt the contents float freely about inside, each time she moved.) That being said, within two months she was out of hospital, a month thereafter, on a phased return to work.

And of the accident itself, she remembered very little (probably for the best, she was told, time and again), except the exact, dreamy point of impact, where everything drained of colour and slowed to the degree she felt suspended, mid-air above her handlebars. Strange, she would think, how such a serene memory of such a cataclysmic event could find the space to even exist, let alone persist.

'Didn't know what to expect to be honest with you. Maybe you just reminded me of someone I've never met,' he said, before pushing forward once again.

'Now you've definitely lost me,' she shouted as she followed, compelled to track his path through the crowd as though tethered by his enigmatic response.

Hugo waited for Daisy to move alongside before leaning closer. With the atmosphere now saturated with lively conversation, he didn't want to shout or repeat himself.

'She's a girl in a song someone once sang about.'

'Oh? Who is she then? What's the song?'

Smiling at her sudden flurry of questions, he was about to tell her but decided not to, sensing yet another opportunity to prolong their conversation.

'Happy to tell you alright but... it'll cost you.'

'Oh? How much... for argument's sake?'

'Hard to say, really. How about... five minutes of your time?'

'Five minutes! That's a bit pricey, is it not?'

'Do you think? Could be the best five minutes you've never spent.'

'Listen to you,' she scoffed. 'You'll be charging interest before I know it.'

Hugo laughed and shook his head, by now hugely impressed with her sharp replies.

'Well, we'll cap it at a drink then, yeah?'

About to agree, Daisy instead paused, adopting a comic, pensive look and, worryingly for Hugo, took some time before responding to his offer. Several uncomfortably long seconds worth of time, in fact. But even so, when her reply finally arrived, it still managed to be far worse than his own far worse, worst-case scenario.

'Actually... I think I'll just get my own, thank you.'

'Aw, you sure?'

'Yes.'

'Positive?' He pressed.

'Uh huh,' she uttered, lips sealed.

Stunned, Hugo turned away to conceal his disappointment, convinced he'd done more than just amuse her. And who could argue? The way she looked at him, how she laughed at his ridiculous comments, the fact she willingly tracked his haphazard route to the bar. She *was* interested. Definitely. But supposing that were all true, for some reason... *she's already with someone? Not into guys maybe? You're a total fecking loser more like...* she said no.

'That's ok,' he said, dispirited, 'I'll grab a barman for you anyway. It's a nightmare getting served here... as if you didn't know.'

Daisy reached out and lightly slapped his arm. 'Hey, I'm just teasing. It's my round... if I ever get the chance to buy one.'

Stunned again, Hugo turned back, this time unable to hide his surprise.

'You serious?'

'Yes, I'm serious! Consider it payback for assaulting you.'

Upbeat and revitalised, Hugo finally made it to the counter's edge. Leaning onto it, he caught the attention of Mike (head barman and all-round aficionado), before making room for Daisy to move alongside. Scanning the beer taps and optics, he decided, somewhat brashly, to have what she was having. Think of it as a lucky dip, he declared. But he didn't feel quite so lucky when she settled on a glass of chilled, white wine. I did ask if you were sure, was Daisy's 'told-you-so retort'. No, you're fine, it's poured now, was his lame response.

Card in hand, Daisy tapped the terminal and handed Hugo his wine before putting her purse away. He drew a deep breath as he looked at her, head to toe for the first time that evening. Beyond attractive, he thought, as she sat, hair up and loosely gathered in a black jaw-grip. Several long, golden tresses dangled freely, and her earrings shimmered like sensual decorations that shook with festive joy each time she moved. Her eyes had the colour of dark chocolate dipped in amber, and her lips, perfectly shaped, were painted a glossy, Warhol red. She wore a pair of faded denims with brown, suede ankle boots, the buckled tops just visible from under the hem of her jeans, and he smiled as he noticed a fluffy yellow pompom, aesthetically attached to the zip of her bag. Sitting under a thinly knitted cardigan, she had a look of skilful, casual elegance, his favourite in a woman, and he struggled to keep his eyes from her.

Daisy lifted her glass and looked up at Hugo just as he

turned away. She guessed he was about six foot, slim, but with strong, gently sloping shoulders. His hair: dark, wavy, almost collar length, was swept back behind his ears, and he was smart but ruggedly informal in a black jacket and jeans. She watched him smile a warm, reflective smile, as he prepared himself for a drink he always considered one up from vinegar, and his accent alone: soft, urban Irish, was to die for.

'So, what's this song you were talking about?' she asked.

'Ah the song,' he said, as he leaned forward, mindful of the noise around them. But before he could elaborate, the area about them suddenly cleared and they found themselves briefly alone. This was a phenomenon unique to bars and the occasional house party. Pockets of space would appear magically, like sinkholes on the Florida coast, isolating those within from all around. And it played right into his hands. Little need now to whisper or conceal from others what they were saying. They were like any young couple on just another night out. At least that's how Hugo saw it, forever the optimist.

'It's called *Lisa Says*, by *The Velvet Underground*. You heard of them, by any chance?'

'No I haven't,' she said. 'But I love the name,' she added, repeating it to herself. 'It sounds so inviting, yet... threatening somehow?'

Hugo was impressed. 'That nails them alright. And *Lisa Says* totally reflects that ambiguity. Think anxious, tapestry of a song, but with a sense of hope woven into it?'

'That's such a lovely description. Are you a music journalist or something?'

'No, I wish.' Hugo sipped some of his white wine and nodded in approval, thinking it wasn't too bad after all. 'Just know a good song when I hear it, that's all.'

11

'What's it about then, this... Lisa Says?'

'Why don't you give it a listen... see for yourself?'

'Now that would be quite odd. Sitting here with earphones in,' she said, looking around.

Unseen by Daisy however, Hugo had actually removed a set of earphones from his jacket pocket. When she turned back, he let them drop.

'Ah well,' he said, shrugging his shoulders, 'better put them away.'

'Oh that's really funny,' Daisy said when she saw them. 'I didn't even see you take them out,' she laughed, as she slapped his arm. 'How did you manage that?'

Hugo smiled as he rewound the long, white wires around his fingers.

'Sworn to secrecy, I'm afraid.'

Daisy waited until he finished winding the earphones before asking him once again what the song was about. Still smiling, he was all set to explain when the sudden, untimely appearance of Katie brought an abrupt end to their rapport. About as welcome as a cold draught, she acknowledged Hugo with the thinnest of smiles, gathered the drinks, then motioned at Daisy to follow her.

Visibly irritated, Daisy grumbled to Hugo, 'looks like I'll be listening to it, then.'

'Looks like it alright.'

'Perhaps we'll bump into each other later,' she said brightly, as she backed away.

'Perhaps. But make it the other ankle next time, will you?'

He watched as she left, remonstrating with her friend and wondering what might have been had Katie not burst in on them. The crowd instinctively gave way, parting in testament like the Red Sea and he smiled to himself for thinking of such an obvious analogy. Then, just before they completely engulfed her, she glanced over her shoulder at him, eyebrows raised. Thrilled with such a fleeting, intimate gesture, he grinned and waved back. But just as she vanished, he suddenly realised... he didn't get her name! He forgot to ask. How could he be so stupid? What if he never saw her again?

Chapter Two

'You were getting on well with... whoever-it-was at the bar,' Katie said, as they made their way back to the table. 'Practically wearing him at one point.'

'Watching us, were you?'

'Only from a distance. I didn't want to interrupt your cosy little conversation.'

'Really? That *wasn't* you interrupting us then. And where actually are we sitting, by the way?' She asked before Katie could respond. 'Mustn't keep Ben waiting.'

Katie smiled at her retort and nodded in the general direction of their table. She watched with admiration as Daisy led the way across the packed lounge, excusing herself with dignity and bearing with grace, the usual sighs of impatience and cliched remarks on women drivers. Suddenly, she shrieked for help as she felt Ben's heavy pint glass, greasy with condensation, slip through her fingers. Daisy reached up and caught it just in time, but tipped it, spilling the contents. She squealed as the cold liquid splashed onto her legs and Katie couldn't help but laugh at her misfortune.

'Oh for goodness sake, Katie. Look at me! People will think I've wet myself,' she snapped, as she stared at the dark patches on her thighs. Wriggling uncomfortably in her seat, she whispered angrily, 'my bum's soaking now.'

Katie quickly put the drinks down for fear of spilling more, shaking as she was with laughter at Daisy's reaction: typically terse, yet overly-dramatic, as if delivered to a packed gallery. She helped Daisy remove her cardigan to cover the stains, and when she sighed and shook her head, it was a clear sign to Katie the credits had rolled on her angry episode.

'So, what were you two talking about?' Katie asked, as she dried both hands on her trouser legs.

'Nothing really,' Daisy replied, busily covering her jeans.

'Nothing really? What, ten minutes of just... staring at each other then.'

'Well, I could think of worse things to do, actually.'

'Fine. If you don't want to tell me then, don't.'

'Oh lighten up, Katie. We were just having a laugh. I'm not about to run off with him. Might catch a movie, though.'

'A movie! Oh excuse the fingers, by the way,' she said, lifting their glasses by the rim. 'Daisy, you don't even know him.'

'True, but just imagine a couple of hours in the dark with him.'

They both laughed at the thought until Katie asked, 'you're not *really* serious, are you?'

'Thanks for that girls,' Ben said, as Katie lay his glass down heavily, spilling yet more of the golden, fizzy contents. 'Whoa, new phone,' he said, quickly grabbing it. 'What are you pair laughing at?' He asked, as he swept the cider away with the edge of his palm.

'Oh, we were just talking about how people meet, you know, what attracts them to each other.' Daisy answered, smirking at Katie. 'What do you think?'

'What do I think?' He asked, taken aback. 'Well... looks first, definitely. It's the hook,' he said smiling towards her. '*And* being fit and active. You have to take care of yourself. So yeah, looks and fitness, I reckon.'

'What about money?' Katie asked.

'Money? Steady now. I'd provide for the lucky girl in my life,' he said, grinning.

Daisy smiled insincerely at Ben as he raised his glass, as if to toast his own sentiment. Is he serious? She thought. Looks and fitness with little else. And does he really expect his 'lucky girl' to sit at home and be provided for... for the rest of her life? That's too long a time to be doing nothing. Actually, five minutes would be too long.

Katie watched Daisy, her best friend for the past fifteen years or so and knew exactly what she was thinking. She was dismantling, word for word, Ben's view of women and relationships. Daisy wasn't that kind of girl. She wasn't put on this earth to be chosen as a trophy wife and paraded at functions and special events as Ben intimated. Daisy would get there on her own or die trying. He would have to accept that, or chalk tonight down to a painful experience.

Suddenly, Daisy leaned forward in a challenging pose.

'So Ben, am I to believe you wouldn't be interested in a rich but dodgy looking divorcee whose only exercise was getting to the car and back?'

Surprised, Ben and Katie glanced quickly at each other, before Katie glared at Daisy as inconspicuously as she could. Her plans for both of them were unravelling rapidly, and to make matters worse, Daisy clearly had her mind on other things, having been caught on more than one occasion scanning the bar, looking for 'whoever-it-was'.

Ben meantime, struggled to find a suitable, coherent response, mumbling instead through a mouthful of cider, 'well, I'm not likely to meet one now, am I?'

'Oh but if you did, and she were a lovely, kind person?' Daisy persisted, her wide eyes demanding a response.

'As Ben said,' Katie intervened, 'that's not likely to happen now, is it?'

'Anyway,' he continued, 'what's it matter?'

'Character would matter, wouldn't it?' Daisy snapped, as she thumped back in her seat, furiously twisting the ends of her hair.

As she reached for her glass, Ben leaned towards Katie whispering, 'is Daisy ok? Think I've pissed her off somehow.'

'She's fine,' Katie lied. 'She's under loads of pressure at work just now, and she's away all next weekend… at her Gran's. It's her eightieth.'

'She doesn't look eighty,' he joked.

'That wouldn't go down well, Ben,' she warned. 'She can get a bit snippy, but only when she's stressed, so don't worry.'

'Yeah? Okay then.'

No, it's not okay at all, Katie thought, smiling as reassuringly as she could. Looking at Daisy, it didn't take a genius to realise she wasn't at all interested in Ben. Mind you, he didn't help his case with his medieval views on relationships either. But people can change their views, can't they? She convinced herself, hoping she could still do the same with Daisy. Now there's a challenge, she thought as she looked at her best friend sitting opposite, still twisting her hair around her fingers. Katie caught Ben's look and returned it with a smile as reassuring as her previous one. Smiling back, he raised his glass in a cheers gesture, then drank heavily before putting it down, slightly breathless as he neared the end of his pint.

'Why don't we drink up and head somewhere else?' He suggested, wiping his mouth with the back of his hand. 'It's too busy in here anyway.'

'Good idea,' Katie agreed, with more enthusiasm than usual, as she noticed 'whoever-it-was' and Daisy had made eye contact and were now waving to each other.

Preoccupied, Hugo took his drink and headed back to his table, distracted to the point he totally forgot it was his round. Returning to the bar, he found himself at the same spot as before, with the same anxious thoughts; how on Earth was he going to find her before she left? The place was heaving to the extent she could easily slip out unnoticed. Several bus parties could come and go and he'd still be none the wiser. And even if he did manage to spot her, how appropriate would it be to gate-crash her private party? He couldn't just barge over and clumsily introduce himself for no good reason, other than he thought she was amazing now, could he?

But as he lifted his drink, he noticed what looked like lipstick at the rim. It took a moment before he realised... this was her glass! They must've swapped them at the bar, he thought as he held it, thrilled that just minutes earlier, her warm mouth delicately left it's imprint on the cool, rounded surface. (Thrilled too, that here was the perfect opportunity to do a bit of 'barging' over.) Looking up, he scanned the bar with renewed optimism, casting his eyes over the sea of heads and shoulders, trawling for clues as to her whereabouts. His sweeping, random approach eventually paid off, when, to his surprise, he caught a fractured glimpse of her through the ebb and flow of the crowd, sitting at one of the smaller, round tables, lounging heavily in her seat and twisting her hair as though bored or angry. Desperate to get her attention before she vanished from view (shouting wasn't an option: Oi! Hey! Eh... excuse me?) he instinctively raised his glass. It worked! His sudden, unexpected act immediately drew her gaze, and as their eyes met, she grinned with delight and waved back with such enthusiasm, it could only have meant one thing. Armed now with 'good reason' and fuelled with nervous anticipation, he made his way across the lounge. Surprised to find no sign of her friends, he squatted down and tucked himself in beside her.

'Hello again,' he said.

'Hello again too,' she beamed.

'Sorry to be a bit of a pain but... I think we must've swapped glasses at the bar there,' he explained, looking back at where they met.

'Oh we didn't... did we?' She asked, looking down at what she thought was her glass. 'Are you sure?'

Hugo pointed to the lipstick. 'That's not my colour. I like a darker red.'

Daisy gasped. 'I can't believe I took your drink. Can I get you another one?'

'No, you're alright. Be quicker swapping them back.'

She slid his glass over, then looked for a napkin. 'At least let me wipe it clean for you.'

'No, it's grand, seriously. It's got a nice... pop art look to it,' he enthused as he held it up. 'By the way, the name's Hugh. Hugh O'Neill. Hugo to my friends.'

'Daisy,' she quickly replied. 'And here, take a seat... *Hugo*.'

'Thanks. Correct me if I'm wrong but... were you not out with a couple of pals?'

'Toilet.'

'Ah right.' Hugo stood and slid onto the chair in one smooth movement before glancing quickly towards the toilets, then in the direction of his table. He knew he'd only seconds to ask what he wanted to ask before her friends came back, or worse, if his lot appeared, looking for him. 'Right well, now that I've got my glass back, you haven't seen my wallet by any chance, have you?' He joked, patting his sides.

'Oh please, I'm not some habitual, petty thief, you know.'

'Just checking,' he grinned. 'Anyway, better get back to that lot over there,' he said, nodding towards his friends. As she turned to look, he seized his chance. 'You don't eh, fancy meeting up again sometime, do you? Maybe next weekend? Just for a drink and a bit of a laugh. If you've nothing else on that is.'

'Oh, I would love to, but I'm so sorry, I can't make next weekend. I'm away from Friday until Sunday evening.... at a party,' she added.

For a moment, Hugo thought she looked a bit disappointed, but reminded himself, with the help of a particularly painful memory, that women can be very skilled in looking one way yet feeling the other. He, on the other hand, almost crumpled with disappointment and was convinced he put it on display for all to see.

'Three days! Party animal you.'

'I wish. No, it's my gran's eightieth, and she lives in Norwich, you see.'

'Eighty, is she? Well, here's to Gran,' he said, raising his glass. 'So eh... what about the following weekend? Unless your gran's like the queen and has another birthday then. You know what they're like, these royals.'

'Ooh yes. And just like the queen, she insists on royal treatment too.'

'I'm sure she deserves it,' he said, by now expecting another rebuttal.

However, far from trying to find reasons to avoid Hugo, from the moment she left the bar, Daisy had been longing to speak to him again. But as she couldn't make the following weekend either, she decided to take the matter into her own hands, taking him completely by surprise (and sparing him the pain of further disappointment).

'I was thinking,' she eventually said, gently placing her glass on the table, 'it doesn't *have* to be a weekend now, does it?'

'Well eh... I suppose not,' he said, calmly as he could.

'How about this Wednesday then… here, let's say…

eight o clock?'

'Wednesday... here... at eight. Seriously?'

Daisy nodded enthusiastically, delighted such a simple act as agreeing to meet for a drink could be so uplifting to someone. 'Yes, seriously.'

Hugo shook his head and sat back, astonished someone like Daisy would allow actually someone like him within touching distance. Barely able to disguise the fact, he basked in the moment until he remembered Katie's cool reception at the bar. He stood quickly, thinking it best to leave before she reappeared.

Chapter Three

'Perhaps he thinks you're some... wealthy heiress or vulnerable young widow, and you're his next victim,' Jane said dramatically, as she was followed by Daisy to her daughter's room. 'Not unheard of by any means,' she added rationally.

'Mum! That's a horrible thing to say about someone. I don't happen to be a vulnerable young widow.'

'Well, I'm your mother and I can say what I like,' she said, as she walked into the bedroom, stopping to pick up a cardigan from just inside the doorway. 'Daisy, this is cashmere.'

Daisy ignored her mother's rebuke and pursued her over the threshold.

'Mum, he was really sweet and so funny. He couldn't have been nicer to me,' she insisted. 'In fact, I think you'd quite like him too.'

'Like him or not young lady, he's still someone who just... came on to you in a bar.'

'He didn't come *on* to me as you say. He was actually very respectful.'

'And what about Ben?'

'Ben? Mum, if you only knew.'

'Oh now Ben's such a lovely young man. So active, really handsome too. And he's so well connected.'

'And so convenient. Honestly, it's like you're selling me off to the highest bidder.'

Jane smiled at her daughter. 'Don't be so dramatic darling. Besides, you two know each other now. You're not complete strangers anymore.'

'Well, maybe I quite fancy a complete stranger. Maybe even more than one.'

'Daisy! What's got into you lately?'

Daisy turned to face her mother who was now

standing by the dressing table, dutifully rearranging its chaotic display and replacing the tops of the perfume bottles.

'Mum! Can you not stand still for a minute?' She demanded. 'Nothing's got *into* me. There's just... something about him, that's all. He's not like anyone I've ever met.'

'My point exactly, darling. You've no idea what he's like. What if he's...'

'It's a date mum! In a crowded bar. I'll text you every five minutes if you want.'

'That's not what I meant, Daisy. There's more than one way to get hurt, you know.'

'I'm not entirely illiterate when it comes to reading people, mum.'

Jane flicked Daisy's hair and pushed it behind her ear, like she always did when they talked intimately.

'You really do think he's worth another look, don't you?'

'That's hardly the most romantic way of putting it, but yeah, he's worth another look.'

'And Ben?'

'Ben's just... Ben, mum. I can't imagine being with him. Surely you understand that.'

Jane sighed and walked over to the bed. Sitting on its edge, she nodded meekly as though yielding to her daughter.

'Yes, of course I do. Sometimes I think I wrote the book on the subject. Maybe I should read it again... if I can find it,' she muttered. 'You know, your grandmother wasn't exactly keen on your father to begin with either. She thought he was rather bumptious and domineering. Which of course he was,' she laughed, 'though not completely,' she added quickly. 'I saw something few others did. So I paid little heed to his detractors. And isn't that just as well, young lady,' she said, smiling at her daughter.

'I just wish you could have found a way to stay together,' Daisy said, quietly.

'I don't know that we could have, darling. It certainly wasn't for want of trying.' Sighing heavily, Jane slumped, as if pulled down by the gravity of their painful separation.

'Your father was a driven man. In so many ways. Work mostly. I wanted something he couldn't give, you see and...' Jane stopped and looked at her daughter who sat, listening intently, having heard little, if anything, of her mother and father's relationship before. Dear, sweet Daisy, she thought. Just look at you, what you've endured, all through your young life. Everything just... happening to you. And when you want to take control, here am I, perpetuating more of what you don't need. Looking around her daughter's bedroom, littered with clothes, make-up, gadgets and shoes, her signature attached to each and every item, she realised it was exactly as her own, thirty years previous. And when she looked back at Daisy, she felt she'd somehow left the room minutes earlier, only to return, years later. Still expecting her daughter, she found someone else in her place. Someone beautiful and blossoming.

'Something *has* changed in you, hasn't it?' She finally said. 'You *do* look different. You're simply glowing,' she whispered. 'Perhaps that's what this young man, this... Hugo saw?' And almost as she said his name, tears rolled freely down her cheeks, falling like sad, little raindrops of realisation. Jane placed her hand over her mouth, closing her eyes tightly.

'How is it a complete stranger could see what I couldn't?'

'Mum, please... don't', Daisy said, sobbing. 'I didn't

mean to upset you.'

'Oh Daisy darling, don't be silly. This isn't about me. This is about you. You without me, standing in your way, my... blocking your every move,' she added bitterly.

Quickly composing herself, Jane wiped her face, then rubbed her hands on her skirt and stood. She knew exactly what had to be done, like she'd known all along what had to be done. But to her surprise, her only surprise was the unexpected sense of release it brought, how unburdened she suddenly felt. Smiling, she reached out to her daughter.

'Come on young lassie, as your father would say. Let's get you looking even more gorgeous... if that were at all possible.'

'Mum,' Daisy said, grabbing her mother's hand firmly. 'I love you. I really do. I love you so much and it hurts to think I can't remember when I last told you. I just wanted you to know, that's all.'

Jane smiled and knelt beside Daisy.

'I know you do, darling. And I you.' Reading between her daughter's words, she added, 'and whatever happens, that will never change. But first, there's the little matter of tonight.'

Jane stood from her hunkered position, wincing as her right knee cracked with the sudden demand placed upon it, and limped as quickly as she could out of the bedroom.

'Mum?' Daisy called, just moments after her mother left the room. 'Mu-um,' she called again, 'what's happening with the dinner?' With no answer, she shouted again, louder and with more urgency. 'Mum! The dinner.'

'Whatever do you mean, Daisy? Dinner can wait, surely,' came the distant reply.

'No. I can smell burning,' she giggled. 'There's something burning.'

It took several seconds before Jane reacted to Daisy's alert.

'The oven,' she screamed, running to the kitchen. Moments later came the distinctive sound of an oven tray, heavy with contents, dropped at speed on to the draining board, followed by a lengthy silence.

'Mum, are you ok?' Daisy called as she made her way to the kitchen.

The room had filled with a thick, blue haze, dense enough to obscure the fairy lights which trailed naturally, like an electric vine around the window.

'Oh, don't come in, darling, it'll stick to your hair,' Jane replied as she emerged from the smoke, phone in hand. 'What about a pizza?'

* * * * *

Hugo entered Dan's, just before eight o' clock, slightly breathless and red faced due to the chilled, winter wind that accompanied him along the way. The warm atmosphere instantly enveloped him and one or two familiar heads nodded, acknowledging his arrival. Hugo nodded back before unbuttoning his coat as he walked across the newly carpeted floor to the bar. Ordering a beer, he glanced up at the clock, just as Mike appeared from the cellar, labouring under the weight of two full crates of bottled lager. Seeing Hugo in the lounge mid-week and not the sports bar clearly surprised him.

'Hugo! On your ownsome tonight,' he shouted, as he shuffled to the far end of the bar.

'No actually,' Hugo shouted back, 'I'm waiting on someone.'

'That a fact, now.'

Hugo was about to respond but instead turned and leant against the counter. He took a long sip of lager and placed the glass on the bar behind him. Taking his phone out, he scanned the last few texts and messages he received that day, wishing he'd added Daisy. If he had, he could well be reading one or two of hers right now. Head bowed, he spared a second to glance at several people leaving. Satisfied he knew none of them, he returned to his phone and the prayer position of the social media enthusiast. But just as he looked down, a certain young lady, beautifully cocooned against the bitter cold, made her way through the doorway before stopping in the foyer on seeing Hugo. The steady blast of cold air on his face forced him to look up and he almost turned away before he realised who was looking back.

'Daisy!' He called, as he leapt from the bar, surprised and amused she chose the one moment he wasn't watching the exit to make her entrance.

'Hey Hugo,' she said, venturing fully in as the doors closed behind her. 'It's so nice to see you. And I'm sorry I'm a bit late. The stupid taxi took forever to come.'

'No worries there. I only just got here myself,' he said, leaning down to kiss her. 'You look... really nice,' he added, as they brushed cheeks.

'Aw, thanks. You look pretty smart yourself,' she said, tugging playfully at his jacket.

But he meant every word he didn't say, for to Hugo, she looked simply stunning, imperially wrapped as she was, in a long, blood red woollen coat and crowned ceremoniously under a sumptuous, Russian-style fur hat. He wouldn't have been surprised if she'd arrived, frosted and cherry-cheeked, in some opulent horse-drawn sleigh.

'Very Romanov, actually,' he heard himself say.

'Romanov! Weren't they all shot?'

'Well, I wasn't going to say anything but... one or two survived,' he whispered.

'Phew, that's alright then. Lucky me,' she laughed, slapping her chest.

Stopping at one of several randomly placed tables, Hugo quickly rearranged the heavily varnished wooden chairs, clearing the way for Daisy.

'Here, let me help you,' he offered as she struggled to free herself from her coat. 'God what a weight. Must be all those jewels in the lining.'

'Yes, it took me all winter,' she laughed, happily playing along with his Russian theme.

'White wine isn't it?' he confirmed, before turning to buy the drinks. Daisy watched as he walked to the bar, then looked around the large, open space which, compared to Saturday, was practically empty. She ran her fingers up through the back of her hair several times, then searched for her make-up and mirror. Satisfied with her look, she was about to check her phone when she noticed Hugo had been served and was returning to their table. She quickly put everything away and dropped her bag down beside her. Looking up as he approached, she caught an entirely different view of him, free as he was from the crowded floor of last Saturday night. Tall and slim, with his confident gait and sixty's style jacket that Dylan or Lennon would have worn equally well, she found him gorgeously handsome. *And* he smelt divine.

Hugo carefully set her wine on the table and sat down, pulling his chair in closer. More ill at ease than he was when they first met, he could only attribute it to applying for a job he really wanted. If Saturday were the application, tonight was the interview, the main event, set before a panel of three and a presentation to deliver. The chaotic spontaneity of last week, where he excelled, now replaced with formality and structure. He was grateful therefore, she plunged first into the pool of pleasantries and small talk that lay between them, breaking the smooth surface and creating ripples of endless replies and routes to conversation.

'Yo there buddy,' Daisy began in a Southern drawl as she lifted her glass and lightly touched his. 'Haven't seen yawl round these parts before. You got a job here or somethin?'

Hugo quickly swallowed a mouthful of lager before laughing at her mimicry.

'Eh no, but I have been known to make the occasional guest appearance. Though it's usually through in the sports bar.'

'The sports bar? I didn't know there was another bar in here,' Daisy said, dropping her accent and looking around for the entrance.

'There is, yeah. We can go through if you like. Grab a game of darts maybe?'

'Darts! No, thank you,' she said screwing her face. 'I can't even bear to watch it.'

'Why's that then?' He smirked. 'No, don't tell me, the tension's unbearable.'

'What's unbearable is never seeing a David Beckham or a Ryan Gosling playing darts.'

'Ryan Gosling, you say? That was him in *Drive*, wasn't it? Good film that.'

'I was thinking more of *The Notebook,* actually.'

Hugo adopted a blank expression.

'Hugo, have you even seen *The Notebook?*'

'Funnily enough no, I haven't.'

'You haven't? Hugo! You must watch it sometime. It's so romantic.'

'Is it now? Must make a 'note' of it then.'

'Oh, very funny,' she applauded sarcastically.

Hugo grinned with satisfaction. Last Saturday clearly wasn't a one-off. This was becoming a serial event. They totally got each other's sense of humour. Confident, he leaned forward.

'So, would it be fair to say you'd watch a game or two... if *they* were playing?'

'Hmm, maybe. If they were in their swimwear, definitely.'

'Swimwear? Now that's never going to happen.'

'One can always hope,' she said.

'Yeah but, we're talking darts here. They'd soon put the old weight on,' he joked, slapping his waist. 'Be like the crew from Wall-E before you knew it.'

'Oh, I loved that film,' Daisy said excitedly with a sad smile. 'I felt so sorry for the little cockroach. How clever was that? Making a cockroach a central character and not just that, one you took pity on.'

'Was it a cockroach? I thought it was a cricket.'

'No. Definitely a cockroach. Crickets don't live amongst urban decay,' she explained seriously.

'Ah, so it was a cockroach. Makes sense that. Yeah, a bold move alright. But it definitely worked, *and,*' he added, 'you didn't know if it was a boy or a girl. Very unusual that, for such a prominent role. Did it have a name, I wonder?'

'Actually, I don't know,' she said. 'I don't think so. It didn't have a speaking part, so maybe that's why. It couldn't say its own name, you see.'

'It made a squeak though.'

'Squeaking doesn't count as conversation.'

'What, even a squeaking part?'

Daisy laughed and slapped the table. 'Oh that's so funny. However, my word is final,' she said firmly. 'Squeaks absolutely don't count as conversation.'

'Well that's me told,' he said, folding his arms.

Grinning to the point of laughing at their ridiculous exchange, Daisy took her drink and settled comfortably in her seat, while Hugo, keen to continue the darts duologue, watched and waited until she lay her glass down.

'Must have a game of darts then sometime. Me and you... in our swimwear. Imagine that,' he laughed.

'I'd rather not.'

'Yeah, maybe not,' he quickly agreed. 'You'd probably hammer me, anyway.'

'I doubt that,' she said. 'I was never what you'd call, competitive at sports? I found most games really silly. Especially football. Grown men acting as they do. Except if they're hot or Italian. Now that's acceptable,' she said, totally unashamed with her stereotyping.

Hugo nodded. 'See what you mean there. Pink skinned, ginger Irish, versus dark, brooding Italian. Not that I like Italian men or anything, it's...'

'There's nothing wrong with appreciating beauty Hugo, be it male or female.'

'No. It's just not something me and the lads discuss on a regular basis, you know?'

'And certainly not in a sports bar, I wouldn't imagine.'

'God, now that would be the last place.'

Daisy smiled, then reached over and flicked the hair away from his forehead.

'I don't see much evidence of a pink skinned, ginger Irishman there,' she said, smiling. 'Nor do you look like your average darts player.'

'That would explain why I can't play like one,' he laughed, thrilled with her tiny gesture of intimacy, and how he appeared to fit perfectly her preferred choice of men.

She'd barely withdrawn her hand when the doors to the lounge suddenly burst open.

Watching as the group approached, he remembered the

last time he got 'involved' with a similar bunch of lads in not *too* dissimilar a circumstance. One of them, hanging on his pool cue like a worn, empty jacket, recognised the girl Hugo was with and proceeded to mouth off that she'd been around the block and back... several times. Turns out she dumped his older brother for driving around the same block himself... several times... and with her in the passenger seat. A matter of detail not relayed to his audience who, like a Sunday morning congregation, sat on their hands, heads bowed and selectively mute. Despite her protestations, Hugo, inflamed with drunken, retaliatory rage got 'involved,' just like the bad old days by Finnegan's barn, across the bridge and up the lane from O 'Grady's.

"Just like frigging Saigon, hey Slick?" he shouts under the spin of the rotors.

"I was in Junior High, dickhead."

He remembers the round wooden table collapsing beneath the weight of whatshisname, the mahogany top snapping off and twisting through the air like a giant coin tossed in anger. Good start, and a clever move... pretending to walk away like that. Then... well, the not so clever dancing and baiting atop the pool table, cue in hand, scything and prodding defensively at anyone who came close, including two of North Dublin's finest. With skulls of granite and fists to match, they quickly conducted business. The transaction didn't last long.

Two minutes later: cuffed and celled.

Two weeks later: tried and convicted.

The charge: longer than a long, thirsty night under his cuts and bruises in a cold, concrete cell.

Balance to pay: three months.

First date as well, he thought, looking back at Daisy.

'So, what have you been up to since last Saturday then?

Anything exciting?' She asked.

'Exciting? Let me see now,' he answered, tapping his chin with his fingers. 'Does getting ready for tonight count?' He joked. 'Thought I'd better have a shower, you know. Change the old shirt as well,' he added, patting his chest.

'Aw, you shouldn't have gone to all that trouble,' she said, as she ran her hand down his arm. 'Nice shirt, though. Very silky too.'

'Thank you. It's Italian... I think. Says Milano on it somewhere.'

'Not Manilla?'

'No, definitely Milano,' he laughed. 'And what about yourself?'

'Well, I thought I'd shower too,' she said, grinning. 'Actually, we had the most amazing day today... Mum and I,' she explained. 'She had to order pizza in. It was so funny. She burnt the dinner to a cinder, smoke billowing through the flat. She came out of the kitchen through the blue haze, like she was on stage or something. Fancy a pizza was all she could say. It was such amazing timing.'

'Your mum sounds great.'

'She is. We're actually the best of friends,' she said warmly. 'And what about you. Do you have family here?'

'No. They're all in Ireland. I've my own place here... in Southwark.'

'Do you? So do we... mum and I!'

'No way,' he said, straightening in surprise. 'You been here long?'

'Oh, it must be ten years or more. And you?'

'A couple of years now.'

'So, if you're from Ireland...' Daisy started.

'How did I end up in Southwark?' He finished. 'Well, dad moved from farming to property a while back, snapped up a few places... including the one I'm in now. I moved over, looking for... I dunno, something different I suppose. I'd a few friends here as well, so it couldn't have worked out better, you know? People I knew, somewhere to stay. I rented the flat off dad to start with, but it's mine now.'

'What, your father gave it to you?'

Hugo indulged a slight smile of irony at Daisy's innocent remark before looking down at his drink. Content as he was, he'd have happily traded the flat and everything else, memories and all, for the chance to reset his so-called new life. To get back to his old life. The life before everything unravelled and broke apart.

'Well, he didn't exactly give it, more... left it to me... in his will.'

Daisy's jaw dropped, her mouth opening wide with horror before she quickly brought her hand up to cover it.

'Hugo, I'm so sorry, I didn't know. How stupid of me.'

'Hey, you're anything but stupid. And how on earth could you have known that? Honest, it's totally ok. Really, it is,' he insisted. 'Ten years though,' he said, switching subjects. 'Can't believe my eyes haven't fallen upon you before now.'

'Maybe they did, but you just didn't notice me.'

'No. I'd have noticed you alright.'

Daisy held her neck and smiled shyly. 'So, do any of your friends live with you or...?'

'That lot? God, no. I'd rather be lonely.'

'Oh they can't be that bad, surely?'

'You've not met them. Anyway, I've got a lodger... an occasional one. She stays when she feels like it, basically.'

'Oh,' Daisy said, taken aback. 'And is she, I mean, how does that actually work then?'

Hugo grinned and leaned forward. 'I could keep this going all night, but it wouldn't be fair to you. No, *'she'* happens to be a cat.' he explained. 'Belongs to one of my neighbours, Eileen. I pop in to see her now and then, pick up some stuff at the shop, or the mail for her. Ninety-two last month she was. I got her a card and took it around. She couldn't believe I remembered. Mind you, I did the same last year, and she forgot I remembered then as well.'

'Oh Hugo, that's so sweet. How lovely of you.'

'Nah, just being neighbourly really. She's been in and out of hospital for a while now and... I suppose I've kind of adopted her cat, you know. Or maybe it's the other way around? Haven't quite figured that one out yet. Anyway, no-one seems to know when she'll get home this time, so...'

'Aw, that's so sad. Does she have any family?'

'Yeah, she does. They don't live around here, though. Her daughter's in Oz, son's in Denmark. Big Lego fan, he is,' he added, grinning.

'Well, she has her adopted son for company now, hasn't she?'

'One way of putting it, I suppose,' he said as he put his drink down. She watched him search for his phone in a mild panic before finding it in the breast pocket of his jacket.

'That's Eileen there... and Whiskey,' he said, scrolling through a few pictures.

'Aw, they're so cute,' she said, reaching over to zoom in. 'Whiskey, did you say? That's a funny name.'

'It is, yeah. Gin would've been better... as in Ginny.'

'Ginny, yes,' she said. 'No, Chardonnay.'

'Chardonnay? Ha. Now that's appropriate... if you had a cat that is.'

'What are you suggesting Hugo, that my life revolves

around Chardonnay?'

'No, God forbid. It just plays a significant part in it, that's all.'

'Actually, it's more a cameo,' she corrected. 'You know, small but utterly memorable. Like Brad Pitt's appearance in that Friends episode?'

'Never watched Friends,' he admitted.

'Me neither,' said Daisy, 'but I remember that one…for obvious reasons.'

'Surprised you do, with all that Chardonnay.'

'Hey! I was only a teenager when I saw it. Anyway, we all drank Vodka back then. Chardonnay was just some girl from Essex nobody knew but everybody heard of.'

Hugo laughed. 'Yeah, we all heard of her as well,' he exaggerated. 'So, same again?' He asked, standing.

'Oh no, please, it's my round,' she said, reaching down for her bag.

'Is it now? Didn't think we were keeping tabs.'

'Well I'm getting the next one, definitely,' she said. 'But could I have a Chardonnay this time... instead of house white, if you don't mind?'

'No problem there. Sure I might even join you!'

Chapter Four

Hugo put his glasses down and looked around as he waited for Mike to reappear from the front bar. By now, several people were filling their coats and checking their pockets as they prepared to leave, and apart from the music, the main source of noise in the bar was from the group who appeared earlier. He watched them narrowly as he stood at the bar, arms folded on the counter, every now and then rubbing his chin and glancing in the opposite direction. A gang of four, they were. Well-oiled and reckless.

'Still here, Hugo?' Mike barked.

'Jesus Mike,' he said jumping, 'yeah... unless you're seeing things.'

'What you for?' He asked, checking his watch.

'Eh, two large Chardonnay if you please, thank you very much.'

'Certainly, Hugo. And what'll you be having?'

Hugo shook his head and smiled as Mike topped both glasses up to finish the bottle, then winced with the noise as he threw it to the recycling bin.

'Don't say I'm not good to you,' he said, sliding the drinks over. 'Nine pounds exactly, Hugo.'

'You see Mike, I told them, but they wouldn't listen. You're an absolute gentleman, so you are,' he declared, leaving behind a ten pound note before carefully lifting both fully-laden glasses. As he passed the group of lads, now casually 'assaulting' each other, as if engaged in some ritualistic, alpha male contest, one of them (the red-faced, head shaped like a turnip one), stumbled into his path, shouldering him painfully in the chest and knocking him backwards. In almost any other situation, it would've been a truly comedic moment as Hugo, flapping and flailing uncontrollably, showered both of them with nearly half a bottle of cold, white wine. Stunned for a second, he skilfully regained his balance, then glanced quickly from side to side, as if looking for an audience and a pool cue (just like the bad old days by Finnegan's barn). But not before the younger man had turned rapidly to square up to him.

'What the...' he gasped, hands out, blinking in disbelief. 'Look what you've gone and done, you bleedin knob-end.'

'Me, a bleedin knob-end?' Hugo hit back, now standing head to head with the slightly smaller man. 'You,' he threatened, 'owe me two glasses of wine...prick.'

'Hugo!' Mike called, 'leave it. They're just going, aren't you?' He suggested calmly to the group.

But in turning to acknowledge Mike, Hugo passed advantage to his attacker who launched himself with furious speed, head-butting him squarely on the left temple. Hugo lost consciousness as he stood, hitting the floor knee first before falling forward and slamming the other side of his head with bone-cracking force against the heavy brass footrest. Mike flung himself over the counter, paying little heed to Hugo's attackers, who by now had dropped their glasses and rushed the doors, fighting each other to escape. Within seconds, he was at Hugo's side, gently shaking him and calling his name. Shouting for someone to phone an ambulance, he called for help to roll him into the lifesaving position. He had to be careful. Chances were Hugo suffered a spinal injury, and if so, moving him could make things much worse than they already were. He needed someone to hold his head as he turned him. Eleanor, the woman who phoned for help, volunteered, kneeling beside them. On Mike's instruction, she kept Hugo's head aligned with his body as they rolled him on to his side, and only when satisfied he was breathing freely, did Mike relax. He sat for a moment, crouched beside Hugo, one hand on his shoulder. Then, remembering why Hugo was in the lounge that night and not the sports bar, he stood quickly.

'Keep an eye on him,' he said, as he walked towards Hugo's table.

Daisy wasn't quite sure what it was she sensed that caught her attention. Something weighty and with significance just occurred. She felt it. Like when her father used to drop those heavy bags of compost from the boot of his car, the house shaking imperceptibly as she watched from her bedroom window. Perhaps they took delivery of something? Not unusual in a pub, she thought, until she saw several people rush to the front of the bar. Curious, she decided to follow them. Rounding the edge of the counter and moving further along, she saw half a dozen customers and staff circled around what looked like a bundle of clothes on the floor, close to the bar. Someone then stood, having been crouched over whatever it was, and walked towards her.

'Mike... is it?' She remembered.

'It is,' Mike replied, as he reached her. Placing his hand on the bar, he drummed his fingers nervously on the smooth surface. 'Daisy, isn't it?'

'Yes.'

'I'm sorry Daisy,' he began seriously, 'but there's no easy way to say this.' Rubbing his chin and looking back at the crowd of onlookers, he was about to explain what he meant, when it suddenly dawned on Daisy why he came over.

'That's not... Hugo, is it?' she asked, as she pushed past Mike, still expecting Hugo to emerge from behind the group, carrying the drinks and a look of bemusement. But as she reached the crumpled figure on the floor, indistinct and motionless, she recognised it instantly.

'Oh my God, it is Hugo,' she cried out, astonished. 'Hugo! Oh my God, what's happened to him?' She shrieked, as she started to lift herself out of her chair in an effort to get closer. Mike quickly moved alongside and gently held her back.

'Let go of me. I have to... let me help him, would you!'

'Careful now, Daisy,' he said, as she tried to wriggle free. 'He's breathing fine and the paramedics are on their way.'

'Paramedics? What do you mean Paramedics? Why does he need a paramedic? Oh no,' she suddenly realised, 'he hasn't been stabbed, has he? Tell me he hasn't been stabbed.'

Mike took a deep breath before answering. 'No. He's not been stabbed. He ran into a bunch of idiots I should've dealt with earlier and...' Mike hung his head, almost in shame. He couldn't believe how quickly things escalated and that as a barman with twenty years' experience, how ineffective he proved to be. 'It was all over in a flash. Before I knew it, Hugo was down.'

'What? They just... attacked him, like a pack of dogs... in a busy bar? How could something like this happen? How?' She demanded, looking at each onlooker, as if searching for complicity.

About to reply, Mike paused before running his hand through his hair, then down to squeeze the back of his neck. 'I'm sure he'll be ok, Daisy... once we get him to hospital.'

'Ok? How is he going to be ok? He's not even moving.' Daisy shook her head as she stared at Hugo. 'I knew I should've got the stupid round. This would never have happened to me.'

Eleanor, herself a mother with a daughter of Daisy's

age, approached and crouched beside her.

'I'm sure he'll be fine,' she said calmly. 'You must believe that.'

'How can I believe that?' Daisy snapped, turning to face her. 'Look at me. I know all about accidents.... and their aftermath.'

Embarrassed, Eleanor looked down. 'How long have you known each other?' She asked.

'Just since Saturday. This was our first date.'

'Your first date?' Eleanor said, clearly surprised. 'We saw you together earlier. You both looked really happy. My daughter even mentioned how close you looked.'

Daisy cupped her mouth and turned quickly to one side. How close they were and what a fun time they were having wasn't what she wanted to hear at all. Glancing sideways at Hugo, still grey and motionless, she began to wonder if he had already slipped away, silent, like an owl at night. She would never even know when it was he drew his last breath. And supposing he did survive, where would the road ahead take him? After all, she knew about accidents... and their aftermath.

Alarmed with such a sudden, invasive notion, she turned back to Eleanor.

'What if he's not going to be ok? What if something... irreversible has happened?'

Saying nothing, Eleanor put her arm around Daisy and gently patted her back. At that moment, two paramedics burst through the doors and Mike quickly briefed them, detailing step by step exactly what happened. Kathy, one of the medics, knelt by Daisy, striking up a conversation as her colleague tended to Hugo. Before long, they had him secured within the stretcher, and although Daisy knew he was in the safest of hands, the sight of him trussed up and set for casualty, somehow deepened her anxiety.

Eleanor appeared again, this time with her phone in hand. 'You must want to call somebody?'

*   *   *   *   *

Jane waited until the taxi was out of sight before walking back to her flat. Jerry, her next-door neighbour, waved as he left for nightshift, and as she approached her door, she looked up, eyes drawn by a sudden spray of light from Jean's living room window. Jean had been in the block longer than the Harris's and had been a regular baby-sitter for Daisy in her younger years. She was a witness to all the major events in their lives, from the day they moved in, to the day William moved out, to the day of Daisy's accident. With her fondness for Daisy and obvious concern for her welfare, she would have been the perfect choice for Godmother, had they felt the need to resurrect such an archaic practice. In saying that, she was one in all but name, even though Daisy referred to her as Aunty Jean. William settled on the 'Jean Genie'. (She had a knack of appearing when least expected or most unwelcome.)

Once home, she turned and leant against the front door, engulfed by the deafening level of quietude in the flat. Walking noisily down the hall, she stopped by her daughter's room, softly lit and evocatively fragrant, dresses and tops strewn across the bed. She stood for an envy filled moment, absorbing the joyful, chaotic scene, before going on to the kitchen. The charred, aromatic scent from the smoke of the burnt steak pie persisted, hanging in the air like a blanket of incense, and though shivering slightly, she left the window open. Deciding on tea, rather than wine, she made her way back to the living room, laying her cup carefully on the small, rickety stool *someone* made at woodwork lessons decades ago. Damn you William Harris, she thought, as she brought her legs up and settled comfortably in her chair.

*   *   *   *   *

Daisy waited for her mother to answer, wondering what took her so long before she realised she wasn't calling from her phone. (Unsolicited calls were generally ignored in the Harris household.) After five or six rings however, Jane eventually answered. Daisy relayed as much as she knew to her shocked mother who, without being asked, prepared to leave as she listened, stepping quickly into her shoes and searching for her keys as she switched the television off. She slammed the door with such force the entire block appeared to shake, compelling Jean above to peer through the curtains at the commotion below. Jane's last word to her daughter as she belted up was to ask where he'd be taken. Guy's, she believed, but... just in case.

Keeping pace with Hugo as he was wheeled out, Daisy looked on as the medics slid him into the ambulance, heavily, like a full drawer in a filing cabinet. Just before Kathy got in the driver's seat she turned and gave her the ubiquitous thumbs up. She'd reminded Daisy earlier *she* was on the case (so no cause to worry), also to tell them at Guy's it was her, Kathy Shearer who brought Hugo in, *and* to not mention the fact it was their first date. They can be funny like that, she'd remarked.

As the ambulance left, she braced herself for the ear piercing siren, until she realised the road ahead was clear. And there she sat, urging her mother's prompt appearance, anxiously aware she had to be at Hugo's side when he regained consciousness. She remembered, all too well, what it was like, waking to a roomful of complete strangers, bewildered to the point of insanity. Time and again, she would squeeze her eyes shut, as if trying to induce a sleep from which she could then re-emerge, free from the nightmarish vision of her broken body. It was several desperately confused hours before familiar faces in the shape of her parents arrived. Several minutes would've been long enough. Seconds even.

She watched as a bus approached with a steady, diesel growl and followed its course down the road, ablaze with light, windows foggy and scrawled upon. Two people left a taxi at the nearby rank and walked away, arm in arm, while in the distance, a siren sounded, making her wonder if that were Kathy, clearing the way for Hugo. It was then that Mike emerged, interrupting her thoughts as he shuffled slowly into her field of view, bearing her coat and Hugo's jacket. With her bag slung like a hold-all over his shoulder, he looked every bit the world-weary traveller keen to forsake all but his own bed.

'I think everything's here,' he said.

'Oh, I completely forgot about them. Thank you, Mike.'

'No worries. You sure you're okay? You're welcome to wait inside if you want.'

Daisy looked back at the premises. 'No,' she replied. 'I think I'd rather wait out here.'

'Of course,' he nodded. 'Well, I'd best get back in, tidy up... call it a night even,' he said, as he shook the ring of keys attached to his belt. 'You know,' he began, turning back to her, 'it's funny how things work out. Last Saturday, I saw Hugo rush across the bar in a panic. Uh-huh, trouble brewing, I thought. But he told me all about it later. Apparently, he'd just a minute to return a glass of wine to a very special lady before she vanished. Now, who on earth do you think that could have been?'

Daisy thought for several seconds before recalling the

moment Hugo appeared at her table with a lipstick stained glass and an awkward question to pose. Mike had inadvertently tied the ravelled ends of unseen detail together, closing the loop on a previous event that led to the moment she now sat within.

'Mike,' she called, stopping him. 'That was lovely to hear, thank you. And for everything you did tonight too,' she said, as she packed the coats on her lap.

Mike nodded his appreciation before making way for several people who were leaving, then headed back in. As the doors closed behind him, Daisy began to wish she had followed him in, but then quickly decided she couldn't have faced it. Not after what happened.

Maybe one day, she thought optimistically. After all, it wasn't Dan's fault. Places are neutral. It's people that deliver the energy, good or bad.

Chapter Five

Anna, the young Polish nurse who'd been a constant presence following Hugo's admission, waited until the team of specialists had left before checking his pulse, blood pressure and temperature readings. *All good*, she said in reference to his vital signs. She was about to leave, but instead stopped and looked at Daisy.

'Perhaps you should get some rest. He will be fine now, trust me.'

Daisy sighed wearily. 'I know. I'd rather stay... just in case he wakes up again.'

'Of course. I understand,' she agreed. 'I wonder if... one moment please, I will be right back,' she suddenly said, as she rushed out, leaving Daisy with a bemused expression.

With the door now closed, the room returned to a calm, settled stasis, in contrast to earlier, when Hugo unexpectedly regained consciousness, startling Daisy. She'd jumped when he opened his eyes and stared straight at her, looking (unsurprisingly) fearfully confused. Pressing the alarm cord repeatedly, the ward sister was first to appear, her impatient look replaced with surprise that Hugo had indeed woken up. Sentient for just seconds, it was time enough for him to whisper her name and recognise his own. And though Daisy had slumped in her chair with concern and disappointment when he drifted back to a deep, heavy sleep, the consultant stepped in to dispel at least part of her disillusionment – *try not to worry, she said. It's a good sign when you know who you are and who's company you're in.*

She watched his chest rise and fall, steady and rhythmic as the tide, comforted now that he appeared to be asleep rather than unconscious. And for the first time that night, she observed his injuries without a sense of shock or panic at their extent. His bloated left eye, blackened to a shade deep as burnt pastry, resembled a stewed, wrinkly plum. His right cheek, red and swollen, carried a cut above the bone where his head hit the footrest, and she could see several stitches through the fine gauze covering, stained brown with dried blood. She worked her fingers gently through his hair, still matted and smelling sharply of wine, then drew them lightly down his face. She believed with absolute certainty he could feel her presence, as she believed she held the power to somehow force recovery upon him. And that's just what she would do. She *had* to. Something had started. Something tiny to the outside world, yet proportionately massive in hers. Something, she felt, which had already taken form and wrapped itself around both their souls.

'Your mother cares very much for you,' Anna said as she sat next to Daisy in the small overnight room she somehow managed to secure. Jane had just left, taking with her Daisy's clothes and an emphatic no to coming home with her. Looking back in only succeeded in reinforcing Daisy's decision to remain where she was, despite the fact they lived just minutes away.

'She does,' Daisy agreed. 'But she worries too much. I mean, can you think of a safer place to stay the night?'

'You are so funny.'

'I was just thinking that of you,' Daisy replied. 'It would be nice to keep in touch... when all of this is over?'

'Yes, that would be nice. But right now, you must sleep. I will come with news,' she said as she stood.

Daisy looked up, smiling gratefully. 'Would you really? You're so kind Anna, thank you,' she said, as she reached for her holdall. 'You're in the right job, that's for sure,' she added, pulling at the bag's contents.

And how right was she? Nursing was a perfect fit for Anna's character: kind, compassionate, unflappable, constantly at hand. And when Daisy wondered if she'd always wanted to be a nurse, what took her down that particular career path, Anna's astonishing reply left little doubt it was absolutely the right decision.

'I cannot remember much *before* I decided to become a nurse so... yes, it would be correct to say I always wanted to be one,' she replied, with a short laugh. Lowering her head, she frowned reflectively before continuing. 'As for why, I would say tragedy was my inspiration. So many people are trapped by tragic events of one kind or another, that is only natural. But for some reason, I felt... liberated?'

Silently intrigued by her statement, Daisy watched as Anna sat back down beside her.

She then told of an incident that occurred many years ago in her native Poland. A catastrophic, life-changing event, with a reach far beyond those directly involved.

'My father was just forty-five years of age,' she began. 'He was fit, healthy, full of life and goodwill. The accident happened one morning as he drove to work. There were few witnesses, but doctors believed he suffered a stroke and lost control of his car before swerving into oncoming traffic,' she explained, using her hand to demonstrate. 'The collision was head on, and two people died in that moment. Two people who awoke that morning and started the day with hope and optimism, but who saw none of the rest of it,' she added with genuine sadness. 'My father was not amongst them, though he was not expected to survive that first long night. It is such a painful memory still,' she said, bringing her hand to her mouth. 'Then,' she continued, 'some... ten days later, he opened his eyes for the first time since the accident and wondered why his face was wet. Unable to lift his arm, he was surprised to see someone standing beside him, tissue in hand, gently wiping it.'

'That was you' Daisy whispered, 'wasn't it?'

'It was. It was me. I was only ten and I went to see him in hospital. He was... dribbling,' she giggled shyly, 'so I tended to him. And when he opened his eyes and saw me, his first words were, *"Anna, oh Anna, my little angel"*. And he cried, as if I *had* descended from heaven... like a real angel. That was the moment I understood. I knew then, what had to be done with my life,' she said. 'It was as if the decision had been made for me, that there were... forces at work?'

Daisy nodded. 'And your father?' She asked fearfully.

'He was sixty last month,' she replied with tears in her eyes. 'And he stood, unaided and embraced all of us present.'

'Your father was right, Anna. You are an angel.'

Smiling, she placed her arm around Daisy saying, 'we are not too dissimilar. Hugo will wake to an angel also.'

'Daisy,' Anna whispered urgently, as she peered around the door to the tiny overnight room, 'come quick, he is awake!'

Propping herself up on her elbows, Daisy squinted through bewildered eyes at Anna's silhouette, heart racing to the point of rocking her upper body.

'Anna? Oh yes, of course. I might need some time,' she said, as she flopped back down on the pillow.

'I am so sorry. I did not think. Can I help in any way?'

'No, that's ok, Anna. But could you give me a minute or two?'

'Certainly. I will wait outside for you,' she said, closing the door.

Fumbling for the light cord, Daisy threw the covers off, pushed herself up and began to unbutton her top.

Looking around for something to wear, several confused seconds passed before she realised she didn't appear to have a change of clothes. She reached for the small overnight bag, more in hope than in certainty. Empty! She stretched over to open the wardrobe, taking a quick look before letting the door slam shut, the spare hangers rattling noisily in protest. Empty! She checked her bag once again before slumping with disappointment.

'Great! Thanks mum. I don't even have a dressing gown,' she moaned. Frustrated, she buttoned her top back up and fluffed her hair before looking for her make-up. A sharp knock on the door was followed by Anna's urgent voice.

'Are you ready yet, Daisy?'

Daisy slapped her thigh, then put her make-up back muttering, 'what's the use? Yes Anna,' she replied loudly.

Anna looked in before pushing the door fully open.

'Why are you not dressed?'

'I don't have a change of clothes. Not even a stupid dressing gown.'

Anna smiled. 'Do not worry, you look fine. And what else would you wear in hospital?'

'But I'm not technically in hospital, am I?'

'No, but you look like you are,' she replied with a short laugh.

'Very funny, Anna,' she said, before squeezing past. On their way back to the ward Daisy looked up. 'I'm sorry for snapping at you like that. I'm just really tired.'

'That was a snap? You have yet to meet my sister.'

As they approached Hugo's room, Anna jogged ahead to open the door, leaving it slightly ajar for Daisy, then stepped back, grinning with excitement.

Hugo raised his head and turned to face the rising sound

that drifted in from the main ward to his private, darkened space. He stared at the figure in the doorway, straining to identify what appeared to be the outline of someone vaguely familiar yet stubbornly alien. But after several intentive seconds, his eyes became accustomed to the subdued light and finally, he recognised who was seated, silently watching him.

'Hey,' he whispered.

'Hey,' she whispered back, as she moved to the bedside and took his hand.

'You look different,' he said, remembering his last view of Daisy as glammed up and fashionably clothed. 'They're not... pyjamas, are they?'

Daisy let go of his hand and instinctively grabbed her collar, pulling it tight.

'Anna, the nurse, arranged for me to have an overnight room.' Looking down at her trousers she added, 'and of course mum totally forgot to bring a change of clothes.'

'Hang on now. You're saying you stayed here... at the hospital... all night? (Daisy nodded.) Now what would you go and do something like that for?'

'Well, I'd already done my hair and there was nothing on T.V. so...'

Hugo smiled. 'So, this is how Ms Harris looks first thing, then.'

'Oh please, don't draw attention to the fact. I'm sure I must look hideous to you.'

'Anything but,' he said, looking at her looking back from under a tangled mass of hair, tartan pyjamas one size too big, make-up on as though hurriedly applied or hastily removed and absolutely gorgeous with it. 'You look great, honest,' he almost gushed. 'But staying here... all night. God, I don't know what to say to you at all.'

She reached for his hand again and rubbed it warmly between hers.

'You don't actually have to say anything.'

'In that case, can I trouble you for a drink?' He whispered, nodding towards the water jug.

'Hmm,' she replied, hesitating officiously, 'I don't suppose a little bit will harm you.'

Glancing quickly at the doorway, she half-filled the plastic beaker and guided the straw towards his lips. Lifting his head, he took one long satisfying sip, before lying back again.

'Thanks,' he breathed. 'Far too hot in here. Not good for your health, hospitals.'

'Yes. We should've just left you where we found you.'

Hugo grinned. 'Wherever that was.'

Daisy gasped. 'Oh no, can you not remember?'

'Yeah actually, I can.'

'Hugo! That wasn't funny.'

'It wasn't, sorry.'

'Actually, it *was* quite funny... now that I think about it.'

'Glad you thought about it,' he said, as he scanned the room, looking for a clock, or some indication of how long he'd been there. 'You don't happen to know the time, do you?'

'Coming up for... six o clock,' she said, tapping her screen.

'Six o clock! You sure about that?' he asked, genuinely shocked. 'I haven't been out that long, have I?'

'Hmm, not quite. You were awake earlier. But only for a little while. I remember pressing that stupid alarm button again and again. I mean, how was I to know it was working? The staff nurse actually snatched the cord from me,' she added, scowling.

Hugo pressed the heel of his hand against his forehead in frustration with his patchy memory.

'So I was,' he groaned. 'Yeah, I see it now. It was a

weird feeling, though. It wasn't like waking up at all. It was more like... coming back to life, you know?'

Daisy nodded. She knew exactly what it was Hugo experienced. The loss of consciousness *was* truly like death itself. You visit a world black as the depths of space and every bit as timeless, with no dreams for comfort nor sentience of any kind. And when you return, you're breathless, utterly confused and totally devoid of sense. As though given birth to.

Gradually, the swirling cloud of random thoughts and foggy images settled like muddied water and his mind began to clear. Soon, recollections of their final moments together surfaced, like tiny, carbonated bubbles, bursting with detail. Daisy listened with fascination as his brain, working like a movie-reel, replayed his memories, frame by frame. She was about to add to the picture when, without warning, he let his arm drop to the bed. Frustrated, he paused mid-sentence, throwing his head back.

'Dammit anyway. Thought it was all coming back for a minute there but...'

'Hey, don't worry about it, everything *will* come back. You've had concussion... a brain injury,' she reminded him, 'so don't force it. You wouldn't run about on a sprained ankle now, would you?' She added, sternly.

Hugo was about to reply, but instead squinted narrowly at her and smiled.

'What are you smiling at? What?' She asked, looking down at her pyjamas.

'Nothing. You just reminded me of mam back in the day, that's all.'

'Your mum! I'm hoping that's a compliment, Mr O'Neill.'

'It is indeed. A fine, strapping farmer's wife, she is.'

Daisy's horrified expression brought a sudden, painful burst of laughter to Hugo, powerful enough even to rock the bed.

'Sorry. But your face there was classic.'

'Glad to be a source of amusement for you, *and* to see your memory appears to be working just fine,' she retorted.

Now that Hugo appeared to be fully aware and mentally robust, Daisy proceeded to tell him as much as she knew about what happened; from the moment he paid for the drinks, to the moment that almost cost him his life, to the one he now found himself in. He listened intently, nodding as Daisy stitched and weaved the details together with calm, sensitive precision. When she finished, he let his head fall heavily to the pillows, as if pulled back with the full, weighty knowledge of what happened the previous night. And when Daisy settled comfortably in her chair, they just looked at each other, silent amidst the growing noise of the awakening hospital. In the distance, the main, power assisted doors to the ward swooshed open, and the sound of several footsteps and collective chattering could be heard. The hand dispensers wheezed protective gel, and the trolleys squeakily announced their presence. Distinctive beeps of computers booting up soon followed, and from the small ward kitchen came the familiar sound of a boiling kettle and clinking cups.

'It must be half six,' Daisy said, straightening in her chair. 'Wakey, wakey, one and all,' she sang happily, as she tied her hair up with the frayed bobble she found in her pyjama pocket. Hugo watched as she skilfully created a pony-tail, twisting the band several times before pulling her hair tightly through it. He was about to say something when an unexpected visitor appeared at the door.

Chapter Six

'And how are you both?' came the thrilled voice from the threshold, startling them.

'Anna!' Daisy squealed before turning around. 'Come in, and yes, we're fine.'

Anna walked in somewhat cautiously, aware she interrupted a private moment.

'If you are sure?'

'Of course we're sure,' Daisy insisted. 'Hugo, this is Anna. She's an angel,' she declared, as Anna looked down shyly.

'It's not every day you meet an angel so, it's my pleasure,' he said, as he looked at her.

Anna was slim, petite and probably not much more than five foot in height. She had long, jet black hair, the sides of which were tied around her head and held in place with a band at the back. She had a dark, fiercely compassionate demeanour, and Hugo thought a couple of wings folded on her back wouldn't look out of place. Black, velvet ones. Not silver.

She almost curtseyed at Hugo, such was her delight at Daisy's delight he was awake.

'It is my pleasure also. I wondered what your voice would sound like,' she said, smiling at Daisy. 'It is so nice to hear it.'

Hugo smiled. 'Not everyone would agree with that but... I know what you mean, thanks.'

Anna ventured closer still and Daisy seized her hand when she came within reach.

'Anna made all the difference tonight Hugo. She was simply wonderful,' she said, just as her voice wavered. 'I'm sorry, I...'

'Do not be sorry,' Anna said. 'It has been a long, difficult night for you also. It is natural to be tired and emotional, is it not?'

Daisy nodded wearily. She'd not felt anything like she felt for longer than she could remember. And though utterly exhausted and totally drained, she was far from collapse, the bewildered state she found herself in being somehow... strangely energising?

'I am so pleased to see you awake and looking well,' Anna said to Hugo. 'You have your colour back and that sense of humour *someone* told me about.' Motioning towards Daisy she added seriously, 'you are such a lucky man to have found her.'

'Don't I know it? Imagine going through all that... just wake up to yourself.'

Anna laughed, then checked her watch.

'I must return to work,' she said, patting Daisy's shoulder. 'It will soon be very busy.'

Did she feel a bit guilty perhaps? Was it just a matter of making sure he was ok? Fix him up, then off to face the firing squad, tied to a chair in the grey, bowled courtyard of Kilmainham.

'By the way, I never actually said thanks for... you know, not deserting me. That was...'

'Well, I couldn't just leave you, could I? Your family's in Ireland, I didn't know any of your friends and... oh, would you like me to call somebody for you? Your mum maybe?'

'No, you're alright. She'd only worry anyway.'

'Are you sure? How about your friends?'

'No, really, I don't want to talk to anybody... anybody else I mean.'

'I know how you feel,' she said, as she yawned and stretched her arms.

'You didn't get much sleep, did you?'

'No I didn't. It was so hot in that tiny room,' she grumbled, pulling at her top. 'And the bed was like a park bench.'

Hugo sympathised with a thin smile. 'Tell me about it. Listen, get yourself home, grab a proper sleep if you can. Things are grand here now.'

'No, I'm fine, honestly,' she replied, as she began to roll her head from side to side.

Hugo raised his eyebrows suspiciously at her. 'Fine? Who you kidding? You're done in so you are. Off you go. Now!' He barked playfully.

'Look! I'm not leaving, ok? I'm absolutely fine,' she snapped, annoyed at how everybody seemed to think she was somehow less capable, but for one obvious reason she could cope without a good night's sleep. Almost as she said it, she looked up and smiled. 'I'm sorry. I can get really snippy when I'm tired. Apparently, I've always been like that.'

'That's ok,' he replied. 'I deserve to get snipped.'

Daisy made a scissors gesture with her fingers at which Hugo clenched his fist, where she then grabbed his hand in hers, wrapping it victoriously before he could react.

'Hey! You're just taking advantage of my current situation.'

'You'll never be quick enough... in any situation,' she gloated.

Hugo smiled at her less than magnanimous retort and turned to look out the window. By now, dawn was breaking, and he watched as the blackness of the mid-winter night slowly gave way to the first milky threads of daylight. The symbolism of the moment didn't escape him either, as it dawned on him too, the significance of everything that happened since their meeting last Saturday in Dan's. He followed the faint outline of a high-altitude vapour trail back to its source, and wondered what was happening at that moment in its pressured airframe as it sped west, travellers seated row by row, flying urgently to a board meeting or happily to holiday. He turned back, satisfied with the pleasure his tiny moment of escapism delivered. Invasive thoughts and fantasy were critical elements in his life experience and sometimes thought alone or imagination set free were reward enough for him. Sometimes, but not always he thought, as he looked at the most amazing reality before his eyes. A reality he somehow *had* to sustain. His life depended on it. His new life. The one that started last Saturday. The one with the tiniest, most innocuous of origins that quickly expanded to universal proportions. It was as if their meeting compared to creation itself. Something now existed that didn't beforehand.

'What do you say to another Chardonnay then... seen as I spilt the last one? Saturday night maybe?' He suggested. 'Not Dan's, though. Somewhere else... obviously.'

Daisy lowered her head, even before Hugo had finished asking what he'd waited all morning to ask. She began to inspect her fingertips, one by one, before picking and scraping at the red nail varnish she'd so meticulously applied the previous evening. After a few moments, she looked up, face etched with disappointment and wearing a faint, almost apologetic smile.

'I'd love to Hugo, but I won't be here. I'll be away... all weekend.'

'All weekend?'

'Yes, I... *we* have to leave first thing tomorrow morning. It's my gran's eightieth,' she reminded him. 'She lives in...'

'Norwich,' he said, as he suddenly remembered. 'Man, I completely forgot about that. Yeah of course, your gran.

Never mind, there's always next week or the following weekend?'

Daisy sank a little further into her chair. This was the very situation she tried to avoid last Saturday night. The one that led to *her* suggesting they meet on the Wednesday. But as she had literally run out of days this time, her only option now was to be painfully honest with him. She couldn't see him next week either. A training course at work. Compulsory and certified. Head office, Bournemouth. And to make matters doubly worse, the following weekend was out, too. She was going through to Bristol with Katie. That's where her friend was from and she hadn't been home in ages. They wouldn't be back until late on Sunday.

Waiting until she finished, Hugo was about to suggest the next again week, or even the next again *following* weekend, but decided he didn't want to be hit with yet another reason (excuse?) for not meeting up. This is a rapidly developing nightmare, he thought. That's practically two weeks. God, I'm at the back of a very long queue here.

'Hell of a schedule that,' he eventually acknowledged. 'Someday then... if you haven't forgotten about me that is.'

'Don't say that, Hugo. That won't ever happen. I do want to see you again. It's just... I don't know when, that's all. But I will call you, I promise. And when I get back from Bristol we can arrange to meet. Maybe the following Wednesday, or better still, the Friday?'

With a weak, disappointed smile, Hugo whispered 'maybe' and turned slowly to his right. Unwilling to look directly at her, he stared through the window at the once obscure shapes he now recognised as buildings, trees, powerlines and chimneys. Shapes once hidden but now bathed in the light of the early dawn, revealing their true identity and form. Yet more symbolism for him to digest, as if he needed it.

'Are you ok?' She whispered, uneasy with his enforced, lengthy silence.

'Yeah, I'm fine,' he lied, 'just a bit... tired.'

In fact, the opposite was true. He felt alert, focussed and fully aware of what had to be done. The urge to obliterate the status quo consumed him. Racing upwards, it rumbled and clattered with a growing intensity, like an oncoming express train, racing from station to station.

'Actually,' he said, suddenly sitting upright, his snap decision ushering back the irrational Hugo of old, 'I'm more tired of this place than anything else.'

Without looking at Daisy, he unclipped the heart monitor, unplugged the drip, then threw the covers back and swung his legs down to the floor, surprised with the warmth as his feet touched it. Getting ready to stand, he positioned both hands either side of his hips, like a weightlifter, psyching themselves up for the big push.

'Hugo, what are you doing?' She asked, alarmed at the sight of him preparing to stand.

'Going home. What do you think I'm doing?'

'Going home? Hugo, you can't go home yet,' she said. 'Please Hugo, don't try to leave,' she begged, as she worked her way around the bed's end to get closer to him.

Ignoring Daisy's pleas, Hugo took one last, deep breath before pushing himself up. Swaying slightly as he sought his balance, he turned to look at her.

'You see,' he declared, arms out, 'some things never leave you.'

Almost fully upright and about to straighten his legs, a sudden noise from outside the room caught their attention.

'It is me again,' Anna said cheerfully, as she pushed a

trolley laden with breakfast through the doorway. 'I am sorry for the delay. I had to bribe the auxiliary,' she laughed, kicking the door closed behind her. Momentarily surprised to see someone standing by the bed, she switched from casual to professional when she realised who it was. 'Hugo, please, return to bed at once,' she said, as she rushed past Daisy.

But before she could reach him, Hugo decided enough was enough and attempted a faltering step towards his locker. His legs however, proved incapable of carrying his weight, and the furthest he got was a couple of feet before he crashed to the floor, hitting it firmly with both knees. The impact split the tissue over the bone and he wavered as he knelt for a second or two, wondering why the floor was wet with a warm stickiness before he fell forward, hitting his head heavily on the solid wooden frame of the hospital armchair.

'Hugo,' Daisy shrieked, watching him fall and feeling the floor shake with the impact. Anna rushed to his side, but slipped on his blood, landing comically on top of him. She reached for the alarm as she lifted herself up and pressed it repeatedly. Checking his breathing was stable, she turned to Daisy.

'He will be fine. I am sure of that,' she insisted, placing a pillow under his head.

'Oh my God Anna, what have I done? This is all my fault. Why couldn't I just...'

'It is no-one's fault, Daisy. He stood when he was not ready to.'

Shaking her head in disbelief, Daisy stared at Hugo, face flattened against the grey, rubbered floor, his crumpled, unconscious figure framed with bloodied strokes and hand-prints, like some macabre Banksy mural.

'I have to go, Anna,' she said, attempting to move

backwards, hitting first the wall, then the bedframe as she moved forwards. 'I have to go before something else happens. We're not right for each other. We can't be. What an idiot I've been, thinking we were,' she said, slapping her armrests.

'Daisy,' Anna said sharply, grabbing her chair with both hands. 'Listen to me. You must not leave. This is an accident. Nothing more, nothing less. Do you understand?'

Running through the door, the staff nurse took one look at Hugo and immediately ran out, returning seconds later with several medical orderlies. Ushered to one side, Daisy once again found herself helpless and horrified as Hugo, for the second time in her presence, was secured to a trolley and stretchered from view. Anna, the last to leave, looked back.

'I will bring news as soon as I can. Please,' she asked, 'wait here. Do nothing until we speak, yes?'

Chapter Seven

Hugo stared at the boxes of light as they raced overhead, following each one till they disappeared from view, then quickly looking up to catch the next one. Glancing to his side, he wondered if the pictures on the walls were in fact windows on a passing landscape, as they too, swept past. But where was everything (he) going? And what mode of transport was he on? A train of sorts? He strained his eyes down as far as he could, but the fuzzy, darkened mounds of his cheeks obscured his view. He wondered why he couldn't lift his head to see past them and tried to raise his hands, but he couldn't move them either. Frustrated, but not overly concerned with his physical condition, he decided not to worry about his immobility and return to his game. Introducing a new element, he would attempt to catch the images and gather them in his pocket for later inspection. Maybe then he could figure out where he was and where he (everything) was going. But just as he resumed his game, he was spun sharply around and propelled to a totally different environment: calmer, spacious and with huge bright lights bearing down upon him. Coming to a halt with a slight jolt, he was surprised to see two people peering over him, one from below and one from above. Not sure which one to focus on, he took the less energetic option and looked down at the smiling eyes of the figure below him.

'Welcome back Hugh,' spoke a familiar voice through the light blue covering of a surgical face mask.

Anna knew she hadn't much time to get all the way down to Hugo, then back up to Daisy before her mother arrived to take her home. Not only that, she was coming to the end of her shift, which her watch confirmed was just half an hour away. Normally a source of great relief and pleasure, it now added to her anxiety. Deciding it was quicker to take the stairs, she raced down the levels to the ground floor, making her way quickly to the ITU, where she paced outside for several long minutes until Hugo arrived back from surgery.

'I wondered how he is?' She asked the staff nurse as she approached Hugo. 'His partner is most concerned. She would welcome some good news.'

'Of course,' the staff nurse said. 'He'll be fine. His cuts are on the mend, though he'll find it a bit painful to walk, at least initially. We also found a small hairline crack on his right cheekbone, which won't really trouble him. He just needs to watch he doesn't knock it again.'

'Yes,' Anna agreed. 'In that case, we will have to tie him down.'

'Whatever it takes. Not that I agree with such drastic measures,' she laughed. 'But no, it's all good really. He was awake earlier, but he's sleeping now. Probably the best thing for him under the circumstances.'

'Thank you,' Anna said. 'May I?' She asked, nodding towards him.

'Yes of course. He won't be here much longer, so don't be surprised if he's whisked away from under your nose,' she said, walking back to her console.

Anna approached his trolley and partly drew the curtain behind her. She leaned over him for a closer look, and like Daisy earlier, drew comfort from the fact he was asleep, rather than unconscious. She brushed the hair away from his forehead, but avoided touching his face, instead looking with concern at his latest injury, the swelling and bruising making him barely recognisable from his right side. Happy he was stable, she was about to leave when a junior doctor, barely in her mid-twenties, slipped in behind her.

'Oh, good morning doctor,' she said.

'Good morning to you too. And how is our escapee?'

'He has not spoken yet. But at least he is still here!'

'Yes, in spite of his efforts to the contrary,' she replied, as she moved to one side to allow Anna out from the bed. 'Let's hope he stays put this time,' she laughed, quietly. 'Two head injuries in one night? That's got to be some sort of record, hasn't it?'

Anna smiled. Wicked as her humour was, the doctor had a point. Hugo did indeed have a valid claim on the record. If such a record existed.

'How long will it be before his partner can visit him?' She asked.

'Not long… Anna,' she said, looking at her name tag. 'He doesn't need a scan, x-rays are clear, except for the right cheekbone, knees sorted and he's only mildly concussed. Are they at the hospital?' She asked.

'Yes, she is waiting upstairs.'

'Hmm, five minutes and you can take her down. They should be fine with that,' she said looking around the unit. 'Unusually quiet in here today,' she whispered. 'Unlike last week,' she groaned. 'Two eighteen-hour shifts, one after the other.'

'Yes, I remember,' Anna said. 'I was here, too.'

'So you were,' the doctor exclaimed, open mouthed. 'I recognise you now. I'm so sorry,' she said as she touched her arm. 'I'm Sarah. Pleased to meet you… again!'

'Anna. Pleased to meet you also.'

'Well,' the young doctor said, rolling her eyes, 'work to do.'

'Yes, and thank you, Sarah. I will go and tell his partner right away.'

This time, Anna headed back to Hugo's room with considerably more haste than when she left it. Unlikely as it seemed, there was a chance Daisy had already left or was preparing to leave, and with Hugo on the road to recovery, stopping her was paramount. Powering up the stairwell, she was right once again in taking the stairs (passing as she did, the packed lift-hall), then thanked her good fortune as she managed to squeeze through the ward doors before they closed. But almost as she entered the room, she knew instinctively Daisy was not there.

'Daisy, are you here? Daisy,' she shouted, as she burst into the shower-room, even checking the cubicle before leaving. Running back into the main ward, she asked her colleagues if they'd seen her. No came the reply. Nobody had seen her. About to run back to the lift hall, it suddenly hit her. The overnight room! She turned and raced down the long corridor towards the small annex. A brief memory block meant she couldn't remember which one Daisy had occupied, but as there was only one door fully closed, she made for that.

'Daisy, it is Anna,' she said, knocking sharply. 'Are you in there?' She knocked again, this time louder and with more urgency. 'Daisy please, are you in there?'

About to try the handle, the door suddenly unlocked and swung open. Daisy smiled on seeing her friend, then backed away.

'Daisy,' Anna said, out of breath with exertion and anxiety, 'I have been looking everywhere for you.' Putting her hand on her chest, she added, 'I am not as fit as I should be.'

Little wonder Anna was exhausted. She had never been as intimately involved with a patient and their partner as she had been with Daisy and Hugo. And along with her usual duties, it made for a most gruelling twelve-hour shift.

'I'm sorry Anna. I couldn't bear being in that room any longer.'

'Of course,' she gasped. That was not good, leaving

you there. I am sorry,' she said, as she sat on the bed.

'That's ok. None of us were thinking straight.'

It was plain to Anna that Daisy had been crying, red eyed and snuffly as she was, strands of hair stuck to the sides of her face, still moist with tears. She held a crumpled-up tissue in one hand, and with her bag on her lap, cut the sorriest looking of sights.

'Did you get to see him?' She asked quietly.

'Yes. We could not speak because he was just back from theatre, but he...'

'Theatre!'

'Stitches only, so do not worry. I spoke with the doctor and there are no concerns for him. She does not believe he requires another scan, and though he has a tiny fracture to his cheek bone, that will soon heal.'

Daisy touched her face, trying to imagine the pain of a fracture to her cheek, wondering if it would hurt to talk, eat or even smile.

'It's funny. This was such a happy little space, now it's the last place I want to be,' she said miserably. 'I don't know what to do, Anna,' she said, as she cradled her face with her hands. 'This has been a total disaster.' Looking at her phone, she added, 'mum will soon be here as well. Maybe I should just... go home with her.'

'Go home! Why would you do that?' Anna asked in disbelief. 'Was it so wrong he tried to leave? Who would want to stay here longer than they felt necessary?'

'You don't understand, Anna. He didn't just want away from hospital, he wanted away from me.'

Surprised, Anna looked at Daisy, but decided not to push for an explanation.

'I do not know what angry words were spoken between you, but I do know we use words as weapons. We hurt because we ourselves are hurt. Hugo is hurt, inside and out, and if you leave him now, like this, there will be no going back.' She took Daisy's hands, gripping them firmly. 'You stayed last night because he needed *you* to wake up to. Is that not still the case? Who would he want to wake up to, if not you? Who?' She pressed, shaking her hands vigorously.

Daisy was surprised at the power of Anna's sudden, forceful gesture.

'Remind me never to get on your bad side,' she laughed as she shook.

'I do not have a bad side. Some not as good as others, perhaps.'

Both girls smiled warmly at each other as they sat in silence, with Daisy wondering what next Anna would say and Anna formulating what she would. Anna then slipped off the bed, and in an overt display of emotion, knelt in front of Daisy before leaning forward to embrace her. She brought her arms up behind Daisy's shoulders, pulling her in.

'You must go to him, Daisy. If you do not, all this pain will have been for nothing,' she said wearily, as she settled into her.

Daisy slowly closed her arms around Anna, giving in to an urge to be held and to hold.

'You've been wonderful, Anna... all night. I don't know how I can ever repay your kindness.'

'Yes you do,' Anna replied, as she pulled back to look at her, 'that is the whole point. You know exactly how you can. You know what you must do for Hugo... for you... for me?'

Daisy stared at Anna, confused for a moment before suddenly realising that she too, had felt their pain and anguish as though her own. She'd spent her entire shift absorbing it as she tended and treated their wounds. She radiated nothing but compassion and equanimity and was now, utterly depleted. If little else, Daisy owed it to her to make amends with Hugo, to complete the final act of their dramatic episode. An act that would not only bring together her and Hugo, but would somehow energise the spirit of her weary friend.

'I didn't *really* want to leave' she eventually admitted. 'I guess I just needed another good reason to stay. And what a perfect reason I have in you, Anna. Thank you... so much,' she whispered. Smiling, she added, 'I actually feel a bit of a fool, now.'

'Do not feel like that. Doing something foolish doesn't make you a fool,' she said, as she settled back onto her calves. 'And you are more than welcome,' she added. 'So, have you collected all your things?' She asked, looking around the room.

'Yes,' Daisy replied, lifting her overnight bag as Anna stood. 'I think so.'

'Well then?' Anna said, as she held the door open.

Before she left, Daisy stopped and glanced back at where she slept, the covers on the bed casually preserving the imprint of a moment from one of the most extraordinary nights of her life. As she ducked under Anna's outstretched arm, she knew the day ahead would be just as extraordinary.

'There we go, Hugh,' the nurse declared, having powered up the monitor and checked its accuracy, 'we're reading you loud and clear... at least your bpm and blood pressure,' he added, grinning. Tapping the saline solution bag, he altered the flow of the drip before pulling the metal stand closer to the side of the bed. 'Not in your way, is it?' He asked.

Electing to say nothing, Hugo shook his head.

Thinking it best to remain a little longer than usual, the nurse picked up Hugo's medical log and scanned it vacantly, glancing occasionally at him. Putting it back, he offered to raise the bed up slightly, but with no response from Hugo, went ahead and raised it anyway. It was then, as he filled the plastic beaker with fresh water and set it down on the empty trolley table, that he noticed the room was devoid of personal items of any kind. No phone, newspaper, pen or book sat within reach. There were no branded drinks cartons, sweets or fruit. No get-well cards stood on the cabinet, and a glance under the bed revealed no slippers, socks or shoes.

'I'll grab a paper for you, pal. There's always one lying around. And if you need anything, or you wanna have a chat, just give us a buzz, yeah? Back shortly,' he said as he left, quietly pulling the door behind him, the soft click of the lock ushering in quietude and isolation. It was exactly what Hugo had waited for all morning. He hated being rude to someone as kind as the nurse, but he knew any verbal response from him would trigger a conversation and keep him from his thoughts. And his thoughts were the only company he wanted right now. He turned to the window. The light from the low winter sun streamed through the glass, scattering the dust and casting a warm yellow glow over everything it fell upon. But Hugo found no beauty in the illuminated scene before him. If anything, he wished he could reach for the blinds and draw them down. He looked away, drowsy-eyed in the warm, silent atmosphere of his room. On the cusp of sleep, he wondered if a nightmare lay in wait, a dark vision of him running with leaded legs across a barren, bleak landscape, pursued by a shadowy, menacing figure. A figure composed entirely of everything he despised about himself. It would be no less than he deserved. After all, he brought this upon himself. And his punishment should be no respite whatsoever, in this or any other world.

Daisy and Anna waited for the lift doors to slide open, Anna arms crossed, Daisy drumming her fingers on the armrests as she stared at the display. Typically, the doors to their right opened first, and they waited as several people, mainly admin staff, hurried out for their nine a.m. start. Reaching the ground floor, they made their way along the busy corridor that led to the ITU. A couple of patients were being trollied into the unit as they approached, and Anna suggested Daisy wait by the long row of chairs as she went in. A moment or two later, she emerged from the ITU looking left, then right. They had just missed Hugo. Frustrated, they made their way back to the lift and returned to the floor they'd just left. The level's familiarity rushed through the open doors like a warm summer breeze, and this time, Daisy left the elevator with a sense of purpose and excitement. Hugo needed her. And for the first time since her accident, dependency shifted to someone else. She charged herself with nursing him back to health. And there would be no repeat of what happened earlier. Not on her watch.

As they approached his room, Anna walked ahead to check his condition before beckoning Daisy forward, something she'd done earlier that morning. She smiled as she saw what she believed to be a calm, settled Hugo, facing away from the window and sleeping soundly.

'Daisy,' she motioned. 'Come, he is sleeping, but he looks fine.'

'I'm not sure, Anna. Perhaps I should wait in the lounge or something. At least till he wakes up?'

Anna approached and knelt beside her. 'No. You need to do this now,' she insisted. 'What is it they say... no time like the present? It *will* be fine, trust me.'

Daisy nodded. Once again, Anna made perfect sense, displaying to the end, the warm rationale of a skilled counsellor or someone considerably older and consequently wiser. If emotional intelligence could be measured, she'd no doubt her Polish friend would pass a scholarship with ease.

Anna smiled as she stood, then swung the door open for Daisy.

'Welcome to your new life,' she said, turning to leave. 'Make it a good one,' she called.

Chapter Eight

Hugo half opened his eyes, fully expecting the bearded nurse to be standing above, syringe in hand and smiling with benevolence. Instead he found... no way, he thought immediately, it can't be. Yet there she was, real as day, studying his face intently but carrying a warm, welcoming smile. He snapped his eyes shut, as if believing they'd intentionally deceived him, that his self-abuse ascended to the level his senses were now complicit, punishing him with a means beyond consciousness itself. Curious, he opened them again. Still expecting the beaming, bearded nurse, he saw that it *was* Daisy, smile broadening with relief he was awake and that he appeared to recognise her.

'Hey,' she said softly, gripping his hand.

Hugo blinked rapidly to shift the watery veil that cloaked his vision. As soon as she appeared sharp and defined, he found his voice.

'Hay is for horses.'

'Hi then.'

He just managed to raise a weak smile before looking down.

'Can't believe you've come back,' he said. 'Honest. That was it, I thought,' he added hesitantly, his voice on the verge of breaking.

Like Hugo, Daisy too, looked away, lowering her eyes evasively before replying. 'I haven't come back, Hugo. I didn't leave. I couldn't do that to you.'

And on hearing her words, his eyes filled and overflowed, propelling hot little tears down his cheeks, where they leapt from his chin to his hospital issue gown. And he wept so much his face glistened, leaving the gown sodden and sticking to his chest. He'd never cried with such abandon before. Not even as he stood by his father's grave under the bleak Irish sky. Not even as he felt his mother's grief clinging like a thick blanket of fog. He cried like he did, because he knew if Daisy had left, the pain would eclipse a thousand such funerals.

'Hey, it's ok,' she whispered. 'Everything's going to be ok, I promise you.' She sighed heavily and looked to one side, respectfully waiting until he composed himself. 'I'm sorry Hugo... for all of this. I feel so... stupid, letting it happen. I don't know why I didn't just...'

Hugo shook his head, squeezing her hand to stop.

'Come on now, Daisy. This was nothing to do with you,' he argued, as he wiped his eyes with the back of his hand. 'Nobody could've stopped what I started. Nobody,' he added bitterly.

'That may be so, Hugo. But you reacted in the only way you could. It wasn't really you in that moment, I know that. Anyway, it doesn't matter now,' she insisted. 'It's not important. Well, not compared to everything else that's happened since we met. Even *how* we met. I mean, how weird was that? Finding each other in a bar so busy you could barely breathe. Swapping glasses like that. Katie and Ben going off to the toilet. What is it with us?' She asked, giggling inquisitively and looking around, as if the walls themselves could deliver an answer. 'Hugo, this has got to be the craziest, funniest, scariest time I've ever had. And I don't want it to end. It's been too amazing.'

She swapped expressions from excitement to one of calm solemnity.

'Someone really special showed me what we have, Hugo. And by showing me what we have, I saw what we could lose. And I'm not losing it. I can't go back to the way things were. And even if I could, what would I go back to? Things are way too different for me now. I've set my course, Hugo. This is what I want.'

Stunned with the sheer emotive force of her proclamation, Hugo inhaled deeply and held his breath for several astonished seconds before breathing out and sinking back into the pillow. Everything he needed to hear he'd just heard. And as he absorbed her words and burned them to memory, he became aware, once again, of the warm, early morning sun washing over his face. For a brief, divine moment, he felt as though he were lowered to a font of tepid water in front of gathered family and friends, cheering his rebirth. How things can change when you least expect them to. We're in control yet we're not. Life sees to that, running as it does at its own pace, delivering random, seemingly chaotic events that determine who and what we are: a missed train, a sudden downpour, a chance meeting in a pub? Not forgetting a mad old dash for freedom, he reminded himself as he looked at Daisy.

'If you think you can weather the occasional mad Irish storm then... who am I to argue.'

'I don't think, Hugo, I know. Anyway, if ever anybody needed a storm in their life, it was me.'

Leaning closer, Daisy gripped his hand with both of hers, as if to prevent his wriggling free once again. She had one key issue to resolve. The 'when to see each other again' issue. Why wait two weeks for that to happen? There was no reason they couldn't spend some time together on the Sunday before her course started on the Monday. And with it finishing on Thursday, they could spend yet more time together before she headed off to Bristol on Friday. Simple.

Hugo smiled at the complexity of the arrangements and began a fatigued attempt at protesting, which Daisy duly dismissed. Her mind was set. It *was* happening. But before he could protest further, she took the decision he'd had enough excitement for the time being and insisted he close his weary eyes. She'd grab breakfast with her mother (due to arrive at any moment with, hopefully, a change of clothes and her iPhone charger).

Closing the door quietly behind her, she looked in the window and smiled as she saw Hugo already sleeping, arms limp by his side.

Nothing lifts the spirits quite like a cooked breakfast and a sympathetic ear, and Daisy left the restaurant completely nourished in every sense of the word, the calm rationale of her mother every bit as satiating as the hot, filled croissants and steaming pot of tea. (Jane had arrived, just as Daisy closed the door to Hugo's room, clutching a bouquet of Lily's, a basket of fruit and a get well card. Creeping silently back in, she left them on the trolley by his bed. Just as silently, Daisy ushered her out and down to the café on the ground floor.)

As they approached the lifts, Daisy tried to calculate the number of times she'd moved between floors that morning, as once again, she made her way back to Hugo's room. She now sat taller in her chair, brimming with excitement and buoyant with anticipation. The vast complex responded accordingly, its corridors no longer narrow and oppressive. The once sharp fluorescents now seemed to bathe the environment with sunlight, and people were less preoccupied, taking time to smile and make eye contact. As they arrived at Hugo's room, Daisy looked through the window and saw him sitting upright, card in hand, the envelope having slipped to the floor. Hugo grinned at Daisy as she entered, followed by her mother.

'Funny card,' he said, smiling at the cartoon image of a man falling down a set of steps towards a waiting ambulance with the words, *don't go falling ill again.* 'Thanks… Mrs Harris.'

'Less of the *Mrs Harris*,' she said warmly, as she accompanied her daughter to his bedside. 'Jane to my friends.'

'Sorry. Pleased to meet you... Jane.'

'Here, have some fruit,' Daisy said, offering Hugo the basket. 'Mum bought them for you... and the flowers.'

'Daisy,' her mother shushed. 'The whole world needn't know. Honestly,' she said, rolling her eyes.

'Mum. Who cares? It was so sweet of you.'

'It was actually. And I love the flowers as well so, thanks very much,' he said, biting tentatively into a black grape, as if the art of chewing had escaped him.

'You're more than welcome,' Jane replied. 'And how are you feeling now?'

Hugo sighed and glanced at Daisy, wondering just how much of his earlier antics and catastrophic aftermath mother and daughter would have discussed. *All of it probably.*

'Much better, thanks,' he replied, as he rummaged about the carton for a softer, juicy strawberry. Realising he had an audience, he paused and looked up. 'Sorry for stuffing my face in front of you, by the way. Here, help yourselves,' he offered.

'No, please, carry on stuffing,' Jane remarked.

'Sounds familiar that, carry on stuffing,' he joked.

'Indeed,' Jane replied. 'But you're far too young to remember the *Carry On* films, are you not?'

'No. I'm actually older than I look.'

Jane frowned for a moment, then laughed. 'Oh, I see what you mean. I wondered what you meant. Perhaps I could have some of whatever it is you're having?'

Hugo smiled, but declined to make any further age-related comments. It was a fine line between sincerity and appearing patronising. Daisy, meanwhile, watched with delight as they traded jokes with each other and fished in the basket for another plump, red strawberry.

'When do you expect to get home?' Jane asked.

'Not sure. Saturday morning maybe? They've decided to keep me in for a while yet.'

'I wonder why,' Daisy said.

'Well, they must do what they must, I'm afraid. Though I'm sure the time will soon pass,' Jane said.

'Yeah, I hope so.'

Jane smiled sympathetically at him, then switched focus to her daughter.

'And speaking of home, young lady, would you mind getting yourself changed?'

'Would I mind? I'm a visitor... get me out of these,' she laughed, pulling at her pyjama top.

He settled back as they left, listening as they debated where she could change, with Daisy insisting she use the little overnight room one last time and Jane replying she couldn't actually insist on anything. Peas in a pod, those two, he thought, recalling his first impression of Jane: slim, pretty, sharply dressed, dark hair tied up. She actually reminded him of someone everybody knew, but he couldn't think who. He could, however, see where Daisy got her looks and mannerisms from, and at times when Jane looked at him, he felt she were more an older sister than Daisy's mother. Something she'd love to hear, no doubt, he thought, closing his eyes. She's gone from pod to pea, he chuckled to himself.

Dreams end

When thought begins

Images melt

And flow like words

Then sense prevails once again

And chaos stays

Hid in den

It was a persistent, rustling sound that caused Hugo to stir, and he frowned with concentration as he tried to identify the source. Though fatigued and reluctant to climb back to sentience, he felt compelled to open his eyes. It was as if the environment demanded his attention. Something urgent and meaningful awaited. Finally, when he did open them, they fell fortuitously on Daisy, looking at him from where she stood, in the centre of the room under a dazzling glitter ball. She was dressed in exactly the same outfit she wore for their first date and looked every bit as radiant and gorgeous as she did then. Giving him time to waken and adjust his vision, she sang ta-dah as she twirled fully around, knee out ballet-like, stopping expertly in the same position she started from. Initially puzzled to see her standing, he soon relaxed, his frown slipping to a wide smile of adoration.

'You meeting someone,' was all he could think of saying.

Daisy smiled and walked over to his bed, the sharp, confident sound of her heels advertising the presence of a beautiful young woman.

'Yes,' she said, leaning down to kiss him. 'You, silly, don't you remember?'

'But I don't get it, Daisy, you're... standing,' he said, just as he woke.

'Only me, I'm afraid,' Jane said. 'I much prefer the flowers on the window-sill after all,' she added, busily re-arranging the stalks by poking the larger ones to the back. 'I'm so sorry for waking you.'

'No,' he said, blinking and breathing rapidly, 'that's

ok. How long have I been…?'

'Oh, about half an hour,' she replied. 'More than enough time for a little bit of housekeeping.'

'Daisy?'

'Toilet,' she answered, nodding towards the shower room. The muffled sound of a flush drew his eyes from Jane, and seconds later, the door slid open, first sticking, then rattling free on its coasters.

'Hugo, what are you doing awake?' She scolded on seeing him. 'You need all the rest you can get,' she said, moving as close as she could before stretching over to kiss him.

'Rest. Who needs rest?'

'You, silly, don't you remember?'

You, silly, don't you…! Astonished, Hugo repeated the words to himself as he struggled to make sense of what he just heard. Like most people, he'd experienced several inexplicable events, the French even coined a phrase for one. But this wasn't a vaguely familiar feeling of something 'already seen', and it wasn't as if he'd just thought of someone who then appeared as though projected from memory. This was different. He actually heard everything she said, word for word, before she even said it.

'I've just had the most amazing dream,' he said, sitting upright. 'I dreamt you just said that. Honest. You were here, seconds ago, and you were sta …' he paused, 'you were dressed like last night and you came over, like you just did, and you said, *you, silly, don't you remember?* Then you kissed me. I saw it all, before it happened. How is that even possible?'

'Shush,' she whispered. 'You just saw what you wanted to see, that's all.'

'No, no, no. It wasn't what I wanted to see at all.'

'Hugo, whatever do you mean? Don't you like me like

this?' She said, as she pulled at her top.

'Yes, of course I do. You look great,' he said as he settled back on his pillows, his excitement waning, along with his attempts to explain himself sensitively. 'Just a crazy dream, I suppose.'

'Aren't they all?' Jane said, as she slid the toilet door closed before gathering her coat and bags.

'We have to go now,' Daisy said, aware of her mother's impatient activity behind her. 'It'll be lunchtime soon, and you *will* gobble it all up. That's an order,' she threatened. 'I'll be back later to check if you have or not.'

Several hours later...

With visiting time drawing to a close and little else to talk about – Daisy's impending trip to Norwich wasn't, for obvious reasons, a topic of conversation – they both sat in silence, occasionally glancing at one another and watching as the ward began to haemorrhage its night-time visitors.

Curiously, everything about them seemed to move with great speed, as if time advanced but left them untouched. Like in a scene from the *Time Machine*, they were the mannequins standing firm against change, as first came the auxiliary followed by the cleaner who preceded the staff nurse who checked the vital signs, before leaving the room.
As eventually would Daisy.

And backing away, she held his hand until the very tips of their fingers were the last to part company.
And then she was gone. As gone as if she had never been there at all.
And everything about him slowed as time readjusted

itself, decelerating to a steady, relentless pace, ushering back a grinding, monotonous reality.

Chapter Nine

Eight o'clock, Saturday night, and the sudden, sharp sound of the doorbell pierces the gloomy silence of Hugo's flat, doing so with such alarming urgency, he immediately decides not to answer. And why would he? He knew it couldn't be any of the so-called 'lads', having warned his friends he'd be lying low for the weekend. And with family hundreds of miles away in Ireland, he couldn't begin to think who might be standing on his doorstep at this time of night. After freezing for a moment, he continued rinsing his mug as quietly and carefully as he could, until it slipped from his hand and smashed against the hard, white ceramic of the Belfast sink. Terrified, Whiskey leapt from the worktop, knocking a glass to the floor, and incapable of reacting, he watched as it fell, jolting with the noise as it splintered on impact. Shutting the tap off, he turned to look at the shards of glass, the jagged stem standing upright as though in defiance, and knew whoever was outside, now knew he was inside. He walked to the couch and sat on its edge, rubbing his chin subconsciously, the bristled resistance of several days growth noisily scratching the palm of his hand. He looked again at the front door and jumped as the bell rang for a second time. A third, prolonged ring finally forced a decision. Reluctantly, he left his seat and climbed the two steps to the small foyer. Glancing at his reflection in the glass face of his father's barometer, he ruffled his hair, then opened the door.

It has to be said, Hugo wasn't one for histrionics, emotional displays or overt signs of surprise, but when his eyes fell upon Daisy, his jaw quite literally dropped, throwing his mouth wide open. He half-expected a T.V. crew and anchor to suddenly spring from the shadows, having orchestrated the mother of all wind-ups. Even greater, if someone had bet the world ending against Daisy appearing on his doorstep that night, then nothing other than a void would exist now between Venus and Mars, such was his surprise. Uttering a word that vaguely resembled her name, he moved to one side to allow her past.

Saying nothing, Daisy negotiated the threshold, then carefully lowered herself down the steps that led to the living area. He shook slightly as he looked out into the cold, dark evening before closing the door. He stared at it for a moment, chilled with the thought he could well have left her on his doorstep, both separated by just two inches of mahogany. He turned and followed her down the steps and stood next to her. She frowned sympathetically as his face came into view, his injuries apparent, despite the subdued lighting.

'Thought you might like a visitor.'

'You thought right,' he said, as he struggled to adjust to the new dynamic forced upon him. 'Here, let me help you,' he offered, as she unwrapped her scarf and undid her jacket. 'I don't get it, Daisy. Your gran's... the party... what's going on?'

'I have no idea what's going on,' she replied, as she wriggled free. 'I just know I had to see you tonight. I was so worried about you and...' She sighed as she looked down at her bag, clicking it open and closed several times before dropping it to the floor. 'Probably more than just worried, actually.'

Hugo smiled and sat down beside her.

'I didn't enjoy last night at all,' she began, describing how the party went, start to finish, dutifully listing all those present: friend, neighbour, family member. (She was good with names. All girls are.) 'And when I went to bed,' she continued, 'I couldn't get to sleep. So I got up

84

and sat by the window, like I always used to. My room at Gran's, well... where I stay when we visit, is at the back of the house,' she explained, 'overlooking the river with the town spreading out beyond. It's such a beautiful view, especially at night. You must see it someday.'

'I'd love to,' he said.

Daisy loved visiting her grandparents in Norfolk as a young girl – even as a teenager, despite the associated mood swings and social media angst. Living as she did in a modern, single level flat in central London, her grandparent's house by comparison, was character laden and huge: three floors, high ceilings, even a servants annex to the rear with separate access and bathroom (Daisy's 'royal apartment' when visiting). It was scary too, which added to the excitement: long, dark corridors, unused rooms, narrow, creaking staircases. The kitchen, with its vaulted ceiling and roughly pointed stone walls, formed part of the original old basement, which to Daisy, made it dungeon-esque and consequently, *super* scary. Outside were several outhouses and a garden that stretched further than she could kick a ball. At the far end of the lawn and buried to its roof, was an old WW2 bunker, which her grandparents used for stacking garden furniture and bags of fertiliser. There was even a well, covered with a metal grill through which stones could be dropped, their fall counted in seconds till they hit the bottom. She couldn't understand why they never made a splash.

'I thought, water equals splashing, does it not?' she said, throwing a puzzled look at Hugo, who sat quietly listening, enchanted with her childhood recollections.

And though her grandparents were always delighted to see her (gran loved preparing her bedroom and baking brownies and fairy cakes), it wasn't so with her father. He would stay just long enough for the most basic of pleasantries before leaving. Daisy knew most of the visits to her grandparents were for 'the wrong reasons', her mother and father needing 'space' to sort things out, something she knew her grandparents knew. She also knew they didn't know *she* knew, so nothing was ever said. And that was the way she wanted it. No mention of her parents added to the magic, especially at night, where she would sit by the window and gaze for hours at the view beyond. In the distance, she could see cars, lorries, buses, all plying their busy little routes under the shimmering, orange glow of the streetlights. And if the moon were out, the river would sparkle as if sprinkled with jewels and fairy dust. Always alone in those moments, she was never lonely, for she kept herself good company.

And then, just weeks before her fourteenth birthday, her grandfather dies, taken from them suddenly and without warning, as if caught in the sights of a lone, distant enemy. That was her first real taste of loss. Never before had she felt such, gnawing, carnivorous pain. She cried enough tears to fill the well at the foot of his beloved garden. She remembered her mother, distraught with loss, her father riven with guilt, and the paradox that was the service – on a day bright and sunny in their darkest ever hour. Her grandmother, gaunt with grief and looking like she was soon to follow her husband, vowed never to see Daisy's father again, a pledge she'd yet to break.

'Soon after, dad left,' Daisy said, recalling her second, bitter taste of loss. 'Mum and I continued to go see gran of course but... it wasn't going to be the same again. Not with granddad gone. And the view from the window was never the same again either.'

She then described how, over time, her mother and

father's relationship completely broke down. She didn't see him for two full years, unsure even, if he were alive or dead. Then, events conspired to make an attempt on *her* life, only to narrowly fail, saved as she was from certain death by an ornamental bush and the intervention of a passer-by. When she opened her eyes several days later, next to her mother stood her father. Dad, oh dad, she cried.

'They still speak to each other, even now,' she said. 'I don't feel any anger towards dad. He's nowhere near a bad man, but he was never going to be a family man either. Now that I know that, we've become closer. Cut your expectations of your father, mum used to say. How right was she? Just have to work on gran now,' she added. 'So,' she said, grinning at Hugo, 'that's my potted history. My childhood in a nutshell. You now know things about me nobody else in the whole world knows.'

Hugo lowered his eyes, as if tipping an imaginary cap with appreciation and humility, honoured she chose him to confide in. And as she talked about her life, he'd felt drawn into it, almost as if he'd lived it with her. He felt he'd watched a Harris family cine movie, its silent images distant and grainy, yet profoundly evocative. Could there be a tiny Hugo squeezed in somewhere between the frames?

'That's a lot to deal with,' he said, toying with the notion their timeline started years, not days ago. 'I know people say things even out, you know, over time and that but... it doesn't feel like it sometimes.'

'Everything does... eventually,' she said. 'I'm still here,' she added rationally. 'I've survived. Who knows, if these things hadn't happened, I might not be here now… with you.'

Hugo listened to her words, nodding in agreement. He knew what she said was right. For some reason, his faith in the blind indifference of the cosmos wavered from time to time. Good or bad cannot be attached to events. They just are. They happen, bursting spontaneously to life, releasing their effect equally and without compassion. Everything that happens, good or bad, makes you who you are. Wishing to change just one thing could lead to changing everything. And changing everything would leave you with nothing.

'So something good has come. And something good happened last night too,' she said. 'It was like... I saw how narrow my life was, how defined and predictable everything had become. It's really hard to explain but... I felt I needed more space? Like I'd grown too big for my life. How weird is that?' She giggled.

Hugo smiled. He drew comparisons with his own life. Only he did things in reverse. His was too wide and filled with angst, so he chose the more covert, narrower path to walk.

'I would've taken the train back, but mum insisted she drive me. She wasn't at all happy but... I couldn't stay there a moment longer. Gran understood though. Well, I hope she did.'

'I'm sure she did,' he said. 'Anyway, there's one person who's *definitely* glad you did what you did, and they're thinking it's like a miracle from where they're sitting. And I know for a fact, they didn't believe in them until now.'

Daisy smiled and took his hands. 'That's another reason I wanted to come back. I love the way you say things.'

'Here, I was gonna offer you a drink earlier, but I couldn't get a word in edgeways,' he said, grinning. 'What do you fancy? Actually, I've only got red... or Guinness.'

'Red's fine,' she said.

Hugo groaned as he rose from the couch, the pressure exerted on his knees painfully stretching the skin.

'Oh, that sounds really sore.'

'Nah. Just a bit stiff, that's all.'

She watched as he hobbled to the small galley kitchen before rooting around for a suitable glass for her, then as he hobbled back with a bottle of Malbec.

'You know,' she said, as she lay her glass down, 'I really didn't want to go out on Saturday night. I was all set to stay in, but Katie insisted. Mum too. A certain person was going, you see.'

'Ah, Mr Ben,' he stated, whimsically.

'Mr Ben,' she retorted. 'I'm sure he's nice enough, not that I saw much evidence of that. But he's certainly not...'

'What you're looking for?'

'No,' she agreed. 'Not that I was looking for anybody,' she quickly added. 'And I wouldn't have gone to that bar to *not* look for anybody either,' she said, laughing. 'Katie wanted to, for some reason. I remember thinking, this is so not a good idea. We could barely get through the doors it was that busy. But guess who insisted on buying the drinks?' She said proudly. 'How fortunate was that?'

Fortunate is not the word, Hugo thought, as he shuddered with the notion of not colliding with Daisy that night, their paths converging with blind precision as they hustled and harried their way to the bar, careering instead into Katie, of all people.

'And isn't it crazy to think I could be at Gran's right now? You'd be with your friends and we'd both be blissfully unaware of what might have been,' she said. 'Well, maybe not blissfully... or even aware,' she added, giggling. 'Do you think things like this happen *all* the time?' she suddenly asked, frowning with the significance of her question.

'I'm sure they do,' he replied. 'I'd like to think the really amazing moments are rare, you know. People come and people go but... to meet somebody...' Hugo paused and scratched the side of his head.

'Somebody you want to be with, so much so, that it aches?' Daisy suggested.

Hugo smiled. 'Yeah. When it hurts like that, you know it's real.'

'Then it is real,' she said. 'Because I've never felt so much pain since my accident.'

'I've been in pain since the moment I met you.'

'Oh don't say that, Hugo. I feel terrible now.'

'Don't be daft. All's well that ends well... as they say.'

'Well, I suppose that's one way of looking at it.'

'It's the only way of looking at it.'

Daisy smiled. 'Perhaps it is. I did, after all, go out with Ben and come back with you. Now *that's* what you call a result,' she declared, clenching her fist and drawing it down victoriously.

Hugo grinned broadly. Daisy was the Jupiter of their Solar System, subconsciously clearing all obstacles from their path and talking them, word by word into a relationship. And he was fine with that. Sometimes emotional cowardice pays dividends, and for Hugo, this was one such time.

'It's such a lovely song, isn't it?' Daisy suddenly said. '*Somebody to Love.* It was on the radio this morning. Somebody to love,' she repeated. 'They so knew what they were singing about, didn't they?'

'They sure did. It's an amazing song alright,' he said, instantly hearing the almost magical, operatic harmonising of a band at the pinnacle of their career. Hugo had always loved the song and it's simplistic, core message. Relationships and experience are what power the human spirit, providing the rich lattice of memories to dwell upon. Few people, if any, look back with fondness at something they bought or owned, but they'll always invoke memories of holidays, time spent with loved ones, their first driving lesson or even where they were on the passing of a genius. But atop it all, sits the need for someone to share it with.

He grabbed the arm of her chair and playfully shook it, smiling as she began to rock back and forth, her head bobbing in time like a little dashboard toy.

'It's funny,' he began as he watched her sway, 'soon as I got home yesterday, I wanted back to hospital. I knew it the second I opened the door. When I put the key in the lock, even,' he added.

For desperate as he'd been to get home, the moment he walked through the door, kicking aside the envelopes and packages that littered the foyer, he immediately longed for the sanctity of his tiny hospital room and the presence of Daisy. Such was the power of his yearning, it was as if every negative emotion he could think of suddenly combined to create a super emotion of such loss, it compared to bereavement. He remained where he stood for several minutes, unwilling to tread further into his flat, fearful each step would take him further from Daisy.

Later, when he gathered the mail, he sat, staring at the envelopes, trying to identify the source by scanning them for clues. He couldn't bring himself to open them, having little will to invite yet more of the world in. The old world. The world before he met Daisy. He switched the tv on, flicking through several channels, then turned it off for the same reason. He scrolled through his playlist. He paced his flat. He boiled the kettle, then let it cool. He'd never felt such a sense of disconnection before. Like a dream, he instinctively understood what was happening, but he couldn't actively alter anything or apply any logic to it.

'Couldn't get to sleep for ages either,' he continued. 'Far too quiet, it was,' he said, grinning. 'I didn't get up till this afternoon, so I missed most the day. Then Whiskey appeared... on the mooch as usual. I'd no cat food in, so I gave her an egg.'

'An egg?'

'Yeah. Sure that's practically chicken, isn't it?' He laughed. 'Then it got dark before I knew it,' he moaned, rolling his eyes. 'There was nothing on tv... as usual,' he added, glancing at it, 'and it's been raining non-stop.'

'Yes, it's been miserable,' she said, as she recalled her own journey to her grandmother's the previous morning. They rarely got above fifty mph, the conditions were that bad. The heavy, incessant rain made the drive dangerous enough, but the spray from the wheels of the huge lorries was deadly. It was like driving through an endless car wash with the wipers on full, but barely managing to clear a view. And being dark and gloomy all day likened it to driving at night, with blinding headlights adding to the confusion. Her mother drove the entire route tight to the wheel, jaws clenched in concentration as she fought the slipstream of the heavy vehicles, leaving Daisy in isolation, alone with her thoughts. And Hugo didn't leave those thoughts all morning. When they eventually arrived, nearly four hours later, Daisy was immediately engulfed with guilt and regret. Though she loved her grandmother more than anyone, her feelings on arrival didn't reflect that. She knew she shouldn't have left Hugo alone; confused, in pain and likely to attempt another escape before his planned release date. And as she looked through the window of her grandmother's sitting room, the day sealed it for her. Mid-day became mid-night, with the wind spattering the rain against the glass repeatedly, every corner of the sky filled with explosive, blackened clouds. The sheer misery of the situation brought an ironic smile to her face, for until last Saturday night, this was the event she'd been looking forward to all year. Now it was the very last place on Earth she wanted to be. And how she punished herself for feeling like that.

'Anyway, that was then, this is now and things are grand. What a difference, seeing your sweet little face has made. It can rain all it likes, so it can.'

'Is it raining? I hadn't noticed,' she joked.

Hugo smiled. He took a deep breath, as if preparing to say something, something he desperately wanted to say (something he never actually believed he'd be in a position to say), but instead paused and looked down. It was like he'd suddenly fallen victim to a silence he seemed incapable of breaking. Daisy watched as he lowered his head before taking a sip of wine. Hiding behind her glass, she decided to break it for him.

'I was thinking... mum won't be home till tomorrow, so I... I really don't want to go back to an empty flat tonight.'

'I don't want you to either,' he quickly said, as he looked up. Clenching his hands tightly together, he brought them to his mouth as though in prayer, giving thanks to a higher power for such timely intervention. 'God no. Stay where you are... please,' he added with a nervous laugh.

Thrilled the final obstacle, the impenetrable bulwark, had been breached, they sat, wrought with anticipation, their hearts pounding like symphonic drums as they gravitated with an almost celestial inevitability towards each other. And not a sound could be heard in the flat. Not the tick of a clock, the drip from a tap, not even their breathing. Finally, Hugo stood. Moving closer, he leant down to kiss first her forehead, then her cheek, then her warm, sweet mouth.

'I can't believe we're doing this,' she said.

'I can't believe I'm asking you this,' he replied, 'but, would you like to get more... comfortable?'

Daisy nodded.

Hugo kissed the back of her hand before leading her through to the bedroom. Saying nothing, he helped her out of the chair and sat beside her on the bed. When she felt ready, she began to undo the tiny white buttons on her blouse, letting it slip from her smooth, rounded shoulders. She unhooked her bra as Hugo pulled his top off in a blaze of static sparks, and once again, he fought an impossible urge to stare at her, as she sat, oozing a shy sexuality, arms drawn instinctively across her chest. She released her hair from its black plastic clasp, then shook her head from side to side before reaching for her necklace, which she started to unclip but decided to leave on. She motioned him closer to help remove her leggings, then watched as he stood to unzip his jeans. As they slipped from his waist, she noticed his heavily bandaged legs.

'Your knees. Will you be ok?' She asked, slightly embarrassed with the notion of how he might injure them.

'These things? Sure they're like knee pads,' he said as he lightly hit them.

He sat back down on the edge of the bed to pull his jeans off, and once free of them, turned to face her. She looked down at her pants before whispering, 'actually, I should have said. Is it okay if we stay like this?'

Straight away he nodded, whispering back of course they could. He knew exactly what she meant. She wasn't quite ready for whatever reason, and for Hugo, that was reason enough.

As they lay back, he pulled the quilt to their shoulders,

and when settled beneath, ran his fingertips across her skin, lightly, as if touching some priceless, fragile artefact once lost to the Aegean, but since rediscovered and presented before him. He cupped her breasts gently with his hand, her hardened nipples irresistible to the tickly centre of his palm, then leaned over to kiss her.

She wrapped her arms around his back and pulled him closer. Pressing her mouth to his, she felt, all at once, his restrained desire, his tenderness, his burgeoning love. It was everything she dreamed of, dipping back into consciousness.

'How wonderful is this?' She whispered.

He shivered in acknowledgement as he rolled his lips over hers, the intense, reciprocal pleasure of the moment contrasting with the awkward tension of their first meeting and his nervous attempts to harry her interest in him. His reward then, a cheeky glance in his direction or a tiny smile fashioned just for him, with not a thought of where things would lead.

Chapter Ten

Hugo padded back from the bathroom and pushed the bedroom door until it swung open. The arc of light that spread across the room swept the bed, and until it shone on her face, he almost believed she'd gathered her things and left in his absence. He even considered the possibility she was never there in the first place, the entire episode an imaginary encounter, echoing his earlier, confused state of mind. But no, there she was, lying on her back, hands behind her head and deep in thought. He slipped effortlessly in beside her, taking care not to touch her with his cold, bare feet, and she waited until he settled before rolling towards him, laying her knee possessively across his legs. Satisfied, she murmured something inaudible as she nestled into his embrace. Hugo returned an equally inaudible murmur as he gazed at her, lying naked to the waist, her warm, curvaceous body resting heavily against his.

'You know,' he began, following several long seconds of silent adoration, 'when I first saw you at the bar last Saturday, I was thinking, surely you have a boyfriend and he'll arrive at any minute and that'll be it. Eh… you ok there, Daisy? He bothering you, he would say, rolling his sleeves up like Spike in Tom and Jerry. Remember Spike?'

Daisy nodded, smiling at the ludicrous nature of a cartoon where animals told a very human story, with gratuitous levels of violence, tales of entrapment, coercion, and the occasional display of conscience and comradery. Poor Tom, she found herself saying once again, as she always did.

'Then I thought you'd probably just get bored of me and engineer an escape route, like only girls can.'

Daisy started to laugh, silently at first, then physically, her body shuddering against his.

'What you laughing at?' He asked, beginning to laugh himself. 'What is it?'

'You needn't have worried. I love funny men. And you were so funny... without realising it. Especially when you were shoved from behind. If you could've seen your own face. Then you thought your barman friend would come straight to us,' she added, 'but he served someone else. I was desperate to laugh, but I thought that would be quite rude. And your luck didn't exactly hold when I ordered a white wine for you now, did it?'

'Is that so? Well, we couldn't have swapped glasses if I chose a beer now, could we? How lucky was that Miss Harris?'

'Hmm, very good point, Mr O'Neill. That makes the glass incident even more significant. Clever boy,' she added, slapping his chest. 'So what did you actually think of me... when you first saw me?'

'Nice... until you spoke. Then I thought you were quite rude. A right madam, actually.'

'Hey!' She snapped. 'I am so not like that.'

'Course you weren't. You were dead cute, so you were. Really funny as well. And you were so... casually attractive with your hair up and strappy top and stuff.'

'Aw, did you really think that?'

'God yeah. I love that look. Especially with your hair up. It's like lifting your dress to show a bit of leg, you know.'

'Like the Can-Can girls?'

'Yeah,' he agreed. 'Or no, more subtle, like Marilyn in the *Seven Year Itch*, remember? Standing above that... air vent thing.'

'Subway,' Daisy whispered.

Hugo sighed as he caressed her shoulders. 'You so

knew you were dead hot, didn't you?'

'Of course I did,' she murmured. 'All girls do. We just don't like boys knowing we know, that's all.'

'Yeah, I get that.'

'Did you imagine being in bed with me?' She asked, burrowing yet deeper.

'God Almighty, I could have worn you, to be honest. But to be fair, just getting to see you again was the target.'

'I so knew it. I could feel you drooling all over me.'

'Drooling? Come on now, I don't think so.'

'Discreet and respectful yes, but drooling none the less,' she said, grinning at his reaction. 'But again, you needn't have worried. I felt the same too.'

'Did you now? And it didn't cross your mind to tell me?'

'A girl has to be fought for,' she reminded him. 'That was the best part. You were so brave with your big wooden club, fighting the competition off,' she giggled. 'Your little feathered display worked.'

'Yeah, it did, didn't it?' he said, proudly. 'Here we are... in my cave,' he added, as they both laughed.

'Isn't it strange... how we make things happen?' Daisy said. 'I mean, just yesterday, this was barely a thought. And look at us now. We *made* this happen. I remember reading somewhere, that if you can imagine something, anything, it will come to be. It will exist, eventually... somewhere in the universe.'

She reached over to switch the bedside lamp off, engulfing them in a near total black, a darkness soon spooned brighter by the hollow, milky light from the frigid full moon.

'The moon looks so beautiful, doesn't it?' she whispered, its ghostly luminescence filtering through the fabric of the window covering. 'As a child, I would imagine travelling there and back in an instant. I would just close my eyes and think the journey.'

'I did as well, but I wasn't quite as imaginative as you. I would fly my own rocket there and back. I thought it was amazing that people actually walked on it, though. I couldn't get over that at all.'

'And how many more thought they did?' She added, laughing.

Hugo chuckled back through the thinning darkness. 'Good one.'

'But you're right Hugo, it *is* amazing that people made it all the way up there, landed safely, then did whatever it was they did.'

'Whatever indeed. Some played golf... apparently.'

'Really? How scientific. Wonder what else they got up to. You don't suppose anybody got drunk on the moon, do you?'

'I'm sure they did. On Moonshine, probably.'

'Oh, very funny,' she said, giving him an appreciative poke in the ribs. 'What exactly is moonshine anyway?'

'Moonshine happens to be the American equivalent of our very own Poteen. It's a type of really strong whiskey from the deep South,' he explained. 'Highly illegal, hence the name, moonshine. Distilled by night under the light of the silvery moon, it was,' he said in a hushed, poetic tone.

'That sounds so romantic. Working by moonlight, deep in the dark, rolling hills of Dixieland.'

'Yeah, very romantic alright, until they were caught, or when they caught someone sniffing around. You ever seen *Deliverance?*'

'Hmm, forget the moonshine then,' she decided as she looked again at the ghostly disc pinned in isolation to the night sky. 'I would much prefer to take a bottle of the finest champagne up there and share that with you. We could watch the Earth rise slowly over the horizon in the blackness of space. Wouldn't that be simply magical?'

'God now, that would be amazing,' he said, thinking what a wonderful imagination Daisy had. Wow. Both of them sitting on the moon, giddy with champagne and watching the world go by... literally. 'And speaking of drink Miss Harris, fancy another red or something else?'

Daisy thought for a moment.

'No, I'm fine thank you. Actually, yes. A cup of tea would be amazing.'

'Tea. You sure? On a Saturday night?'

'Yes. And just with milk please,'

'Ok, tea it is,' he said, as he reclaimed his arm from beneath her head. 'Close your eyes,' he warned as he reached for the light.

When he returned with two steaming hot cups of tea, Daisy was already sitting up, pillows behind her fluffed and stacked, her thin nylon top clinging loosely to her shoulders. Taking a moment to stare at her from the doorway, he found it hard to believe how attractive she really was. And not just her looks. He was loving her quirky imagination, how colourfully expressive she was, how she switched moods and topics at the drop of a hat. Dizzyingly confident and as comfortable in her own skin as was possible to get, she was the ultimate tonic for the weary, disillusioned soul he'd become.

He heeled the door closed before walking over and laying the cups down. Once in bed, he turned to her, just as she turned to him, making them both laugh.

'Look at us, if you could,' she said, 'sitting in your bed on a Saturday night, sipping tea, of all things.'

'Here. What's wrong with my tea?'

'You know what I mean,' she said, as she carefully

checked the temperature with her lips before taking a sip.

'Ooh, what a perfect cup of tea,' she oozed. 'Is there no end to your talents?'

'It's an Irish thing. People think our national drink is Guinness, it's actually tea.'

Daisy smiled and looked around Hugo's bedroom, properly, for the first time that night. Slightly larger than expected, she found it (unsurprisingly) functional in layout and plain in appearance, with light coloured walls and carpet to match. The doorway was angled inwards, cleverly eliminating one of the corners to create an interesting architectural feature, and along the same wall ran the fitted wardrobe, complete with sliding doors, one of which was wedged open with the heel of a trainer. Across the room, a chest of drawers stood beneath the window, which was concealed behind a set of dark red curtains, and tucked away in the corner, sat a chair piled with clothes of all sorts: jeans, shirts, boxer-shorts and socks. Even a couple of tea towels and... was that an oven glove? She wondered. Apart from the bed itself, the only remaining items of furniture in the room were the two bedside cabinets, similar, but not identical to each other. On the wall behind his bed, hung an aerial picture of a vast, tree covered crater, and to the right, a large map of Manhattan, with pictures of familiar buildings and landmarks joined by lines to the map, showing their location. From a 'through the keyhole' perspective, the space was entirely male – but for her presence and discarded clothing.

She liked that. Introducing a female element. To his room. To his life.

'I meant to ask you,' she suddenly said, prodding him in the ribs, 'what made you change your name to Hugo? It sounds... French,' she mused. 'Is there a Gallic connection there, somewhere?'

Hugo laughed. 'No, the only French in me is the Beaujolais I have occasionally. I just thought Hugo Neill sounded better than *Hugh* O'Neill, that's all. A bit more stylish, you know,' he added. 'It's not official or anything. It just felt good kicking boring old Hugh into touch.'

'Yes, I quite like the name Hugo,' she declared. 'Very continental. But what about poor Hugh? I hope he's ok. I'd love to meet him too.'

'Not sure about that now. He's quite shy, you know. Probably jealous as hell.'

'Jealous? Ooh,' she said, 'he's not here is he, hiding in a cupboard or something, just... waiting and watching?'

'That's actually really creepy,' he said, the thought of a maniacal relative hiding in the cupboard, however absurd, making him cringe. 'I wondered where that bread knife went. Hope you'll be ok tonight, out there on the couch.'

'The couch! Oh, I don't think so, Mr O'Neill. I've a feeling you won't want me out of your sight tonight.'

'It's that obvious, is it?'

'Yes, it is and... oh my God, it's becoming obvious again!' She shrieked, as she inadvertently brushed against him.

'Sorry, but that's nothing to do with me,' he explained lamely. 'That's eh... Hugh. He quite fancies you as well, by the way. Just so you know.'

'That,' Daisy started slowly, as she pushed herself away from him, 'was the creepiest, most disgusting thing I've ever heard. Suddenly the couch seems very appealing. Ugh,' she shuddered. 'That's the worst, Hugo.'

'Sure is,' he replied, happily. 'We're a good team, so we are. You cast the line, and I plumb the depths,' he said, yawning.

With his last few words almost incoherent, Daisy looked up and caught his red, bleary eyes looking down through tired, narrowed lids. She gently touched his bruised face and ran her fingers down to his lips, where he playfully bit them.

'You look absolutely shattered. What a horrible time you've had.'

'Yeah well, could've been worse, you know.'

'I know, but that doesn't make it any less of an ordeal,' she said, as she snuggled back into his embrace. 'You're the last person something like this should have happened to. Nothing like this will ever happen to you again. I'm going to look after you from now on. I promise.'

Chapter Eleven

Wow, Hugo thought when he opened his eyes and turned to see Daisy looking straight at him, head on hands and wearing nothing but a warm, welcoming smile.

'Good morning, Mr O'Neill,' she whispered.

'Morning, Miss Harris,' he replied. 'You been awake long?'

'No,' she said, shaking her head. 'Just a few minutes. You must've been dreaming. Your eyes were twitching and your breathing was quite fast too,' she said with fascination.

'Can't remember if I was,' he said, as he rolled on his side to face her. 'Feels like I'm dreaming now, though.'

Daisy smiled and flashed her eyelids slowly in appreciation.

'Me too,' she said. 'Though I never dreamt I'd be whisked away by a tall, dark stranger, let alone wake up to him.'

Hugo put his arms around her, pulling her in closer.

'You did a bit of whisking yourself,' he murmured, as he kissed her forehead, then the cold tip of her nose before reaching for her lips. He grinned as he lay back down on the pillow. 'More than a bit, I'm happy to say,' he added. 'Here, do you fancy breakfast in bed?'

'No, thank you. I can't eat straight away. Makes me feel sick for some reason. Tea would be lovely though.'

'You sure?'

'Yes. Tea, first thing... always,' she instructed. 'Coffee, mid-morning onwards. Remember that,' she ordered.

'Yes mam,' he replied obediently. He waited until she lifted her head before retrieving his arm and swinging his legs to the floor. 'Back in a sec,' he said as he left the room.

With the door closed, she rolled her head lazily across the pillow to face the window, where the low winter sun cut through the dark fabric, creating a thin sheet of light as fine and precise as a laser. Feeling a sudden, overwhelming urge to throw open the curtains, she sat up, groaning in pleasure as she stretched her muscles after hours of sleep induced inactivity. She found her clothes, lying where they fell, and after hooking her bra and buttoning her blouse, shifted cheek to cheek to pull her trousers up. The chest of drawers was well within reach and once standing, she shuffled towards it. With her hand on the surface, she swept one of the curtains aside, instantly flooding the room with a light of such intensity, it seemed to roar its presence. And as she stood, bathed in sunshine, she almost believed the day outside to be mild and spring-like, until she saw the twinkling frost on the slates and tiles of the neighbouring buildings.

'What a beautiful day,' she whispered, as she stared through the window at an outside world locked in the still, silent grip of winter. Turning her head towards the door, she caught the distant rumble of a kettle from the kitchen, along with clinking cups and cupboards closing. She smiled as she realised there were few places in the world where she felt as she did now, where she could travel to such wonderful moments in blissful solitude. And this was one such place, a vessel in which they would set sail and begin their journey to… wherever. Bon voyage, she thought happily.

As he stood, tapping his fingers and watching the kettle boil, Hugo heard the unmistakable sound of the cat flap and quickly moved to one side, waiting for his tiny tenant to appear.

'Gotcha,' he called in ambush, as she fell victim to his warm, over-friendly grasp. He shook her small, indignant head gently in his hand, before dropping her to the floor. She circled his legs like a shark: darting, twisting and pressing for food, all the while nudging him towards the fridge. 'What have we got here, then?' He asked as he scanned the interior. 'How about another egg?' He suggested, as she stood on her hind legs, pawing the air frantically. Seeing there were only two left, he settled on milk, half filling her bowl. When she finished, he grabbed her just as she tried to escape and carried her through to meet the new pretender to her throne, murmuring and tickling for extra reassurance. Tapping on the bedroom door, he waited for an answer.

'Hugo, what's with the knocking?'

He poked his head around the door as he held firm to Whiskey, now tensing with fear.

'Someone here to see you,' he said as he pushed the door wide open.

'Oh, it's Whiskey,' she squealed. 'I forgot all about her. Here, bring her over,' she demanded, hands out.

However, ears flattened and overcome by panic, she swiftly turned from a ball of fluff to a nest of brambles. Clawing free from Hugo's grasp, she jumped to the floor and slithered under the bed in one single movement.

'Ow, you little bugger,' he yelped. 'That was sore. Obviously not used to seeing another female in here.'

'Well, that will have to change, won't it?' Daisy said emphatically before leaning forward as far as she could to look under the bed.

'Right then, better get your tea,' he said. 'You two be alright together?'

'We'll be just fine,' Daisy said, as she looked around for something with which to tease Whiskey out from under the bed. Finding a pen, she wiggled it over the side of the frame, and before long, a curious little white tipped paw appeared, snatching wildly at it. Having grabbed her attention, Daisy then dragged the pen back and forth across the floor, several times, hoping to tempt her out. Annoyingly, but predictably, Whiskey remained where she was. Grumbling in frustration, Daisy threw the pen down, made for her chair and left the room, just as Hugo arrived with the tea.

Hugo set the cups down, next to their wine glasses and made himself comfortable on the couch. Once again, Daisy enthused about the tea, this time insisting Hugo explain exactly how to prepare the perfect cup, an explanation he duly delivered – along with a bit of Colonial tea making history. Milk first, *then* tea poured from the pot. That way, the tea didn't stain the fine bone china, he explained. And, crucially, Assam for the morning: strong and peaty, Darjeeling for the afternoon: light and citrusy. Remember that, he instructed.

With the talk then turning to Daisy's looming work commitments and her leaving for Bournemouth first thing the next morning, they decided to make the most of the rest of the day. Southwark Park they would visit, for a cold winter's stroll through the tranquil, tree lined avenues, a wander around the monuments, then onto the deafening chaos of the nearest Costa, after which they would slowly wind their way back to her flat. And after that, he didn't want to know.

'Right, better get dressed,' he said, downing the rest of his tea.

'Could you get my socks and boots when you're through?' She asked, 'and the travel toothbrush?'

'Anything else?'.

'No. Yes, actually! Could you put my socks on for me?' She petitioned sweetly.

'No, I've got my own ones,' he shouted from the bedroom.

'I so knew you were going to say that,' she yelled back.

'Yeah, I knew you knew,' he replied, as he dutifully returned. Kneeling in front of her, he shook each sock out before lifting her left foot by the heel. 'How'd you manage to get them so perfect?' He asked, looking at her flawlessly painted toenails.

'With the greatest of difficulty,' she replied. 'Though mum does help sometimes,' she admitted. 'Maybe you could do them for me one day. Have you got a steady hand?'

'As a rock,' he replied.

'What are you smiling at?'

'Nothing. Just never ceases to amaze me the effort you girls put in to looking good, that's all.'

'Aw, so I look good then, do I?'

'You, Miss Harris, look amazing,' he said, as he pulled the other sock on, then helped her into her boots before zipping them up.

* * * * *

Daisy peered over her large, bowled cup, watching him sit, deep in contemplation, like some modern-day Greek philosopher, chin in hand and staring blankly beyond everything in view.

'What's on your mind?' She asked.

He sighed impatiently as he waited for the clamour of the coffee shop to dull, then signalled his relief when a near silence suddenly broke with a timely, mute explosion.

'Dunno, really. I was just thinking it's, well...'

And once again, Hugo stopped short of saying something he desperately wanted to say, in spite of the moment screaming out for it. She was the most amazing girl he'd ever met, he'd not slept since last Saturday night, her name alone raced his heart, and despite the short time they'd spent together, he was utterly convinced he couldn't be with anyone else. His was already a life-long commitment.

That's what he wanted to say, but he thought it too heavy a sentiment for such a tiny moment to carry.

'It's been a mad old week, hasn't it? One minute we're down at Dan's, the next we're in hospital,' he laughed. 'Last night was amazing, though,' he added seriously. 'That was like, so unexpected. I think that's the best thing that's ever happened to me. Honest,' he insisted. 'And waking up this morning and not having dreamt the whole thing was the next best thing, I can assure you. Or maybe it is a dream, is it? In that case I wouldn't want to wake up. Keep me under!' He almost shouted, before ducking out of everybody's sight.

'Aw, that's really sweet, Hugo,' she said. Leaning forward, she whispered mischievously, 'sounds like you've fallen for me?'

'Pushed, more like.'

'Now who would do something like that?'

'Who indeed,' he replied, as he smiled at her.

'You mean that someone is me?' She asked, reacting with bewildered sarcasm as she looked around. 'Well, ah never,' she drawled. 'Yawl knew something ah didn't.'

Hugo laughed, impressed again with her hilarious mimicry.

They both sat back, smiling at each other before suddenly frowning as the deafening hiss of steam and relentless, metallic clanging of the café re-emerged.

'Will you be ok… next week?'

'Course I will. Like I said, things are grand now.'

'Well no, not quite. You still have to watch what you do,' she reminded him. 'Hugo, the doctor told you that…

wait a minute,' she suddenly realised, sitting upright, 'what did you promise to do tomorrow?'

'Yeah, phone the doctor,' he recited, as though in primary school.

'Please do it Hugo. I'll be so worried if you don't.'

'Look, I said I will, and I will. Promise. That nice?' He asked, as she tucked into the scone, coating her top lip with clotted cream.

'Bliss,' she replied, as she licked it off.

'This looks familiar,' Hugo observed, as they ambled along the private road that led to Daisy's apartment block. 'Is there a courtyard in there, by any chance?'

'Yes, there is,' she said. 'Come round the side, I'll show you.'

Daisy punched her PIN on the keypad before swinging the heavy gate open, allowing them entry to a beautifully manicured and landscaped courtyard. The space was about the size of two tennis courts with a dozen or so raised flowerbeds, each built from railway sleepers and decorative bricks. Several naked cherry trees, stripped of leaves, stood in small groups with ornamental conifers planted amongst them, providing varying shades of green and yellow for year-round colour.

'Very nice,' he said, as he strolled between the beds and strategically placed seating areas. 'You manage all this by yourself?' He asked, smiling back at her as she followed.

'Oh, it's never ending.'

'Here, I'm sure I was at a party in one of those flats over there,' he said, as he pointed towards the far row of doors. 'A few years ago now, but...'

'Hmm, unlikely,' she said, burrowing in her bag for her keys. 'There are dozens of apartment blocks like this in the area.'

'Really? Maybe not, then,' he said, as he followed Daisy in through the back door. 'Hey now, this is a fair size old kitchen! You could fit my whole flat in here.'

'Well, we eat in here too,' she explained, nodding towards the glass table with four yellow melamine chairs positioned underneath.

Hugo nodded approvingly as he looked around the gleaming, state of the art space. With the exception of the hob and oven, all other appliances were concealed behind smooth, off white unit doors. The sparkling, twin-bowled sink sat under the window and in the corner was an expensive looking enamel mixer.

'Who likes to bake?' He asked, as he carefully lifted it, unsurprised with its weighty quality.

'Mum,' Daisy replied. 'You would kill for her olive and sundried tomato bread.'

'No, I'd prefer to ask her instead,' he replied, smiling. He ran his fingers along the smooth, oak work top as they made their way from the kitchen to the back corridor, where Daisy pointed right to the bathroom before leading him to the main hallway, which ran at least twenty feet to the front door.

'Wow, this is impressive,' he said. 'Looks nothing like this from the outside.'

'That's what everybody says.'

'How the other half live,' he joked.

'Dad pays the mortgage actually, but never say that to mum ... ever.'

'Never say what?'

Daisy smiled as she led him to the living room (first telling him where the other doors led to, her own bedroom included). He dropped his jacket to the floor and fell stylishly into the nearest of the two couches facing the television. Suddenly he sat up, an all joking aside look on his face.

'I just remembered. Your mum. She'll be back soon, won't she? We'll have to get our story straight. She's bound to wonder where you were all night. What if she asks even? God,' he groaned, flopping back heavily.

'Oh don't be silly. Mum would never embarrass us like that. Anyway, in the unlikely event that she did ask, I would have to be... entirely honest with her,' she giggled.

'That's not funny, Daisy. You're her daughter, for Christ sake. It'd be like a crime to her. They'd have to cordon the flat off and everything.'

'A crime,' she squealed, slapping her thighs and laughing at Hugo's imaginative escalation to criminality. 'Hugo, mum knows exactly how I feel about you, and last night was *always* going to happen... sooner or later. In our case sooner,' she said, as she approached the couch. 'Can we stop talking about mum now please? She'll be here soon enough.'

She lifted herself out of her chair and dropped onto the cushions, settling in beside him. Before long, she began to wriggle about awkwardly.

'This isn't comfortable at all,' she complained. 'Let's lie down,' she said, sitting up to remove her boots. Hugo forced his off without untying the laces, then lay along the full length of the sofa. Moving out to make space for her, she snuggled in behind, burying herself between him and the back of the couch. Resting her head heavily on his chest, she sighed deeply in contentment. 'Mum always leaves Gran's around mid-day, so she'll be a couple of hours yet,' she said, as she glanced up at the clock before lowering her head again. 'Hmm. It's like last night, all over again,' she whispered.

Hugo nodded as he ran his hand slowly down her body, stopping at her hips and contemplating whether or not to squeeze his fingers under the tight, elasticated waistband. Daisy however, had thoughts of a different nature, thoughts prompted once again by 'what ifs' and negative stereotyping.

'You do know,' she began drowsily, 'that some people would have expected, or even preferred, Ben here with me today. Had things been different last week, he could well have been,' she added, almost casually. 'Of course, I can understand perfectly well why. We'd have made *such* a lovely couple, wouldn't we? All boxes ticked. Everything in its place.'

Hugo smiled at her venomous comments. They carried a deadly humour that resonated perfectly with his own. Of all things about her that appealed to him, her humour was higher up than most and on a level with the very best.

'That's a good one,' he said. 'Yeah, I like that. You and Ben, the perfect couple,' he toasted. 'And I suppose the same people would view us as the *odd* couple?'

Daisy nodded silently. Hugo was most astute.

'Well,' he continued, 'if being normal's what some people expect, then here's to being odd,' he declared. 'And for the record... if anyone asks, I didn't see you as someone in a wheelchair either. And I don't,' he added. 'I just see this girl who's fortunate enough to have met me,' he said, concealing a huge grin and biding his time until Daisy raised her head combatively, only to catch his smile before laying back again. 'Seriously though,' he went on, 'nobody would've said a word if we'd met *before* your accident, would they? Aw look at them, sticking together, they'd say. So what's the problem meeting after it and 'sticking together'? We did it in reverse. So what. Relationships aren't governed by a compass. They don't know east from west or up from down, do they?'

This time, Daisy pushed herself almost fully upright. Propped up on her elbow, she stared directly at him, as if searching for some contradictory facial expression. Finding none, she dropped back down.

'That was such a lovely thing to say, Hugo. You're too good to be true, you know that?' She added. 'And that begs the question, where on Earth did you come from, Mr O'Neill? Well?' She demanded, slapping his chest.

'Ow, from a little farm in the middle of nowhere.'

'That's not what I meant, silly.'

'Southwark, then.'

'Not that either. You're just making fun of me now.'

'No, I'm not. I'm having fun *with* you. There's a difference there, you know.'

Daisy smiled. 'I know. I just love the way you say things, Hugo. You're like some classic novel come to life. So many choice words,' she whispered, 'and the spaces in between,' she added, alluding to his knack for perfect timing and a clear depth of character.

In response, Hugo ran his fingers up through her hair, gently scratching and massaging her scalp with his nails. As she squirmed with pleasure, he smiled to himself, satisfied he found something she clearly enjoyed which required little energy to execute.

'Hmm, you can't possibly know what you've done to me, Hugo.'

'And you, Miss Harris, have no idea what you've done to me.'

'Tell me then.'

'Words can't describe it,' he said, as he pulled her closer and pressed his lips to hers, slowly and sensuously rolling over them, as if searching for entry to a sacred place, a small chapel of love and adoration. Pulling back after several seconds, he finished with a tiny, delicate peck. 'Thought it best to show you.'

'Hmm, you thought right,' she said, closing her eyes and sinking deeper into the soft surroundings. 'This big old comfortable couch was always my favourite,' she whispered, remembering long winter evenings as a little girl, lying under a fleecy blanket with a bowl of treats, a Disney film playing and her mother cooking in the kitchen. Always looking in with a little something extra, she occasionally stayed and stole a flump or two, both sitting warm and excited under the covers. 'Even more so now,' she added quietly. Hugo smiled and grunted softly in agreement before closing his eyes.

Chapter Twelve

'Only me,' Jane shouted, as she backed in through the front door. 'What a day,' she added loudly, as she lowered several plastic bags filled with party leftovers carefully to the floor. Throwing her keys onto the hall table, she smiled when she heard Daisy's voice.

'In here mum. Hugo's here, too.'

'Lovely,' she replied, trying not to laugh. She'd caught sight of Daisy and Hugo through the living room window as she walked back from her car, both of them stretched out on the couch. For everybody's sake, she thought it only fair to noisily announce her presence. 'Give me a minute,' she said as she hung her coat up, then went to the bedroom, where she dropped her bags on the bed before kicking her shoes off. The journey back from her mother's was as tedious and energy sapping as ever, and she looked longingly at her bed, desperate to flop, face first onto it. She felt she'd done little else but drive all weekend, thanks in part to Daisy's desire to be with Hugo, a decision that not only doubled her driving, but effectively ruined her enjoyment of her mother's big day. 'No rest for the charitable,' she muttered, before walking to the living room. As she suspected, Daisy and Hugo were now sitting up with a generous distance between them, watching T.V. Daisy held her arms out to welcome her mother as Hugo stood respectfully. It was a nice, friendly introduction that ensured the ice was well and truly broken. And of the night before... absolutely no mention.

'Daisy, he's no idea where everything is. How mean of you,' Jane said in response to her daughter readily agreeing to Hugo's offer to make them all tea.

'Cups and pot in the unit above the kettle, and the

teabags are in the jar on the worktop. Hmm, I think it says tea on it,' she instructed sarcastically. 'And the fridge is the second last cupboard on the left. Oh, and spoons are in the top drawer. Where else would they be?'

Hugo grinned, knowing full well what she was up to.

'I'll bang on the wall if I need any help,' he said, looking back in.

Jane followed the sound of Hugo's footsteps down the hallway before turning to face Daisy. She wasn't surprised she'd spent the night with Hugo. The more devious side of her nature compelled her to ring their landline number several times over the course of the night. No answer, meant no one at home. And Daisy inadvertently wearing the same outfit the following day merely confirmed what she suspected. But in truth, Jane wasn't interested in the detail of their night spent together. Not that Daisy provided any more information than the fact they spent most of the night talking (knowing Daisy as she did, she believed that to be true), and that sometime after midnight, they fell asleep in each other's arms. No. Their relationship was now very much bigger than their one night spent together, something Jane and *her* mother talked about as they tidied up in the party's aftermath. And though her mother made perfect sense with everything she said about coming of age and letting go, Jane couldn't erase the sentiment she'd either constructed herself or seized from somewhere, long ago.

For one relationship to flourish, another has to wither.

'I could tell, almost from when I first saw him, that he really, really liked you,' Jane eventually whispered. 'And now I know how you feel too. It's actually quite beautiful to witness,' she said with more composure. 'Two young people coming together, building something, working to a plan they haven't yet seen. Who knows what you'll both construct? But I do know one thing. Whatever it is, it'll be magical.'

Daisy held her arms out, inviting her mother's embrace.

'Well, I want you to remember one thing, mum,' she began emotionally. 'I wouldn't be who I am or where I am without you. You're part of this too. You are,' she insisted as she hugged her tightly. Jane smiled as she rested her head on her daughter's shoulder thinking, if only that could be true.

As he waited for the kettle to boil, Hugo switched the light off and stood by the sink, looking out the window. A boiling kettle always seemed to instigate a pensive moment for him, and he watched as darkness slowly enveloped the courtyard. Devouring first the cornered areas, it soon spread over the entire space like some catastrophic oil spill, smothering everything in its path. Several lights flickered on across the square, and he stared intently at the windows for signs of activity. He wondered if anybody, anywhere, could possibly be in his position right now; standing and staring through a stranger's window, being the topic of a conversation taking place just yards away, watching as night arrived like an all-consuming entity. It was irrelevant he would never know. It was a question without an answer, and to him, that was fine. Sometimes not knowing was more inspirational than knowing. It kept the cogs turning and the wheels of thought in motion.

He then heard the sound of movement in the hallway followed by some chatter. Quickly, he filled the teapot and set it on the table. Just as he sat down, the kitchen door swung open and Daisy entered, ducking under Jane's outstretched arm.

Jane sipped and listened as Hugo (*again*) explained the

procedure for the perfect cup of tea, nodding with interest as Daisy offered her own views on the subject. Already it seemed they knew so much about each other, things of little consequence, but with no less relevance than those deemed important. They shared a humour many couples could only dream of, and at times, it appeared their time together could be measured in months, rather than days. She could feel the attraction growing between them, like tiny tentacles reaching out, unseen but immensely powerful, twisting and binding, drawing them together – each tentacle a story, a smile, a shared experience or something indeterminate.

'You'll stay for dinner, won't you?' Jane suddenly said.

'Yes, he will,' Daisy answered for him. 'Do we still have some of that curry in the freezer?' She asked her mother. 'Is there enough for three? You do like curry, don't you?' She asked Hugo.

'Eh yeah, I love curry,' he replied, 'but I don't want to put you out or anything...'

'Nonsense,' Jane said, as she stood. 'It'll take just minutes to prepare. Daisy, can you do the rice?' She asked, as she searched the freezer.

'Can I help at all?' Hugo offered, amidst the sudden rush of activity.

'You can set the table if you like,' Daisy said, before flicking down a packet of Uncle Ben's with a spatula.

'Nicely done,' Hugo said, as he watched.

As he arranged each place setting, the microwave beeped complete and Jane transferred the contents to the pot. Soon, the kitchen began to fill with the sweet, aromatic smell of homemade curry. With the microwave free, Daisy prepared the rice before searching for some Nan bread.

'Ooh, look what I found,' she said, sitting upright with

a plate of her mother's olive and sun-dried tomato bread, which was tucked away at the back of the fridge. 'We'll have this instead,' she decided.

'Red or white?' Jane asked.

'Eh, I'm not sure,' Hugo said.

'Aw he's overwhelmed,' Daisy giggled. 'White, of course.'

'White's good,' he said, just as Jane found a bottle of Riesling in the fridge door and handed it to him. Cutting the heat, she carefully filled a serving dish with the curry before spooning in the remainder of the sauce. Daisy followed suit with the rice, then checked on the bread in the oven before tipping it into a basket.

'Right,' Jane said, looking around, hands on hips. 'Almost there. Oh do sit down Hugo,' she said.

'Thanks. This looks and smells amazing,' he said. 'What a team you are,' he added, as he squeezed to the back of the table, the curry, rice, crusty bread and bottle of chilled, white wine laid out in front of him.

'That's sweet of you to say,' Jane remarked, as she dimmed the lights and set a candle in the centre of the table.

'We've had years of practice,' Daisy added, as she filled their glasses.

'So, you're from Dublin,' Jane said, as she brought the remaining dishes over to the sink.

'Eh, County Dublin actually. A small town called Ballyboughal to be exact. Just to the north of the city?'

'That sounds lovely,' Jane said. 'We lived in rural Norfolk before we moved to Norwich. It was such a beautiful area. So peaceful.'

'Was it now? Mind you, I wouldn't say we were rural as such. We weren't that far from the city where you couldn't see it glowing in the night sky. You could actually hear the roar of the place as well. I remember sitting in the wheat fields at night, just watching and listening, desperate to explore the streets.'

'Yes, cities have that effect,' she agreed, as she slid the plates into the sink. 'They draw you to them, whereas you escape to the countryside from them.'

Hugo nodded. 'That's true alright.'

'Although, in saying that, I'm really quite happy where I am.'

'You wouldn't go back then?' Hugo asked.

'At this moment, no. Maybe one day.'

'Now if you don't mind me saying, you sound a bit…'

'American?'

'Yeah, American.'

'Well, my father was from Philadelphia. Actually I was born there myself.'

'Really? Some city, Philly.'

'Have you been there?'

'I haven't, no. I just love the east coast cities. They're amazing places. The architecture's something else, especially the early skyscrapers. They're like giant, Art Deco monuments. Even the railway stations are something else.'

'They are indeed, although I don't recall seeing any of them first-hand. I was only two when we left for Norfolk, you see.'

'Now that's a hell of a move,' he said, as he rinsed the soapy plates with cold water. 'Philly to Norfolk. I'm thinking American Air Force?'

'You'd be thinking correct,' she laughed. 'RAF Lakenheath to be precise. Home to the 48th. Dad was an engineer. He was posted there in sixty six.'

'Sixty six? Memorable year that.'

'So I gather,' Jane laughed. 'Something about football?'

Hugo looked around, then turned back whispering, 'they'll never let us forget, you know.'

'Indeed,' Jane replied.

'Anyway, it's nice to know something *else* actually happened in sixty-six,' he joked. She looked at him, puzzled. 'Your moving over here?' He reminded her.

'Oh, of course. I'm not at all with it today'.

Hugo smiled a 'don't worry about it smile' before continuing. 'So, I take it you eventually bought a house in Norwich and settled there?'

'Yes. Germany was an option, but after Anne was born, mum and dad decided to stay where they were. And mum's still there,' she said.

'Is she now? In the same house?' He asked.

'The very same,' she answered poignantly.

'That's nice,' he said, as he positioned the last of the dishes on the draining board.

'What's nice?' Daisy asked as she returned from the bathroom.

'Oh hiya,' he said, spinning round to face her. 'Just saying that I didn't know your gran's been in the same house all these years.'

'Yes, it's our family home… technically,' she said. 'Though for how much longer, I don't know.'

'Daisy! Whatever do you mean?'

'Oops. Me and my big mouth.'

'Daisy!'

On the cusp of retorting 'Jane!' (a response she frequently used in disagreements with her mother over the years), she decided to hold back. This was bigger than the unholy state of her room. Bigger too, than social media overuse. Boys even.

'Don't say anything to Gran, mum,' she pleaded, 'not that she said not to say anything. But don't anyway, please.'

'Of course I wouldn't, darling. What has your grandmother been saying?'

Hugo looked at both of them, then turned back to the sink, deciding any form of activity was better than none in the midst of this micro family crisis. He picked up the dish cloth Jane dropped in surprise at Daisy's revelation and started to dry the dishes with as little noise as he could.

'It was when you popped out for soda water or tonic or something,' she began. 'I wanted her to know how I felt and why I needed to come back,' she said, glancing at Hugo. 'I was worried she'd be upset, but she was fine with it. In fact she insisted I do it. I was so grateful I gave her a big hug. And then, totally out of the blue, she started talking about her own life.' Daisy sighed heavily before continuing. 'She sees things differently now, mum. Everything's too big and… unmanageable. She can't remember the last time she was upstairs, the garden's simply huge, she doesn't see Anne much and... I think Bill and Margaret moving last year upset her too,' she added. 'And the new road with all those roundabouts simply terrifies her, houses springing up like mushrooms all over the place, strange faces everywhere. She doesn't know any of her neighbours now, either. It was really sad, listening to her. I want her to be happy mum, but I'd hate to see her leave. I don't know how I'd feel, never seeing her house again. It's like... part of me. Part of us. More than a part, actually,' she added, quietly.

Jane stood, back against the worktop, staring at the floor. Though shocked at what she heard, she wasn't entirely surprised.

'Are you ok?' Daisy asked.

Jane nodded, but was left to wonder why her mother felt it necessary to skip a generation with news of such significance. Or was it really that significant? She asked herself. How many eighty year old women living alone and far from family would consider something similar? Entirely logical, downsizing to a smaller, more manageable house. Or a smaller, more manageable life, to be more precise. How cruel, that after years of glorious expansion, the point in one's life is reached where everything starts to cool and contract, layers built up are stripped away, things undone and discarded… like evolution in reverse. She looked up and smiled at her daughter.

'I'm fine darling. We'll talk later,' she said. 'It's just not what I need right now. What I do need is a long, hot bath. So if you both excuse me?'

'Of course,' Hugo said, stopping what he was doing.

Turning to him, Jane said, 'it was lovely to see you again, and looking so well too,' she added, as they brushed cheeks.

'And you,' he replied. 'Oh and, thanks for dinner. Daisy was right. Your Med breads to die for.'

'Med bread?' She repeated, puzzled. 'Oh yes, I see,' she laughed. 'You're more than welcome. And Daisy, tomorrow… remember?'

'Yes mum,' she answered.

'Oh yeah,' he said, stopping suddenly and turning to walk back to her. 'I almost forgot. Actually no, I didn't almost forget at all,' he admitted.

Daisy frowned, unsure what to expect.

Hugo leaned forward, placing both hands either side of the doorway, satisfied her confused demeanour meant she'd no idea what he was about to say.

'I have to be entirely honest with you about something. And okay, I know it's only been a week but… something seriously strange is happening here. Good strange. Like, really good strange,' he emphasised. 'And I was thinking it can only mean one thing,' he said, as Daisy held still, rigid with expectation. 'Daisy Jane Harris, I actually think I love you,' he declared, as he gently tipped her head by the chin and kissed her, then pulled back, leaving her lips parted in stunned surprise.

But before he could move from reach, she seized his face in both her hands and returned a heated, more urgent kiss.

'Oh Hugo, I love you too!' Wriggling with excitement, she added, 'you so know how to thrill a certain girl.'

'I do? Now that's what you call a result,' he said, straightening up. 'Seriously though, I wanted you to know before you left. I'm not the most direct person in the World when it comes to things like this, so... you know, I...'

'Hugo,' she interrupted, 'shut up. Just leave me with the 'I love you' part, okay?'

Hugo smiled. 'Yeah, okay. Until Thursday then.'

Daisy lingered in the doorway, listening as the sound of his footsteps receded. She blew a long, passionate kiss from the tips of her fingers into the night, hoping it would somehow find its way above the dark, twisting streets of the capital to Hugo. Whispering until Thursday, she backed away from the door and closed it. As she moved slowly down the hallway, she was suddenly reminded of all that occurred and everything they endured within the timeframe of a single week. They had surely earned the right to begin their journey, to proudly display their tickets for inspection, paid for with near disaster and the insane pace of events. She smiled, hugely satisfied, as she realised they'd out-manoeuvred everything and everybody cast before them as obstacles. And she decided next week might not be so bad after all, not least because it made Thursday all the more appealing.

The harsher the Winter, she remembered, *the sweeter the Spring.*

Buoyed with Hugo's touch and emotional declaration, she was about to enter her bedroom, but instead, carried on to the bathroom. She grinned mischievously as she waited outside the door, listening to the harmonious sounds from the water studio (a title she bestowed upon the bathroom as a young child), and her mother's occasional sigh beneath the soft whirr of the fan.

'Mum,' she shouted through the bathroom door, startling her mother and literally causing a splash. 'That's Hugo gone now, so you don't have to worry about putting your make-up back on.'

'Ha de ha. Maybe he'd like me au-natural.'

'Mum!'

'Make-up, darling, not clothes, make-up.'

'Hmm?'

'Daisy, I'm old enough to be his mother.'

'Not quite, mum. I'll have to watch you, clearly,' she warned, as she hurried away, leaving her mother to protest to herself.

Chapter Thirteen

Hugo left his flat, pausing briefly to lift his collar, before setting off down the cobbled lane. He couldn't believe the speed with which Thursday arrived, having expected the week to last an eternity, the days to drag as arduously as Scott hauling men and equipment across the white wilderness of the Antarctic. The reality, as it happens, was very different. Last Sunday seemed only minutes away, and the image of Daisy bidding him goodnight from her doorstep felt as if it occurred just moments ago. Nevertheless, Thursday it was, and with Daisy back from her course, they'd agreed to meet at 'Cooba', a cocktail bar like no other (Dan's was mooted but quickly dismissed... for now).

Throughout the afternoon, heavy, rolling clouds swept overhead, blanketing the city beneath a vast, thermal cover and lifting the early morning frost. Soon, small pools of surface water sprang to life, glistening like molten metal under the orange glow of the street-lamps. He walked lightly and with care as he felt his footing give way on occasion, but quickened his pace when he reached the main road and the smooth, broad pavements. Slowing as he approached the bar's gaudy neon signage, he squinted into the distance, thinking he might catch sight of Daisy, but with no sign of her, he decided to make his way in. Entering the bright, tunnelled foyer, he knew full well what to expect, but was pleasantly overwhelmed when faced with it. The sharp, techno-beat went beyond sound, its frequency making the premises throb and pulsate, while the warm, sweet aroma of freshly chopped fruit and exotic spirits soaked the environment with a distinctive, tropical scent. Already the bar staff were busy preparing row after row of cocktails, with some delivering to numbered tables, others returning with trays of empties. Looking around, he guessed the place was about half full and was about to choose one of the many free tables when, for some reason, he glanced casually to his left. He almost looked away before he realised who was smiling and waving furiously at him. He jokingly looked behind him before heading over, waltzing with restrained composure between the tables.

'Well, hi stranger,' he gushed, leaning into her embrace as he kissed her. 'Had a feeling you'd be here.'

'Hi to you too! It's so lovely to see you,' she beamed.

'And you,' he murmured against her cheek. 'You haven't been here long, have you?'

'No. Just ten minutes or so.'

'You've been busy,' he said, removing his jacket as he nodded at the two Margarita's on the table.

'Well, what was I supposed to do, just sit here? Mind you, that would've been an experience in itself. How amazing is this place?'

'Yeah, it's something else alright. I've never seen another place like it... anywhere,' he added, as he got himself seated and comfortable.

The neon theme continued inside but was restricted to the bar area and much more subtle. Small LED's twinkled in the tiled floor, and the semi-circular bar appeared to hover, as if landing or preparing for take-off. Polished optics with dozens of spirits clung to the glass walls, where coloured lasers shone down through the base of the bottles, while above, neat rows of sparkling glasses dangled freely. The tables were small, round and coated in clear resin with tiny up-lights embedded, which the customer could choose to illuminate or not. Bucket style chairs, dynamically coloured, sat about like large pieces of cubed fruit, and the music that played sounded as if it were only just produced and downloaded.

Contemporary beyond belief, or amazingly retro with a futuristic twist, if Jamaica fused with Cuba and launched a space station, then undoubtably, this is what it would look like. The scientific pursuit of fun and entertainment on an astronomical level.

'Here, have you seen this?' He asked, as one by one, he flicked the table lights on by means of small, rubberised switches on the outside edge.

Daisy gasped as she stared at them.

'Ooh, what a great idea,' she said, as she positioned her drink above one of the lights. 'How beautiful is that?' She added, as the glass itself seemed to burst into life, her eyes widening, as if they too, were desperate for a taste of the action. She moved her glass from light to light across the surface before lifting it. 'So, shall we?' She asked.

'Be my guest.'

'Hmm, now *that's* a Margarita,' she said, the flavours sparking and bursting with the same glittering intensity as the coloured spotlights. 'Lovely,' she whispered, licking her lips.

'Best in town,' he said.

'I could so get used to this.'

'Let's make it our new local then.'

'What about Dan's. Don't they do cocktails?'

'Only in cans.'

'Oh, I love this song,' she suddenly said, putting her drink down and looking up for the source of the sound as she recognised the track; a catchy little number driven by a hard, electronic beat. Silently singing, *excuse me, can I please talk to you for a minute,* she swayed in her seat, then slid her head in impossible fashion along her shoulders, keeping a near perfect rhythm.

Hugo smiled at the comedic nature of her movements and how quickly she supressed any feelings of self-consciousness.

'Come on, join me,' she insisted wickedly, holding her hand out.

Hugo reacted with mild horror.

'You serious? I've got zero co-ordination.'

'Nobody has zero co-ordination. Come on, it'll be fun.'

'No chance. I've never been able to control my body. It's got a mind of its own. And I certainly can't do that.'

'Do what?'

'That... thing with your head.'

'This,' she laughed as she accentuated the move, then further complicated matters for him by gracefully rolling each shoulder in time. 'Come on,' she said, grabbing both his hands, 'we'll do it together. But wait till the main beat returns.'

However, on return of the verse, Hugo completely mistimed and only just managed to execute a vague sideward nod. Daisy, meanwhile, executed her manoeuvre with such precision and timing, he felt his effort laughable. And laugh she did, her shoulders shaking almost uncontrollably.

'Yeah well, told you I had zero co-ordination.'

'I'm beginning to believe it,' she said as she settled back, breathless with laughter. Looking around the venue, her eyes drifted towards the bar area, now a bustling hive of activity. Underneath the huge, brightly lit gantry of lights and drinks, several bar tenders, busy as bees, energetically prepared an assortment of cocktails. Daisy watched as they lay them on the counter, each an art form with its own distinct glass, colour and adornment.

'This place shouldn't work, Hugo,' she suddenly announced, turning back to him, 'but it absolutely does. It all works... somehow. It's like... everything is blended to perfection.'

'It is yeah. Just like a cocktail. In fact, the place itself is a giant cocktail.'

'Yes, it is! It's exactly like a cocktail,' she replied, as she fought the paper parasol for control of the glass, finally catching the salty rim with her lips. 'You know, you're really rather clever,' she whispered between sips. 'It's a real humorous intellect. I like that.'

'Do you now?'

'Uh huh.'

'Well, seen as we're entering a mutually appreciative stage, I'd have to say that,' Hugo leaned forward mid-sentence, 'you're no intellectual slouch yourself. Good craic as well.'

'Ooh now, what's this before my eyes?' She asked, having just returned from the ladies. Hugo had fortuitously beaten her back to the table, quickly setting down two long-stemmed glasses, brimming with the colours of warm sunlight and tropical fruit.

'Well, sticking with tequila, which incidentally happens to be fairly healthy for a spirit, I thought you'd fancy the one and only tequila sunrise, as popularised by the Eagles, Cuban asylum seekers, and sun-worshippers the world over.'

'You so thought right,' she said, as she positioned her glass over the spotlights for yet another micro light show. 'This is too much,' she said with a serious frown, switching to astonishment as she sipped the cool, iconic liquid. 'Oh wow. This is...'

'Yep. Paradise in a glass.'

'Oh my God, I've never tasted one this good before... ever,' she insisted. 'And yet, I don't actually like Tequila. Strange, isn't it?'

'Yeah, weird alright. It tastes great with everything... except itself.'

'So, what's healthy about Tequila, then?' She asked,

taking another long, cool sip before laying her glass down.

'Everything... apparently. Good for digestion, fat burning, circulation. It's supposed to be a powerful mood enhancer as well... so they say.'

'And who would 'they' be?' She asked, grinning.

'*They* would be the makers,' he answered, grinning back.

'There's a surprise. But hey, who cares. My moods lifted already.'

'Eh, you've only had one.'

'I know. What a lightweight.'

'Or a cheap date.'

'Hey!'

'Kidding.'

'Oh I love this song too,' she said abruptly, as she moved to the rhythm of yet another of her favourite tunes, this time a re-mixed Eighties classic.

'Don't even think about it,' he warned.

'I wasn't going to,' she retorted. 'I don't mind dancing here… all by myself.'

Hugo smiled at her play on words.

'So, you all set for the weekend?'

'Hmm, kind of. Just a few things to throw in a rucksack. Katie's coming round after lunch, so I've got all morning to get ready. The train leaves at four, gets in about half five. Her mum and dad will pick us up from the station. They're really lovely.'

'What's the plan for tomorrow night?'

'Dinner with Katie's mum and dad,' she answered. 'I think her sister will be there too. She's home from Uni. Reading week,' she laughed. 'Like, does anybody actually *read* anything on reading week? I think not,' she scoffed. 'Then, out on the town on Saturday night. Maybe even look for a cocktail bar. There must be one in Bristol, don't you think?'

'Big place, so I'm sure there must be.'

'I'm teasing you. We'll just go for a meal. Nando's probably, then home.'

'Don't be daft. Away and have a ball,' he half insisted.

'Aw, you're so sweet,' she said, 'but Nando's is fine. And then,' she added excitedly, 'Sunday night, and I'm all yours. One hundred, million percent.'

'One hundred percent's fine,' he laughed.

'Well if it isn't the one and only Hugo Neill, back on his feet... or his arse more like it,' the voice boomed.

Hugo glanced quickly at Daisy before spinning round in his seat.

'Jack my man, Diane. How's things?'

'Great bud, just great. How you doin'?'

'Ah, getting there, you know?'

'Taking its time, is it not,' he joked, on seeing Hugo's injuries.

Diane slapped his shoulder. 'Jack.'

'What?' He asked. 'Just saying is all.'

'We only heard yesterday,' she said apologetically.

'What a bunch of little bastards eh?' Jack continued, as he stared at Hugo's face. 'They get them yet? Probably not. The old bill aren't interested unless you're stealing something or trolling someone.

'True enough. Eh, Daisy, this is Jack and Diane. Jack, Diane, Daisy.'

'Nice to meet you Daisy,' Jack said, grabbing her hand. 'Proper nice,' he said to Hugo, on the quiet, but loud enough for Diane to hear. Rolling her eyes, she noticed Jack staring at Daisy's wheelchair and subtly elbowed him, catching him in the ribs. Jack jumped slightly before breaking into the opening guitar riff of a certain rock classic. Badly. Like really bad karaoke. Only worse. 'Dahhh, dahh, dah, dah, dah... dah-dah...'

'Don't worry, he always does that,' Hugo informed a bewildered Daisy, later explaining that Jack was born in nineteen eighty two, the year 'Jack and Diane' was released by John Cougar. Thirty years later, when Jack met Diane, the song became their 'official' anthem. On Jack's insistence, it has to be said. Diane thought it rather laboured.

'Glad you're feeling better Hugo,' Diane said, as she lightly patted his shoulder. 'What a thing to have happened.'

'Yeah, should've seen it coming but... must've had my eyes closed,' he joked. 'Didn't know where I was for a few days, you know, headaches and that but, grand now, thanks. So, where you two heading?'

'Simone's,' Diane said. 'Jack's treat, isn't it?'

'Yeah, my treat, so she chooses the dearest bloody steakhouse in town.'

'Ah, she's worth it, is she not?' Hugo reminded him.

'Tell you later,' he said, winking.

'You see what I've got to put up with?' Diane moaned, as she turned to Daisy.

'Oh, I can see that alright,' Daisy laughed, as she raised a brow in Hugo's direction.

'Jesus, talk about ganging up. I'm outta here,' he muttered. 'Nice meeting you Daisy and eh, good seeing you up and about, bud.'

'Yes, and we must have a night out sometime,' Diane added.

'What about the wedding?' Jack said. 'We'll see them there. You're going aren't you?' He asked, turning to Hugo.

'Eh, yeah, we are, I think,' he replied. 'Just the reception, though.'

'Yeah, like you, me and everybody else.'

'Dave and Carol Ann are getting married in Bali,' Hugo explained to Daisy.

'Oh how lovely,' she said. 'What a dream start to life together.'

'Nah, don't fancy Bali,' Jack said. 'AYIA NAPA,' he roared.

'Jack, shush,' Diane snapped. 'Come on, we'll be late. Sorry guys. Table's for 9.'

'Ok, ok. Chow,' he said, playfully punching Hugo's shoulder. 'Later bud.'

As they walked away, Diane looked back, smiling warmly as she waved at Hugo.

'They're really nice,' Daisy said.

'Yeah,' Hugo agreed, 'they're alright.'

'I think Diane quite likes you,' she said, as she chased her straw around the glass before gathering it with her lips.

'What you mean?'

'She *likes* you, is what I mean.'

'No, she doesn't. Well, not in *that* way.'

'What way would that be?' She asked, smirking.

'You know like… ah hang on now, I'm not going there.'

'And where would that be?'

Hugo laughed awkwardly as he reached for his drink, while Daisy, grinning now from ear to ear, took a sideways step.

'So, is Jack one of your 'darts' friends?'

'Jack? No. Only met him last year. Anyway, he's barred from Dan's.'

'Barred! What for?'

'Dancing on the tables, none of which could take his weight.'

'He is a big chap, isn't he?'

'Very.'

'And how long have you known Diane?'

God, he thought. She's not letting go of this, is she?

'Eh, a few years now.'

'A few years? So you knew her before Jack?'

'Yeah, I did.'

'I see,' she replied, nodding studiously.

'Oh you see now, do you?' He said, finishing his drink and laying his glass down. With little else to do with his hands, he resorted to rocking the glass on the surface before scratching the side of his face and rubbing his chin. 'Ok,' he sighed, 'you win. We went out a couple of years back... but only for a few weeks,' he quickly emphasised (as if the fact should carry some significance). 'She moved up to Derby. Something to do with work, I think. I had to go back to Dublin, cos I hadn't actually moved over here by then, and it just sort of... fizzled out, really. So it was hardly...'

Daisy smiled triumphantly.

'I knew it,' she gloated 'I totally figured that out. And she still has a thing for you. But don't worry Mr Casanova, I think it's really sweet,' she giggled. 'Jack doesn't know, does he?'

'Eh, no, clever clogs, he doesn't.'

Daisy leaned over the table whispering, 'don't worry, your secrets safe with me.'

'Here now, don't even joke about it.'

Still whispering, Daisy added, 'what I'd really like to know is what she sees in him, I mean... compared to you? I'm sure he's really nice, but...'

'Jack's alright, once you get used to him. They're actually well suited, the pair of them. They don't look too deeply at anything and they're always out and about.' Leaning forward, he added, 'he's eh, legendary, apparently... in a certain department.'

'Oh,' she said nonplussed. 'I thought it was the other

way round, big boy, small manhood.'

'Hmm, not always.' he said. 'Promise me one thing though.'

'What?'

'Don't ask me how I know.'

'I wouldn't want to,' she shuddered. 'And Dave. Is he a Lord of the darts ring too?' She asked with cinematic sarcasm.

'Dave is, occasionally of the ring,' he laughed.

'But not Carol Ann.'

'No, not Carol Ann.'

'And how do you know her?'

Hugo was about to answer, but unfortunately swallowed the wrong way, forcing him to clear his throat – something Daisy immediately seized upon as being diversionary. With a look of genuine disbelief, she simply said, 'oh no, not Carol Ann as well.'

'Well,' he started, having decided it was best to come clean, avoid the third degree and move on, 'we were a bit drunk one night. And it *was* actually one night, so...'

'Hugo,' she said in astonishment, 'I wasn't actually being serious. Oh my God, you were rampant back then. Was no woman in London safe from you?'

'Actually yeah, they pretty much all were. I bored most of them to distraction. Suppose I just wanted company really.'

Daisy shook her head.

'Clearly I'm more perceptible than they were.'

Hugo looked at her, confused.

'You're anything but boring, Hugo.'

'Ah right... thanks. By the way, that wedding invitation? It says, Hugo *plus* Partner.'

'Hmm, I'm not sure, Hugo. I wouldn't know anybody there and…'

'And you'd knock them all for six, no doubt about it.

Anyway, you'd be with me,' he reminded her.

'Yes, and half your ex's.'

'All the more reason to show me off then,' he argued. 'Wait till they all get a load of you as well.'

'You don't mean that.'

'I don't mean it. You serious? Look at you. Gorgeous, sharp, funny, caring…'

'Go on,' she giggled.

'Well... if you *must* know, you've only been in my life a week yet... you're already the best part of it,' he said quietly and with palpable honesty.

'Oh Hugo,' she cried, as she reached across the table. 'I was just expecting you to say I was clever or something. That was so sweet.' Squeezing his hands, she added, 'of course I'll go with you. When is it?'

'Saturday the twenty-third. Eight till late.'

'We'll go for nine.'

Chapter Fourteen

Hugo walked up to the front door of Daisy's flat and rang the bell. As he waited, he looked around the quiet cul-de-sac, finding it hard to believe that in the three weeks or so since they met, this was the first time he'd actually called for her. About to ring again, he stood back on hearing what he assumed to be Jane approaching, then quickly ruffled his hair for his preferred, unkempt look.

'Hugo, how lovely to see you,' Jane said, 'do come in.'

'Thanks,' he replied, as he brushed cheeks with her. He waited until she closed the door, then followed her through to the living room, choosing the couch opposite to the one he and Daisy cavorted on a couple of weeks ago.

'Let's have a look at you,' she asked, before he sat.

Hugo obliged by removing his coat to reveal an off-black, fitted suit with a crisp white shirt and coloured tie. Indicating a twirl with her index finger, he spun round awkwardly for her.

'Very smart,' she said, as she approached and picked one or two pieces of fluff from his lapels, before smoothing them down with the tips of her fingers. 'I'll let Daisy know you're here.'

Hugo sat down, pulling at his collar which felt at least half a size too small. He undid the top button, then tightened his tie back up to cover it.

'Mu-um,' he suddenly heard. 'Where's Hugo? Tell him to come through. I'm decent now.'

'Honestly, Daisy,' Jane muttered, as she walked back to the living room. Poking her head around the door, she said, 'Madam will see you now.'

Hugo laughed. 'I'm honoured,' he said, standing. He walked across the hall and stood for a moment in Daisy's doorway, watching as she sat, sideways on her chair and leaning into the mirror. Aware of his presence, she twirled around.

'Just the person,' she said, spinning to a halt. 'Ooh Hugo, look at you,' she gasped. 'What a lovely suit. Come here,' she ordered.

Hugo smiled. 'Yes mam. By the way, its goin back tomorrow,' he joked as he picked at it. 'But enough about me,' he added, as he absorbed the glorious imagery in front of him. 'You look... amazing. Absolutely gorgeous, in fact. Hollywood royalty, even.'

'Aw, do you think?' She said, as she threw her arms above her head, twisting and turning her hands as if dancing privately and provocatively for him.

It was, most certainly what he thought. And if he could deliver more superlatives, he would. Time and again, Daisy took his breath away, but this was a time like no other. She really *was* as he described. Reclining like some A-List movie star, she was dazzling to behold in a black, sequinned evening gown, her long, blonde hair cascading like liquid gold over her bare shoulders. Even before he approached, the warm, sweet smell of her perfume captured his one remaining sense.

He leaned forward and lightly kissed both her cheeks, then pressed his lips against hers. About to abandon himself in her embrace, she shifted to one side.

'Right,' she said officiously, as she gently pushed him away. 'I have a very important task for you to perform.'

'Task? Don't tell me, a decent cup of tea, yeah?'

'Tea?' She grimaced. 'I don't think so. We're on Prosecco tonight. No, this task requires a steady hand and a degree of artistry.'

Hugo frowned for a second or two before suddenly remembering what she meant by a steady hand.

'Toenails, yeah?'

'Yes. Kneel, Sir Hugo.'

Hugo pulled his trouser legs up and dutifully knelt before her, then sat back on his calves, shifting for comfort.

'Towel,' she pointed (to cover his thighs), before selecting a deep purple varnish. She placed both feet on his legs and pressed down gently, tapping lightly with her big toes.

'Right then,' he said, as he began to unscrew the top, 'where's the little... paint brush thing?' He asked, looking around.

'Don't be silly. It's part of the top.'

He smiled as he removed the cap, then dipped the tiny brush back in before wiping the excess on the rim.

'Hold still,' he said, as he selected the big toe on her right foot. At first, Daisy giggled with his touch but, like all girls everywhere, proved herself fully capable of enduring any form of tickly or painful contact in the name of any form of beauty application. Hugo deftly moved from toe to toe, touching just once, the skin around one of her nails with a tiny sliver of varnish, which he meticulously wiped away. Lifting her left foot, he proceeded every bit as diligently, finishing on the tiniest of nails, which required the most delicate touch of the brush. Task complete, he lifted each foot by the heel and blew over her toes.

'All done,' he said, as he sat up, impressed with his achievement. It was then that he caught Daisy's affectionate smile of appreciation.

'Thank you,' she mouthed. 'That was so sweet. And they're perfect,' she added as she wiggled her toes.

She lifted her feet off his legs and dropped the towel to the floor, by now littered with everything from tops and tissues to used tufts of cotton wool, squashed and browned, like toasted marshmallows. She turned to the mirror and angled it as she prepared to paint her lips, the last act to perform, other than looking for her heels. As she finished sketching the outline, Hugo positioned himself behind her, and saying nothing, took the lipstick from her hand. Fully aware of his intentions, she pouted her lips as Hugo, watching her image watching him from the mirror, delicately coated them. Just as he finished, she took his hand and slid the lipstick over her open, rounded mouth before closing her glistening lips around it, wholly unaware her mother was watching from the doorway with a glass of wine. It took several seconds before Jane realised exactly what her daughter was simulating, her eyes widening in shock as it registered. She turned away quickly, leaning against the doorframe, hand on her chest.

'Daisy,' she gasped, as she made for the kitchen. She searched for her shoes and slipping into them, returned to the bedroom, making as loud a heeled noise on the tiled floor as she could. She smiled when she saw Hugo had straightened up and moved away. 'Hugo, I should've asked. Would you like a glass of wine too?'

Daisy couldn't believe they missed Dave and Carol Ann's biggest moment of the night; the romantic dance, the choreographic equivalent of tying the knot, followed by the cutting of the cake. For someone as well rehearsed and organised as she, to miss such a key moment was, in her book, inexcusable. (To not even consider the notion that eight p.m. had some significance was possibly even harder for her to take.) But once she'd been introduced to everybody and 'sank' a few, she soon relaxed and began to enjoy herself. Hugo's friends in particular couldn't have been nicer. She and Sam, who proudly introduced himself as Hugo's best friend, took to each other straight away. Michael and Pat, two of Hugo's oldest friends, were clearly inseparable and so naturally funny, she felt they could have provided entertainment for the night itself. She loved the way they interpreted for each other on her behalf, where occasionally one would protest *"sure that's not what I said at all"*. *"No, but you meant it"*, the other would argue. Then there was Jack. Boisterous East Londoner and wannabe pub landlord who, as usual, found something to moan about—the table being 'miles away' from the bar for a start. And the bride and groom; Dave, less vocal than the lot of them, but no less handsome and charismatic, and Carol Ann, whom Daisy thought looked remarkably like one of those upbeat weather girls she recognised, but never caught the name of. She looked beautiful in a tight-fitting mermaid style dress and a wispy, delicate veil held in place with a diamanté tiara. Daisy couldn't keep her eyes from her, nor could she stop herself thinking Carol Ann's look was probably the one she'd adopt for her own big day. But that was *strictly* between her and herself, she thought, as she watched her cross the dancefloor.

She looked around the venue, compact but beautifully proportioned, with space for a hundred people or more. Guests arrived by lift, or down a grand, sweeping staircase leading to a pair of art nouveau style doors, which opened onto the function suite. The dance area featured an exquisite wooden floor laid in a herring bone style, with decorative, wrought iron columns positioned at each corner. Spotlights picked out the huge wall mirrors and other reflective surfaces, and the music played just above the excited chatter of the guests. Each table carried a stunning floral bouquet, with complimentary bottles of red and white, and the impeccably dressed staff, barely noticeable, were always at hand.

About to check her phone, Daisy was suddenly joined by a jaded but exhilarated Carol Ann, busy working her way table to table and trying desperately to find something different to say to each guest.

'Daisy,' she said, as she slipped in beside her. 'I'm sorry. I haven't had a proper word with you yet. How rude am I?'

'Oh no, you're not at all rude. You've got loads of people to see. By the way, you look absolutely beautiful, Carol Ann. And what a gorgeous dress,' she added, close enough now to study it and run her fingers over the sparkling satin fabric.

'Aw, thank you Daisy,' she replied. 'But hey, what a stunner we have here, eh? Just look at you,' she said. 'Love the dress, by the way. Jimmy Choo's as well,' she remarked, as she caught sight of her heels.

'Mum's actually,' Daisy admitted.

'Yeah? I'm wearing something of mum's too, but I can't show you here,' she laughed. 'But really, isn't Hugo a lucky old devil? What is it about the Irish, eh?'

'I feel just as lucky, actually.'

'Yeah, Hugo's lovely alright.'

'This is such a beautiful place,' Daisy said, looking around. 'I had no idea it even existed. It's Perfect for a wedding. Is it Edwardian or something?'

'No idea, Daisy, but yeah, it's the business alright,' she agreed. 'Cheers dad,' she said, as she raised her glass roughly in his direction. 'Thanks for coming tonight, by the way. Nice having all our friends who couldn't make it to Bali.'

'I can't believe you got married in Bali, Carol Ann. What was it like?'

'Daisy, it was un-be-liev-able,' she said. 'Honestly. We were there for just five days, but…oh my God, what a beautiful place. It was hot, but not unbearable and everybody was so friendly and…' she sighed, reliving some moment she'd yet to describe. 'We got married standing on an old, rustic wooden pier, which was actually in the hotel grounds, so no photo bombers in sight,' she added, laughing. 'We couldn't have wished for a better setting though, the clear, blue sky, the sea behind us, the white sand, the palm trees.'

'Aw, it sounds wonderful, Carol Ann. Here's to you both,' she said, raising her glass.

Diane then appeared and joined the toast.

'Cheers too,' she said, 'or three, as it happens.'

'Cheers Diane,' Daisy said. 'Please… sit down.'

'That was the intention, Daisy. I'm whacked. Here, has someone had a swig of this?' She asked, holding her glass. As Carol Ann turned to look, Diane seized her chance, hugging her best friend tightly.

'She's bloody gorgeous, is she not?' She gushed, as she followed up with a heavy, prolonged kiss on her cheek.

'I was just saying that!' Daisy said. 'And what a beautiful dress,' she added. 'It's just... heavenly, Carol Ann. I can't take my eyes off you.'

Diane and Carol Ann looked at each other, then back at Daisy, smirking mischievously.

'Oh stop it, you two. I only meant it was a beautiful dress, that's all.'

'Stop what?' Carol Ann asked.

'I think it's heavenly too,' Diane admitted. 'But I wouldn't get my left leg in it. *You'd* look divine though,' she said to Daisy.

'She'd look divine in a bin bag,' Carol Ann added.

Daisy shook her head.

'I'm not saying another word. I couldn't possibly win with you two on my case.'

Daisy then noticed Diane studying her and Carol Ann closely, as a dressmaker would.

'Your dresses would fit each other like gloves. Why

don't we hit the loo and swap them? Imagine the reaction if you came out, looking like each other.'

'No, that would bring bad luck,' Carol Ann said.

'Who says?' Diane asked.

'Everybody says,' she replied.

'Rubbish. You make your own luck in life. You don't import it.'

'I'm worried now,' Daisy interrupted, visualising a forced costume change.

'Oh now, don't you worry,' Diane said. 'You'll be fine... after some more of that,' she added, nodding towards the bottle.

'That's not making me feel any better,' Daisy said, now looking distinctly fearful.

'Aw, that's so cute,' Carol Ann said. 'You look so sweet and vulnerable.'

'Do you think?' Daisy asked, grinning. 'I've worked so hard on this look over the years.'

Diane and Carol Ann looked at each other, then burst into laughter.

'Have we just been played there, Caz?'

'Looks like it.'

'Never even saw it coming.' Diane said.

'Me neither. The sweeter they are, eh?' Carol Ann acknowledged, before lifting her glass. 'To Daisy,' she toasted, 'who played us both as skilfully as a fiddle.'

'At least he's guaranteed a lift home now,' Jack said, laughing at his own joke and encouraging his audience to follow suit. Being a big, overpowering man, most reluctantly complied. 'Wait'll you see, she'll have a set of arms on her like me before you know it,' he continued. With a muted response to his remark, he held his arms up in a Charles Atlas pose. 'Like this, look.'

'That what you think, Jack?'

Jack turned quickly to see Hugo standing right behind him.

'Hugo, speak of the devil. Come on in,' he said, motioning him towards the ring.

'I don't think so, Jack.'

'Ooh, we're not good enough for you, are we?' He replied, wriggling his fingers under his chin, an expression Hugo absolutely hated. At that point, everybody else shuffled awkwardly and looked down, saying nothing. But not Jack. He squared up to Hugo.

'What's your problem, Hugo?'

Hugo thought of several 'appropriate' things to say, but realised there weren't many people alive Jack wouldn't take out to preserve his ego, and Hugo wasn't sure if he was part of that particular club or not.

'Screw you Jack,' he settled on, before heading off to the bar.

Jack turned back to face his friends, closing the ring once again and muttering dismissively to himself. He finished his pint and looked at the empty glass, then up at the bar. Sam noticed his intent.

'Here big man, I'll get this.'

'Whatever,' Jack replied.

Sam, with a handful of glasses, tracked Hugo's enraged path to the bar and squeezed in beside him.

'You ok?' He asked.

'He's a total arse, so he is,' he spat back. 'I'm pissed off now Sam, and I can't even do anything about it.'

'No. You did something, Hugo. You walked away, and that was the right thing to do. Sure you can't win when he's in that kind of mood.'

'I can't believe he'd take me out over that. And he bloody well started it. What's up with him lately?'

'God knows, Hugo. He's been a pain all night and

Diane's just leaving him to it.'

'Daisy was right. What on earth did Diane see in him that we all missed?'

Then he realised he'd been away for longer than intended and strained to catch a glimpse of Daisy at their table. He almost jumped when he saw Jack's huge frame towering above her.

'Jesus Sam, he's over at the table.'

Sam spun round, scanning the area near the dance floor.

'Who, Jack?'

'Yeah. I'd better get over there.'

Sam grabbed Hugo's arm.

'Hang on, Hugo. He's not likely to have a go at Daisy now, is he? Play it calm and see what happens. From what you've told me about Daisy, she can more than handle the big twat.'

Hugo nodded and relaxed. Even Jack wouldn't be so stupid. And if he were, Daisy would probably make light work of him anyway. He looked at Sam and smiled. He was a good friend, level-headed, totally unbiased and completely non-confrontational – being five foot eight, slightly built and ginger necessitated that. Sam was great in heated situations, particularly like the one just past, partly due to the fact that people like Jack viewed him as 'not worth the effort'. Not that Sam was concerned. He was happy to lie just below the radar – a space relatively risk free and one that offered a unique perspective on life. Sam knew things about people few people knew he knew. Rumours and anecdotes, gestures and glances all fell to him from above, unwittingly discarded by those who disregarded him. Sam, therefore, was a good person to have onside. In his own words, he drank and he knew things. Hugo liked that.

Jack, unsettled with the awkward silence that followed the incident, glanced repeatedly over at Daisy, watching as she sat by herself. Not having a pint glass to hide behind added to his discomfort, and with Hugo over at the bar, he made his decision. Without saying a word, he left his circle of acquaintances and walked over to Daisy's table, making his presence known by pulling out a chair.

'Hey Daisy.'

Daisy looked up. 'Hi Jack,' she replied. 'Oops, just as well we're not on a plane.'

Jack frowned for a moment, then laughed as her joke registered. She was alright, he thought. In fact, she was alright to the point he began to cringe inwardly at the jokes he made at her expense. He wondered if he could tone down the more explicit of them, or even avoid mentioning them altogether. But he knew to get this particular job done properly, he'd have to repeat them verbatim, apologise and hope that was the end of it. And if that was no less than she deserved, it was *exactly* what he deserved.

'Mind if I sit?'

'Of course not,' she answered, turning to face him. 'So, what's up, Jack?'

'You alright there, Daisy?' Hugo asked, as he arrived back from the bar.

'Yes, why wouldn't I be?' She replied. 'I've just been talking with Jack and everything, I can assure you, is fine. So please, can we all be friends again?'

Jack stood up.

'Sorry Hugo. I was well out of order earlier.' Looking down at Daisy, he smiled, adding, 'she's top drawer, man.'

As Jack held his hand out, Hugo glanced at Daisy,

wondering what on Earth she said to defuse the situation.

'She is that, Jack,' he said, grabbing it. 'And no worries, apology accepted.'

'Just as well for you we didn't come to blows, eh?' Jack suddenly barked, 'You'd be back in Guy's before you knew it,' he laughed, as he lightly punched his arm. 'Later, bud.'

Hugo nodded goodbye and sat down beside Daisy.

'He had to get that in, didn't he? You see, you can never quite be sure with Jack. It wouldn't take much for him to...'

'Oh don't worry about Jack, Hugo. You're *totally* safe now,' she said, grinning. 'Like I said, I'm going to look after you, remember?'

Midway through the night and with everything at full swing: drink flowing, music blaring, dancefloor packed, the reception almost descended into total chaos. Three or four children found themselves a large bag of party poppers and proceeded to frighten the life out of the elderly guests with their indiscriminate 'popping'. In the explosive aftermath, clouds of (supposedly non-flammable) paper-esque ribbons drifted across the venue, some floating lazily onto the tables before combusting on contact with the Bali themed candle holders. Amused, Daisy watched as staff frantically gathered the streamers and patted out the flames, while parents apprehended and chastised the tiny culprits – but not before they'd burst several glitter filled balloons, dusting the premises with flecks of silver paper which seemed to find their way everywhere. Daisy had already flicked showers of the glittering particles from her shoulders and was busy fishing some from her drink, when she noticed Diane bursting through the double doors, stopping only to acknowledge a familiar face before making her way over to their table.

'Hi guys,' she said, dropping to the seat as she reached for the wine. 'May I?'

'Of course,' Daisy said, pushing her glass over. 'I'll join you.'

Diane sighed, then took a long sip of wine before shaking her head as she lowered her glass.

'I just met Jack outside the gents. He's off home. Best place for him just now.' Looking at Daisy she added, 'I can't believe what he was saying about you, Daisy. I'm flipping well mad at him. Disgusted, actually.'

Daisy reached over and lightly patted the back of her hand.

'Hey, I've heard much worse, trust me. But he did apologise, Diane, and I know he meant it, so don't be too hard on him. I'm totally fine... really. So's Hugo, aren't you?' She asked, turning to him.

'Yeah,' he said with less conviction. 'The trouble with Jack is he plays to the audience, and before you know it, he's in a situation where he can't back down. He's had a skinful as well, so that doesn't help things,' he added. 'But it's cool, seriously. If Daisy's fine, I'm fine.'

Diane smiled gratefully at them. She wouldn't have been surprised had they both raged at Jack's behaviour, so she found their charitable response all the more welcome. Lowering her head, she leaned forward.

'Look,' she began, almost in a whisper, 'I know I shouldn't be saying this but, can you two keep a secret?'

Daisy and Hugo looked at each other before looking back at Diane, nodding.

'We've been trying for a baby,' she said.

'Diane, that's wonderful,' Daisy squealed. .

'Well, it ain't wonderful yet. Trying's the operative word. We've both been having tests to see why I'm not conceiving. I got the all-clear. Plenty of happy little eggs in the basket yet,' she said. 'But Jack,' she sighed, 'well, his count is low, which is a surprise, cos everything else is working well. Forgive me for putting it like that,' she added. 'So IUI, here we come. No idea if that will work. We get three shots, then it's private,' she explained. 'Look, I'm sorry he's been a pain. More than a pain, bloody awful, actually. But he *is* really cut up about this. He's worried he won't ever be a dad, and that would make him the only one in his family. So fingers crossed it works. But don't say a word, please.'

'Diane, we would never say anything, ever,' Daisy assured her.

'Stupid fool me. Of course you wouldn't,' she said as she stood, smoothing her bodice with the palms of her hands. 'Look, he may have apologised, but he's not out of the woods yet. He's getting it later... big time.' Squeezing Hugo's shoulder, she reached over to kiss Daisy's cheek. 'Thanks guys,' she said as she made for an exuberant Carol Ann dominating the dance floor.

After she left, Hugo turned to Daisy. 'Still no excuse for his behaviour. Partly explains it, I suppose. I mean, it can't be easy hiding the fact your tadpoles can't swim to save themselves now, can it? God, that's brilliant, so it is. Wait till I tell everybody,' he said, taking his phone out. 'Joking,' he quickly added.

With Jack gone, Hugo's friends flocked to the table, appearing from nowhere like birds to the feeder, hungrily rejoicing in the absence of a razor-clawed family pet. Unsurprisingly, the talk turned to his comments from earlier, but with Daisy, Hugo and Sam saying nothing, the rest of the table left the subject, drifting away on the lightening mood. Carol Ann then appeared with two extra bottles of wine: white and red, and left them with Daisy.

'A gift for my favourite table. Say nothing though,'

she hushed, finger to lips, before vanishing.

'Aw, thank you so much, Carol Ann,' Daisy called after her. 'She's so lovely,' she said, turning to Hugo. '*Red* wine, anyone?' She joked, as she stashed the white wine by her side.

'Actually, I think I'll have white,' Hugo said.

'Not this time,' she replied, holding tight to the bottle.

'In that case, we'll all have red,' Pat shouted, 'except your man there. Sorry Hugo, but if you leave for the bar now, sure you might get a drink before midnight.'

'Oh all right,' Daisy relented. 'You can have one. Where's your glass?' She asked, just as Hugo grabbed the bottle and emptied a sizeable amount into his lager. 'Oh that's clever. What a waste of white wine.'

Hugo grinned and took a healthy swig, then immediately wished he hadn't.

'Jesus, that's awful,' he groaned, as the rest of the table clapped the surface, shouting, 'neck it, neck it, neck it.'

Hugo took an even healthier swig. 'God, it's still awful,' he said, looking around for something to spit in.

Daisy shook her head, then produced an extra wine glass.

'Don't say I'm not good to you. Anyway,' she added with a satisfied smile as she filled it, 'that's for earlier.'

'Sure what exactly were you up to earlier?' Michael shouted.

Daisy waited patiently for the laughter to subside.

'Hugo,' she said, pinching his cheek, 'has the softest of touches.'

'Don't be saying things like that now,' he pleaded, as they erupted once again.

'Sure that's down to the pink rubber gloves he uses,' Pat said, joining in. 'Keeps his hands all lovely and soft,' he joked, rubbing his together.

'Yeah, only thing is... he's never washed a dish in his life,' Michael roared.

'Oh, I wasn't talking about dishes,' Daisy suggested seriously, adding to Hugo's discomfort and raising the decibel level at the table to such a height, that people across the suite looked over in curiosity.

'Just one more before you go, hand on heart,' Diane promised, as she hauled Hugo to the dancefloor for the third time in an hour. When it became apparent what the song was, the space soon filled with couples holding on to each other, the number not quite pacey enough for individual antics. Daisy looked on, grinning at Hugo simulating being strangled by a clearly buoyant and emotional Diane. She then started to laugh as they spun erratically around each other, the stand-out couple on the dance floor for all the wrong reasons, both of them enthusiastically incapable. Hugo admirably held his own until the end and bowed respectfully at the songs conclusion. Diane would have none of it however, and lunged forward, hugging him tightly. She blew a kiss at Daisy before looking around for another partner, willing or not, as yet another of her favourite tracks started.

After a quick scan to check they'd left nothing behind, either on the chairs or under the table, they headed for the exit, saying goodbye to several familiar faces on the way out. Just before entering one of the lifts, Hugo noticed Sam making his way back from the gents.

'Hey, Sam,' he shouted as he saw his friend. 'Wondered where you got to.'

'Nature called and I answered,' he laughed. 'That you off now?'

'Yeah, that's us away,' he said. 'We'll see you again sometime.'

'You will indeed, Hugo,' he said, as they both slapped

each other's shoulders. 'By and large, this was a fairly good night.'

'It was,' Hugo agreed. 'Eventually.'

'Sure meeting this girl here was the best part of it,' he said, as he leaned over to kiss Daisy's cheek.

'Aw, it was lovely meeting you too, Sam. We must meet again soon.'

'We will indeed, and eh, don't forget what we talked about now, Daisy,' he said as he winked indiscreetly at her.

'I'm already on it,' she replied, as Hugo frowned at both of them.

'What are you not to forget?' He asked.

'If we told you, we'd have to kill you,' Daisy replied, giggling.

Hugo nodded, before suddenly realising what they were both concocting. God, as long as it's not Katie, he thought. That wouldn't be fair on poor old Sam. On anybody, even.

Chapter Fifteen

'Nobody could survive on Mars like that. Not even Matt Damon. And he's *very* well equipped.'

Hugo laughed. 'Yeah, a bit fanciful alright, growing potatoes on Mars... and not an Irishman in sight,' he said, as he switched the DVD off, then reached for the wine bottle.

'Things escalated far too quickly as well. It was the same with Gravity. I like a slower build up to the big event, *and* more of a back story,' she added, critically.

'Listen to Ms Scorsese there,' he retorted, waving the bottle in front of her.

She shook her head as she stretched and yawned before falling sideways onto the space he vacated. Too slow to react, all he could do was shout in frustration as she coveted his seat, spreading over it like a hot blob of tar.

'Hey,' he growled, grabbing her. 'Be off with you. That's my patch.'

'Squatter's rights,' she protested, as he attempted a forced eviction. 'Ow! Don't Hugo, that's really sore.'

'Sorry,' he said, rubbing her wrist. 'Want me to tickle you instead?'

'Don't you dare.'

'Well, I won't if you have another one. Come on, you might as well finish it... before it gets warm.'

Daisy laughed. 'That's the best excuse for finishing a bottle of wine I've ever heard.'

Looking wearily at the time on her phone, she succumbed once again. 'Go on, then,' she said, reluctantly. 'A small one!' She shouted, as he emptied the bottle, filling her glass almost to the rim. 'Hugo, I've got work tomorrow. Honestly, I've never drunk so much since I met you.'

'There you go then. Being with me is just one long, endless party, isn't it?' He said, as he passed the glass to her.

'Pity I can't remember any of it.'

'Like the wedding?'

'Don't remind me.'

She hadn't fully recovered until midweek, and any reference to alcohol prior to Wednesday made her dash to the toilet or reach for the nearest watertight receptacle. Worryingly, she couldn't quite remember clinging to the last bottle of white wine, the story of which Hugo relayed with such conviction and attention to detail, she felt must be true. He took equal pleasure in reminding her that *she* was the one who hauled him into her flat in the early hours, where an amused, but slightly awkward Jane sat in the kitchen with both of them, as they greedily consumed the bottle of wine she'd opened earlier. Hugo could barely remember getting home, which was sometime after three. One up from Daisy however, who struggled to remember events beyond the reception.

Sitting forward, Hugo lay his glass on the table and looked at her, lying semi-comatose, head resting heavily against the arm of his couch. Like a cat, she lazily opened an eye in response to his movements.

'So, what do you think then?' He asked, as he muted the tv and lifted his glass. He'd 'floated' the idea of them going over to Ireland for a few days after dinner, but worried it was a bit ambitious – jetting off on holiday after only a few weeks together, not to mention the little matter of the hotel. He couldn't assume she'd be happy to share a room either.

Groaning as though in pain and with considerable effort, Daisy pushed herself upright and squinted at Hugo, hair plastered to the side of her face. She reached for the large, yellow scatter cushion and wrapped her arms around it, resting her chin on its edge. She'd adopted this, the biggest one, as her 'comfort cushion'.

'Hmm, I've been thinking about that,' she began, frowning. 'I'm not sure I'd like to,' she said, her reply proving more than just disappointing for him. He was about to respond with a list of concessions, but she held her hand up, palming him to silence. 'As I said,' she continued authoritatively, now sporting the widest of smiles, 'I'm not sure I'd like to... I'd love to,' she squealed.

'What? No way. You wouldn't, would you? Seriously? *(she nodded furiously)* God Almighty, you had me going there.'

'Yes, of course I would. What a lovely surprise,' she said, playfully elbowing him. 'So looking forward to meeting your fam, too.'

Hugo grinned. 'Yeah, they should be out by then. Hang on, will you be able to get off work?' He suddenly remembered.

'Hugo, I've got loads of days to take before April. I haven't had a holiday in a year, remember? When were you thinking of going?'

'Next Saturday, back on Tuesday. And here's the thing. It'll be over Valentine's as well,' he added, flushed with excitement. 'How romantic's that, eh?'

'When's Valentine's Day?'

'When it always is. The fourteenth of Feb.'

'The day, dummy.'

'Sunday. And there's loads of hotels in and around the airport as well, so...'

'Oh yes, I forgot. The hotel. What did you say about us having two rooms again?'

'Madam shall have her own suite, should she wish.'

Daisy dropped the cushion and beckoned him closer.

'As if,' she said, as she grabbed hold of him.

Chapter Sixteen

'I was getting ready to go home, well... back to London, when mam came into my bedroom and sat and watched me pack. "Is that you going back, Hugh," she asked, as if hoping I'd change my mind, you know? It didn't feel right, leaving her like that, but I had to go. Yeah, I had things to get on with but, I wanted to get away as well. I'd been there nearly two weeks and...' He shook his head and sighed as Daisy listened impassively. Taking a sip of black coffee, he decided he didn't want that particular taste and reached for the tiny milk jug. Pouring a little in, he spooned it slowly and methodically through the dark, tarry liquid, listening as the cup seemed to chime with nostalgic reverence.

'Then she started talking about dad, what he was like and that. And it was nice to hear, actually. Sort of... therapeutic, you know. It was dad's idea to switch from farming to property, then into holiday lets. He was quite the entrepreneur, selling off farmland, snapping up property down the docks, cashing in years later. Mam was no slouch either,' he stressed. 'She was with him all the way. And things were much harder for her, you know, having kids to mind and everything. Then of course the obligatory, 'where they met story', which happened to be on O'Connell Bridge, back in the summer of fifty-nine. Mam and her friends were in Dublin for the day. Must've been a Saturday,' he guessed, looking to one side. 'Anyway, there they were, four girls up from the country, shopping and stuff, just having a laugh, you know. They were crossing the bridge when this street photographer stops them. Now I don't know how he managed it, but Dad somehow ended up in the picture as well! The original fifties photo bomber,' he said, grinning with pride. 'Well, he might have been persuaded to join in,' he admitted. 'Great picture, though. Dad, arm around mam, smiling like a big eejit. Her words, not mine! And out of the four girls, she's the only one looking up at him, killing herself at something he'd said. She can't remember what it was, though. Pity, that. But he must've made a good impression, cos he saw her home later that evening. Turns out, she only lived a couple of fields away! As the crow flies,' he added. 'It was ten minutes by car. Dad joked he was going that way anyway. Luckily for him, Mam had as good a sense of humour! Anyway, the rest, as they say, is history.'

'Hugo! That's an incredible story. Your mum and dad met because of this... street photographer. What if your dad had been held up elsewhere, or if he crossed the street? What if he said no to having his photo taken?'

'Yeah, I wouldn't exist,' he replied casually. 'None of my family would. We wouldn't be here today, chatting over a cup of coffee. Who knows what you'd be doing right this minute, but I wouldn't be here. Not a thought, memory or fragment of me anywhere.'

'Oh my God. That's really scary,' she said, suddenly understanding how fragile everything was. She understood the impact of chance events on relationships – they were the prime example, with all the tiny events and decisions that conspired to bring them together. But what hadn't occurred to her was the impact those same events had on *actual* existence, how they dictated life and death, determining with an almost divine quality who should exist and who shouldn't. 'It makes you wonder who we have to thank for being alive, let alone being here today... with each other.'

'Everything and everybody, basically. It's all connected. The entire universe. But you'd go mad trying to make sense of it all. For a start, look at that photographer. Barely two minutes in the existence of one single person out of hundreds of thousands of people in Dublin that day. What was his life like that morning in Dublin? Why did he stand where he did? Why did he ask Dad to join in? Street photographers never do things like that. How did he even get there? If he took a bus, what was the traffic like? Did the driver run a red light, or slow down to let a little old lady cross the road and, if that were the case, what about that little old lady? What propelled her to that moment in time and space that made such a difference, helping to create me twenty years later?' Hugo looked down at the dregs of coffee as he swirled them around in his mug, debating whether or not to drink them. 'Can you imagine the odds on something like that happening? How do you even calculate it? All the millions of variables in the life of just one person. Trillions to one, I bet.'

'My brain hurts now,' she said. 'But, we made it... in spite of chaos,' she added, laughing.

'Yeah, in your face universe,' he said, finally deciding to drink the last of his coffee. 'Fancy another one?' He asked, as he stacked the cups and saucers before hooking the tiny milk jug, creatively sculpted as a farmyard urn, around his little finger.

They'd only just arrived in the charming Irish town of Howth, disembarking at its delightful little train station. Ornate and colourfully adorned with winter flowers, it was staffed with people so friendly and comfortable in their positions, that Daisy felt the place imaginary. "Mind yourself now," came the call as she left the train. "Where you fella's from," was the question on ticket inspection. "Howya," was the greeting as they passed the turnstiles. Were it not for Hugo pushing forward, she would have stopped and talked to each and every one of them. Once out of the station, they worked their way along the main road to the harbour front, where luxury villas stood next to their Georgian counterparts which sat alongside shops and bars hewn from centuries old warehouses. Aged and fiercely proud of its heritage, the bustling, contemporary atmosphere blended perfectly with the ancient activity of sea borne trade and all things nautical, proving the town was equally proud to be forward thinking and modern. They decided on a chic little coffee house with Wi-Fi and cakes. What more could a girl want? Daisy thought as she entered, already checking her iPhone.

'Ooh, you're so bad,' she said, as he slid the enormous Danish pastry towards her. 'I'll never eat all that.'

'Sure I can help you there,' he said, lifting his coffee. 'Bon Appetit.'

Daisy smiled and raised her cup. 'Bon Appetit back. Oh, and cheers to that photographer too. I'd be talking to the wall right now, were it not for him.'

Hugo laughed. 'Indeed.'

Having consumed the pastry (with a little help from Hugo) and the few remaining crumbs which she gathered by fingertip, Daisy pushed the plate to one side and leaned forward, eagerly insisting on some more stories from the O'Neill family archives. Hugo smiled, having anticipated such a scenario. Saving what he considered to be the best for last, he proceeded to tell her the truly remarkable story of the day his father stumbled across a tragic, bungled robbery at a North Dublin bookies, swollen with takings thanks to the Cheltenham festival. Hugo had been shocked to silence as he sat on the bed listening to his mother's recollections of the events of that day, humbled to tears when she handed him something that had such enormous sentimental value, it could never be calculated.

Dublin, nineteen seventy two, and a glorious Spring day saw Michael O' Neill walk back to his car following a particularly gruelling business meeting. His associates had decided to grab some lunch at the Gravediggers pub by Glasnevin cemetery, but Michael opted to return home to the farm. He couldn't wait to lose the shirt and tie, relax and attend to whatever needed attending to. With most things hovering between nearly done and just started, he was rarely short of a task to undertake. Being perpetually active, was how he relaxed.

Jacket slung over his shoulder, he was within sight of his car, which he'd left on Phibsboro Road just along from Crossguns bridge, when he noticed the police car across the road, sitting outside a bookmakers, doors open and parked as though abandoned. Curious, he stopped for a closer look. That was when he heard it. Being a farmer, he knew immediately it was a shotgun. He also knew there were few, if any, reasons to discharge one in a built up area. The obvious reason alarmed him, and instinct told him to back away. But Michael O'Neill was old school, a man of honour and integrity, and doing nothing wasn't an option. Decision made, he rushed to his car, threw his briefcase and jacket on the rear seat, then crossed the road. As he approached the bookies, two police officers suddenly appeared at the entrance, one, a young female making a desperate attempt to get to the car and the other, a sergeant who turned to confront whoever it was behind them.

'Dad didn't know the Sergeant had already been shot. But it looks like the poor fella knew it was fatal. That's why he tried to save his colleague. Then the gunman fired again, took the side of his face off. Some of the shot hit the woman as well. Right in the neck. Dad recognised the gun; an old sawn-off double-barrelled thing, so he knew

163

he'd fired his last round. He just... ran at him, shouting and waving his arms and that. The guy wisely bolted. And I mean wisely. You ever seen 'Taken'? A big, uncompromising man was dad,' he reflected.

Surveying the scene before him, Michael knew there was nothing he could do for the Sergeant, but the woman, clinging to life, had reached the car and propped herself up against it. He knelt beside her and took his tie off, where he rolled it up and pressed it to her neck, then grabbed her hand and swapped it with his. She'd begun to gargle and choke in her own blood, so he carefully brought her forward to help her breathe. He hadn't noticed that a crowd had gathered, forgetting even that he'd screamed for an ambulance. It was unusually hot for a spring day and the sun beat down upon the blood soaked scene, its heat tempered by a light, persistent breeze. Lorry's, buses, cars all trundled past, and from the corner of his eye he saw someone check their watch, as if late for an appointment. Jackdaws squawked from high in the beech tree across the road, its leaves emerging like a billowing, green mist, and a graceful swan broke free from the slimy green surface of the nearby Royal Canal, majestically taking to the air. And he saw the indifference, he felt the omnipresence, he understood the unrelenting nature of everything, its interminable cycle terrifying, yet resplendent. There was nothing to life but the desperate urge to cling to it. There was no cruelty or benevolence, no predetermination or blissful afterlife. Just life and death. On and off. In and out. And in that moment, he knew he was right. A simple, God fearing farmer, no longer would he be.

'He thought she was like, trying to tell him something, so he leaned closer, but she could hardly breathe, let alone talk. Then she tried lifting her arm to touch him but... she hadn't the strength to do that either.' He sighed and shook his head, as if the news he was about to relay to Daisy had only just reached him. 'By the time her hand hit the ground, she was gone. She just wanted to connect in some way, you know, to show her appreciation. She knew what he tried to do for her, and even though he couldn't...' Hugo paused, clenching his teeth together. 'Even though he couldn't save her, at least her final moments were peaceful ones, thanks to dad. His kindness was the last thing she ever experienced,' he added, smiling sadly. 'I'd like to think what happened earlier was totally eclipsed, you know, because of dad being there. That's why it's important someone's with you when you die. It's the last thing you see in this world and the first thing you remember in the next. It's what you take with you... if you go anywhere, that is.'

Hugo's thoughts turned to Sunny, his spaniel, lifelong companion and best friend ever who died just as he came home from school, as though he too, had been clinging to life long enough to say goodbye. Two days he spent slipping away, momentarily surprising everybody with a sudden lease of life. Then, that afternoon, a final breath drawn, a tightening of his little body, and he was gone. Not a human tragedy by any means, but the death of a special being, nonetheless. Hugo cried for days, hating everything and everyone. He knew what he felt, but being twelve, couldn't get close to expressing it in words, instead, using his emotions as a weapon, targeting those around him. He buried his beloved Sunny, close to the woods by the edge of the field of barley where they spent their summer days, hunting and fetching, marking it with a huge granite stone he could barely lift. No one was allowed to attend his sad little ceremony, but Kathleen stood and watched from a distance, tears streaming down her dirty little face. He heard her scream, "I loved him too, you know. I loved him too", she said, as she approached cautiously.

'So, he just sat there, holding her, soaked in blood. Then he thought of their families and that crushed him. Mam said he wondered if he'd be the one to have to tell them. Funny, the things you worry about,' he said. 'Anyway, the following year, on the day it happened,' he added, 'mam and dad received a bunch of flowers from her family. Spring ones, along with a laminated photo card with a little message. It's an Irish thing,' he explained. 'Mam gave me the card after he died. Imagine that, he kept it all those years.'

Hugo then took a deep breath and prepared himself for what he was about to say. 'In her darkest final moments, you were an angel of light and serenity. God bless you and your family for evermore,' he recited, somewhat hesitantly, but pleased to have done so verbatim. 'Beautiful, sad words,' he added quietly. 'Liz, by the way. That was her name. Liz Osbourne, just twenty-four years of age. She joined the police at twenty-two. The sergeant, Frank, was forty-eight, kids and everything.' He sighed, shaking his head very slightly before adding, 'I'm gonna say their names all the time now. Keep them real.'

Hugo looked up at Daisy, almost for the first time since he started the story, and saw her face, grief stricken and wet with tears.

'Hugo,' she started, quietly and slowly, 'that's the saddest thing I've ever heard. Those poor police officers. And your dad. What a wonderful person he must've been,' she whispered. 'And you knew nothing of this till after he died, when your mum told you?'

'Not quite. We'd heard there was a robbery and that two police officers were shot, but we were sort of led to believe dad arrived too late to do anything. We'd no idea the trauma of the whole thing. It seemed like ancient history as well, you know. The seventies! God, that long ago?' He said, grinning. 'So the enormity of what happened evaded us completely. And it *was* enormous. Someone else could've died that day. Then what?'

Hugo looked through the large window of the café towards the east wall of the harbour, and recalled a stubbornly vague memory of him running along its promenade as a child, ice-cream in one hand, stick in the other. Who was that little fellow running to or running from? How old was he? Did he know how fortunate he was to even be there? Wrestling with the recollection, he searched for ancillary clues that could complete the picture and make sense of it all. Frustrated he couldn't, he drifted back to the present just as Daisy leaned towards him.

'What actually happened to your dad... if you're okay to talk about it?'

Hugo smiled. 'There's not that much to talk about,' he said. 'Very sudden it was. He hadn't been feeling well for a while and mam was constantly at him to see about it, at least have a chat with the doctor, which of course he didn't. He'd been a bit breathless in his last few days, struggling with things he wouldn't normally have struggled with. Clear warning sign really. Then one night, that was it. Poor mam,' he sighed. 'She went to bed the usual time but woke up about 2am. Dad hadn't joined her so she went downstairs and... there she found him, where she left him, in his chair. Heart attack. Probably around midnight.'

'Hugo, I'm so sorry.'

'I know, thanks,' he replied, touching her hand. 'It was one of those... life before and life after moments, you know? Everything stopped at that point, then re-started.

But different. Darker. And I know none of us got to say goodbye to him either, but at least they all saw him every day. I hadn't spoken to him in over a month.'

'You had your life to lead, Hugo. And you were on your own too. Your dad would've known that.'

'Yeah, I know but, if I'm honest with you, it wasn't that I was too busy or anything,' he admitted, 'I just found it hard to talk to him, you know? So naturally, I kept putting it off. I'll call him tomorrow, I'd say, no... the weekend, no... next week! Hard to talk to indeed. Maybe it was me that was hard to listen to. Either way, I should've made the effort. But that's me, isn't it? And that's what I've got to live with,' he added. 'Funny how mistakes you make haunt you forever, yet good things seem to... vanish in time.'

Daisy was about to challenge his last sentiment, but instead held his hands, squeezing them in recognition of his painful admission.

Hugo looked up, smiling weakly. 'Hey, I'm sorry, I...'

'Sorry! What on earth are you sorry for?'

'Well, I've been going on and on all morning. Not exactly uplifting now, is it?'

'Hardly,' she retorted. 'This has been an amazing morning, and we still have the rest of the day... and tomorrow!'

Daisy leaned closer and gently tugged both his cheeks.

'And another thing. We girls don't want excuses for emotion. Ever! You get that?' She demanded, as she reached under the table for her bag.

'Yeah, I get it.'

Noticing some activity out of the corner of his eye, he turned to see two young lads staring through the window at him, laughing hysterically and pulling their own cheeks. Very funny, he thought, before looking away for fear of encouraging them. Seconds later, they appeared at the next window along, now fully in view. This time he laughed, whereupon they issued a thumbs-up before moving on, shoulder charging each other and occasionally looking back.

Oblivious to what was happening, Daisy busily reapplied her make-up, only briefly looking up when she heard Hugo laugh.

'What are you laughing at?'

'Nothing,' he shrugged as he gazed at her. 'Just a couple of lads making faces through the window, that's all.'

'Oh,' she said, disinterested.

Watching with fascinated affection as she traced the outline of her mouth with a dark red liner before filling in with her customary bright red lipstick, he felt a sudden, overwhelming urge to reach across the table, grab her gorgeous, round face with both hands, and press his mouth to hers. That would give those lads something to gawp at, he thought. Thrilled with the notion, he licked his lips, subtly, just as she smacked hers together on a tiny square tissue, which she glanced approvingly at before folding neatly and tucking away. Catching his stare, she glanced once again over the tiny, enamel backed mirror.

'What?' She asked, this time faintly irritated.

'It's still nothing, honest,' he answered. 'I just love looking at you.'

'Me too. I mean, I love looking at you too,' she giggled, 'not me. Well... sometimes me, I suppose,' she said, grinning in the mirror.

'So, Miss Rembrandt, do you think you'll be done anytime soon, like... today, maybe?'

'Hmm... two minutes,' she said, twisting the mascara top.

Hugo sat back, then immediately sprang forward, feigning impatience like a small child. He couldn't wait to 'hit the old pier' once again and marvel at the sheer wonder of the place: its scale, astonishing views, the living history underfoot, the magnificent, fortified lighthouse sitting proud at its tip, fully half a mile out to sea.

And to Hugo, it wasn't a gamble that Daisy be sufficiently impressed to make the long journey down the vast granite promenade with him. She'd be well up for it. He knew that.

And who knows, he might even stumble across some of his discarded memories, catch up with that little fellow he caught sight of a few minutes earlier.

His last statement spurred a confused but intrigued Daisy into action.

Chapter Seventeen

Crossing the road, they made their way towards the relatively bland and uninspiring section of quay that led to the huge east wall of the harbour. Wondering where Hugo was leading her, Daisy frowned suspiciously and began to question whether or not she would enjoy the experience as much as he insisted she would. But as they passed the silent, out of season ice cream van and squeezed between the rows of cars, the great pier suddenly and dramatically announced itself, looming with the visual equivalence of an orchestral movement. Daisy was taken aback at the scale of the massive structure, which reached further out to sea than she thought possible. It was enormous, she declared. So much so, she could barely see the end of it.

Like a grand ocean liner from the golden age of travel, the promenade pointed seaward as if set for sail, only never to raise anchor, her voyages fuelled instead by dreams. The elements too, powered the nautical illusion: the strong, relentless headwind, the waves rushing past, flags like frenzied gulls, flapping furiously. Greased ropes and rusty chains hung from the white tipped capstans, and the boarding steps, now cast in stone, led to the water's edge, where absent launches ferried phantom seafarers ashore and back. One could almost hear the entity grumble and groan, feel even, its heavy movement as it sought to break free and gain momentum.

She shielded her eyes as she strained to take in everything laid out before her. 'Is that a lighthouse at the tip?' She asked.

'It is, yeah. That's where we're headed. Think you can make it?'

'Think I can make it,' she retorted, as she donned her sunglasses and pulled her ski hat over her ears, leaving just her lips and the icy tip of her nose exposed. Pulling her jacket tight against the wind, she followed Hugo as he strolled along in front of her.

Despite the elements, the pier was busy with people from all walks of life: tourists, locals, merchants, touts 'encouraging' holiday makers to board tiny, brightly coloured boats for sea trips around the coast and out to the islands, stripped of colour and silently awaiting visitors. The chilly, persistent wind that reddened their faces, numbed their ears, and though the low winter sun cast little warmth, it sprayed out a wonderful light, bathing all in its sharp, crystal clear luminescence. Everything in view sparkled: the tips of the waves, the shiny metal mastheads, the bronze capstans, the polished portholes of the bobbing yachts. The shimmering, visual spectacle blended with the unmistakeable salty smell of the sea, and the soft, rhythmic clanging of rope on metal was capped with the occasional sound of a ship's bell. A feast for the senses, it was the most compelling of places for Hugo, and it mattered not that he hadn't returned in many a year, he would always feel drawn to it – despite the loose pledge he made with Kathleen never to return. He turned to face Daisy, where she smiled and reached her hand out. Grabbing it firmly, he playfully dragged her along the bumpiest section of the pier.

'Oh, you do have a wicked side to you, don't you, Mr O'Neill?' She said in a shaky voice, as she laughed at the sound of it.

Before long, they passed the regimented rows of the marina which dominated the waters within the harbour, stopping at the section of pier that swept gracefully inwards, like a giant, protective arm, flexing its muscle protectively over its sheltered space. The elbowed midpoint, they were now within clear sight of the lighthouse, perched furthermost at the fingertips. It's function now reversed, rather than warning them away, it seemed to draw them closer.

'Is that another promenade up there?' Daisy asked, pointing to what looked like a second, elevated walkway, where fewer people, almost all of them teenagers, opted to walk.

'Yeah, sort of,' he replied, smiling to himself at the sight of her pompom moving in rhythm with her head. 'It's basically the top part of the wall, which then slopes down to the sea on the other side. We used to go fishing there, years ago,' he added, as he acknowledged a passing young couple with triplets, each identically dressed, legs kicking excitedly in sync. Waiting until they passed, and before Daisy could react, he suddenly ran towards the upper walkway. Jumping as he reached it, he scraped for a foothold, then pulled himself heavily up the near vertical, granite edifice. Standing atop with self-satisfaction, he breathed deeply and shouted above the wind.

'Woo-hoo, that was tough. Haven't done that in years.'

'Bravo,' Daisy clapped. 'There's life in the old dog yet.'

'Less of the old... and less of the dog,' he yelled back. Looking towards the sea, he saw several people milling about the rocks, some casting lines over the water, others scouring the salty little pools between the boulders for cockles and mussels. He shouted to her as he pointed to the base of the slope. 'Told you. There's a few people fishing there. They're off their heads,' he added under his breath, as he watched some almost lose their footing on the slimy, moss-covered stones. In saying that, he couldn't quite suppress an urge to follow suit and do a bit of 'scouring' himself. Like he used to. Kathleen, too.

173

Kids made great 'scourers', he remembered. And though the fleeting memory was a painful one, it brought a tiny, recollective smile to his face – and a certain tune to mind.

Grinning, he spun back to face Daisy before spontaneously belting out the first few lines of *Molly Malone* (who, as it happened, wheeled her own wheelbarrow through streets broad and narrow, filled with those very same molluscs). When finished, he lowered himself down using his heels as brakes and jumped the final few feet before walking over to Daisy. A group of passing American tourists clapped and cheered, and Hugo accepted their applause by bowing towards them. 'Thank you very much,' he said, Elvis-like.

'Nobody told us live entertainment was thrown in,' the lead American said to his friends as they approached.

'Live maybe, not so sure about entertaining,' Hugo said.

'Oh no, we loved it,' he joked. 'You folks from around here?'

'I am, yeah. Daisy here's from London.'

'Is that right? Tell me, my friend,' he continued, 'this place is huge, but Howth itself is a small town. Why so?'

'Trade and mail, basically. Known the old Brits though, they probably had troops in mind as well. We Irish were a right old handful,' he laughed. 'They built an even bigger one at Dun Laoghaire, just along the coast,' he added, pointing south.

'More troops, right?'

'Something like that. Where you from yourselves?'

'Boston, buddy. You been?'

'No, I haven't. I'd love to, though. Take in New York, Philly as well. Maybe next Valentine's,' he said, smiling at Daisy.

'Hey now *that's* romantic,' he said as he slapped Hugo on the shoulder. 'You two folks want a Valentine's photo?'

'Actually yeah, that would be great, thanks,' he said, handing the American his phone as Daisy removed her hat and sunglasses. Offering to return the favour, one of the tourists gave Hugo their camera; an expensive, over-complicated SLR. Just point and shoot, a confused Hugo was told, much to his amusement. There was a time in Ireland saying something like that could get you arrested... or worse.

'What are your plans for the rest of the day?' Hugo asked.

'Golf at... Sutton, is it?' He replied, turning to his friends for confirmation. Yep, someone shouted. Clontarf tomorrow, someone else added.

'Perfect weather for it,' Hugo said, feigning interest. Mark Twain didn't go nearly far enough. Golf wasn't even a good walk spoiled for him.

'Sure is,' the American agreed. 'Well, it was a real pleasure talking to you folks. You have a nice day and take care,' he said genuinely, as the group nodded and collectively turned.

'That was so sweet of you,' Daisy said, as the Americans ambled away. 'No one's ever sung to me before.'

'And no one's ever listened to me,' he said, as he crouched beside her, perilously close to the pier's edge, the slop of waves as they rebounded from the harbour wall, clearly audible. 'These are great,' he remarked, scrolling through the photos. 'Here, have a look' he said, as he shielded the screen for her.

Hugo logged out and put his phone away before making himself as comfortable as he could on the hard, granite flagstones. And for a few moments they just sat, content, like a pair of restful, dusty lions on the scorched plains of the Serengeti, lazily watching the activity around them. Boats of all sorts were busy chugging back and forth, with some making for the dark waters of the open sea and the promise of raising sail to the wind. Several children raced along the promenade towards the harbour's mouth for the chance to wave at the pilots as they passed, and a beaten, rusty fishing boat limped across the basin to the distant west wall and the critical care of its maintenance yard.

'You know,' he began, having absorbed the entire scene in front of him, 'they couldn't have known what this place would *ultimately* be used for when they built it, could they? I mean, it's a day-tripper's paradise now, but originally, it was a dirty old working harbour. Easy to forget that, isn't it?' He added, now leaning heavily against her.

Daisy nodded thoughtfully. 'So when was it actually built?'

'During the reign of the Prince Regent so, two hundred years ago... give or take a year or two. He wouldn't have seen anything like it, anywhere,' he said proudly. 'The biggest man-made basin of water on the planet. Packed with ships from... everywhere.'

'That must've been some sight,' Daisy said, as she tried to imagine the vestiges of modern life absent, instead, the harbour brimming and bristling with sail and mast from all corners of the empire, vessels loading and unloading wares hauled by horse, cart and human hand.

'Yeah, it would've been,' he agreed. 'I think his footprints were cast here somewhere. The Prince, from his first visit,' he explained. 'A few handshakes on the quayside before shooting off to Dublin Castle for affairs of state, then on to Slane Castle for an affair of a different kind.'

'What do you mean, an affair of a different kind?'

'Lady Conyngham. His mistress and true love, apparently. They say he had the straightest road in Ireland built... just to get there and back as quick as he could.'

'Oh, how romantic,' Daisy sighed. 'All that effort for a few brief moments with someone you truly loved. If it's true, of course.'

'Course it's true! His coach is in a museum somewhere. They call it his passion wagon, if you know what I mean,' he added, standing up to loosen his legs.

'Ooh, I know *exactly* what you mean,' she said, looking around to ensure no one was within hearing range. 'All that frolicking about in a shaky horse-drawn carriage. Hmm, not unlike a train, if I recall,' she added.

Bemused, Hugo stopped and turned to face Daisy, before walking slowly backwards in front of her.

'Eh, a *train*, you say? Would you care to like... elaborate on that?'

'Not particularly,' she answered, nudging him off the subject.

'Fair enough,' he replied, after a short pause. 'Anyway,' he continued, distracted but undeterred, 'that was the Prince Regent for you. And then there's Captain Bligh, no less. Harbour master at Dublin he was. Redesigned the whole port. Chartered the waters around here as well.'

'Really?' Daisy asked, surprised such an iconic English maritime figure helped shape the nautical landscape of the Dublin bay area. 'Dublin must've been very important for the British, was it?'

'*Very* important it was. Dublin was second only to London in power and influence back then. In fact, we were the *first*, second city of the empire. Other cities claim the title now, which is totally pointless without having an actual empire to be second in,' he laughed. 'But we were the first. Put us top of the social calendar as well. Even then it was a mad, party city,' he laughed. 'And then, almost overnight, the party stopped.'

'Why, what happened?'

'It's complicated, but the act of union in 1801 did most the damage. The Irish houses of parliament were mothballed and London assumed direct rule. With that, went Dublin's political influence and social standing. The empire was protecting itself in a way that was impossible to challenge. No need to start a war. They just changed the law. Typically British, wasn't it?' He added. 'After that, the wealthy and influential just... drifted away, leaving behind their grand Georgian mansions, most of which were carved up and rented out to the poor and the destitute. Eventually, Dublin became home to the world's first inner city ghetto. Really,' he insisted. 'Long before New York or anywhere else. We went from session to recession in a matter of years.'

'I find it hard to believe they could do something like that. Especially with all the effort and investment put into places like Howth. It's almost as if they cut their nose off to spite their face, isn't it?'

'They didn't give two hoots. Job done, so to speak. You see, it wasn't about money. They'd plenty of that. It was about power. Dublin had to be put in her place, which she was, and before long, she became the forgotten city. Everything seemed to bypass it, including the industrial revolution. And while the Victorian era brought all sorts of opportunities to other cities, huge public buildings and stuff, it just didn't happen here.'

'Do you think they knew the effect that this ... Act would have had?'

'I don't know if they did. They wouldn't have cared anyway,' he added. 'So yeah, they beat us alright, but they couldn't defeat us. We love this city. It's ours, you know, in spite of the English influence. We built it.

Crafted it with big Irish hands and then filled it with musicians, storytellers, authors, playwrights. You may wonder where you are when you're downtown in other cities around the world, but when you're in Dublin, you know you're in Dublin. It's unmistakeable. That says something about the people here, you know.'

He slowed to allow Daisy time to catch up.

'But there's no acrimony now. Not that there was much of that anyway. You see, the empire by that time was just a big soulless machine. Who could you blame?' He asked, holding his arms out, as if beseeching thousands of onlookers. 'Who could you write to? Don't forget, the empire controlled you lot as much as it did us. You were victims too, you know. The whole world was. So why keep whinging about it,' he added, smiling. 'Especially on a day and in a place like this.'

'That's really very generous of you, Hugo,' she remarked. 'I've only been here a short time, but already I know generosity fills the hearts of all Dubliners, the Irish too. It's in your DNA. All of you.'

Hugo wandered over to Daisy and hunkered down beside her.

'What are you up to now?' She giggled, looking around as he took her hand.

'Well now Daisy, on behalf of the people of Ireland and *especially* the people of Dublin, I would like to say, that was a wonderful thing you just said. It actually makes me want to cry.'

'Really? Oh Hugo, you're so soft and wonderful,' she said, pinching his cheek. 'You always make me want to cry too,' she said.

'I don't, do I?' He asked, surprised and alarmed.

'Yes. But for the right reasons.'

Saying nothing, Hugo stood and walked around behind

Daisy, gripping the handles firmly.

'Now, let me assume control for a minute,' he said, as he prepared to push her. 'Stop it now,' he warned, as she tried to deploy the brakes. 'I'll tip you into the harbour there like a bag of rubble,' he threatened.

Daisy gasped. 'I can't believe you just said that. I'll have to watch you,' she muttered, as she allowed herself to be propelled the rest of the way.

Soon, they reached the long row of concrete workshops situated across the promenade from the tiny boatyard, where several yachts and smaller boats sat, upended and helpless outside their natural environment. With the lighthouse in view, Hugo dropped his pace on seeing the American tourists, milling about the imposing structure, taking photographs and slapping the smooth granite walls, the sharp crack of contact audible above the wind. Slapping was a pre-requisite for all who visited the harbour. Never enough to simply gaze, there had to be a physical element involved, a connection made. Slapping created a separate route to understanding the unyielding permanence of the structure sight alone couldn't.

But rather than continue directly on, Hugo took Daisy by surprise and turned right, taking the path to the same level as the upper walkway, which led to the curious, curved wall that surrounded the seaward side of the lighthouse. Like some impossibly steep football terracing, it was broad enough for two to walk upon before widening as it stepped sharply down. At the wall's end, the blocks curled in on themselves as if clutching something unseen, creating a wondrous little pedestal, the furthermost point on the pier. The perfect place to sit, he decided. If they could make it across the no-man's land of cracked paving, dips and bumps.

'Isn't she a little beauty?' the American said, as he appeared, seemingly from nowhere.

'Hey,' Hugo replied. 'Yeah, she is.'

'Is she still operational?'

'No, not anymore. Classed as a 'day marker' now or something, so she still serves a nautical function. They light her up occasionally... just for show.'

'Right. So, she'll never shine again. Not for shipping purposes anyway,' he added poignantly as his friends approached, some scaling the steeply stepped wall like a troop of rock apes.

'She still earns her keep, though. Apparently, any ship that passes a lighthouse has to pay a fee, regardless of weather or anything,' Hugo said.

'Is that so? Jeeze, a lot of money to be made in a place like this.'

'Eh, boats don't count, I'm afraid,' he laughed. 'What do you think of the new one, then?' He asked, as he pointed to an entirely functional concrete pillar, similar in height to its older neighbour and with a large light bulb attached. Looking like a giant, red tipped matchstick, it was set on a new stretch of causeway that metastasised from the tip of the pier like some malignant, unsightly growth.

The American shook his head.

'What's wrong with it?' Hugo joked.

'What does the new 'lighthouse' remind you guys of?' He asked his friends.

'Anyone got a light?' Someone shouted back.

Hugo laughed. 'Here, I couldn't ask another favour of you, could I?'

'Another photo, right?'

'Yeah, thanks... if you don't mind.'

After handing over his phone, Hugo crouched beside Daisy, where all three waited patiently for a strong gust of wind to abate. Just as the American lined up his shot, Hugo suddenly stood.

'Actually, hang on a minute, can you?' He asked, before turning to Daisy. 'Can we stand for this one... if you're up for it, that is?' He added. 'Just it's... I don't know, it seems fitting somehow.'

Looking down at the rough, uneven surface, strewn with gravel and flaking mortar, Daisy's initial instinct was to insist on remaining where she was, but Hugo's sudden burst of enthusiasm (and the fact he rarely asked anything of her) persuaded her otherwise. Nodding, she took her hat off, slid her sunglasses into it, and along with her hand-bag, dropped them to the ground. Holding Hugo's hands, she rose from her chair and took a couple of steps before falling stylishly into him. She wrapped her arms around his neck, and as he held her by the waist, they began to sway, as if dancing provocatively, cheek to cheek. It was a moment as exhilarating as the one that carried their very first kiss, and as they stood, clinging to each other, everything around them slipped to insignificance, leaving them in binary solitude at the centre of their very own universe.

The tall American grinned broadly, fully aware of what he was witnessing. After a few seconds of deliberate pause, he barked his order.

'Hey... smile, you two.'

Instinctively, they both turned to face the camera, and in doing so, unwittingly created the perfect pose for a picture so perfect it would leave them stunned when they viewed it later. The American, still grinning, crouched for several 'creative' photos, then called for them to look at each other as he zoomed in for the final portrait.

'Aw man, you guys look like royalty. Beautiful,' he oozed, as he took the last snap. He quickly scrolled through the images before walking over and handing Hugo his phone. 'That was real sweet, folks,' he said. 'By the way, the name's Sam. Sam Malone.'

Hugo raised his eyebrows on hearing the name. 'Seriously? And you're from Boston as well!'

Sam nodded. 'Sure am. Funny thing is, it's been twenty years since the last episode, and it still gets a laugh.'

Daisy settled back in her seat, looking at both men, utterly confused.

'You over here for long?' Hugo asked.

'Oh, about two weeks in all,' Sam replied. 'Mostly for golf, but this time I intend to visit County Clare. See where the ancestors hailed from. My great-great-great grandfather came from Ennis. Thomas Malone. He emigrated to the US in April, Eighteen Forty-six,' he said precisely. 'Though not through choice. He was wanted for stealing food during the famine and, would you believe it, for destroying evidence through consumption. But, like I say, they never caught him.'

'Destroying evidence. Really?' Hugo asked, as Sam nodded. 'How did he mange to get away?'

'He fled to Cork the very same night, and with the help of a family friend, found passage on a boat bound for Boston. One of the many 'coffin' ships, as they called them.'

Hugo explained to Daisy the use of the term 'coffin' ship and what it meant for those aboard; wretched emigrants, forced across the unfathomably vast ocean, half-starved and wracked with disease. And upon reaching their brave new world, they found it rife with old, colonial ways (it wasn't just the wretched emigrant who sought passage to the new world). Yet somehow, despite the hardship and discrimination, many found success, weaving a rich, new fabric from the very worst of threads reserved for them. (It is said the Irish had but two things in their favour: sheer weight of numbers and spoken English.)

183

'If he'd been caught,' Sam continued, 'it was the penal colonies for him. Transportation as they referred to it.'

'The penal colonies! For trying to feed himself?'

'Yes mam. Harsh times they were, especially in County Clare. No dispensation given, whatever the circumstance. Normally they would be hanged, but the authorities hit upon the idea of forced labour. Tens of thousands were sent to the US, but after the war of independence, as many again were sent to Australia. The famine gave them good cause... in their eyes.'

'You wonder how people could do things like that to others. Sending fellow human beings away from their homes and their families. Even having to flee for their lives. That was almost a death sentence too, wasn't it?'

'In many ways mam, yes, it was,' he agreed. 'But luckily, Thomas not only survived, he prospered, and I figured the least I could do was to celebrate that and pay my humble respects to those less fortunate.'

'That's a lovely thing to do,' Daisy said.

'It sure is,' Hugo agreed. 'And you know something Sam, he'd appreciate the gesture, no doubt about it. And he'd be proud to know part of him made it home after all these years as well.'

'He would, yes, and that's very kind of you both to say.'

'What do you hope to find in Ennis?' Daisy asked.

Sam sighed and shrugged his shoulders.

'Not too sure. I would hope to find the family home but, failing that, just to walk the streets he walked before his life changed forever. That would be something. Who knows, if I walk for long enough I might even tread upon one of his footsteps,' he added emotionally. 'And of course, the Central Fire Station. Now that's a must.'

'Ah, a firefighter,' Hugo said.

'In Boston, yes. As am I, my father before me and before him and so on, right back to Thomas. My son as well. That's him in the Red Sox cap,' he said, pointing towards the group.

'Oh I love firefighters,' Daisy said, as she looked for the tell-tale hat amongst the tight-knit pack of heads. 'I think you're the most amazingly brave people.'

'Is that so? Well, we have our moments, I guess,' he said, smiling.

'That's actually news to me,' Hugo announced with a slightly uncomfortable laugh as he glanced at both of them. 'I'm in the wrong job, clearly.'

'Oh no,' Daisy argued. 'You're in *exactly* the right job.'

Sam roared with laughter at Daisy's riposte, before checking his watch.

'Well folks, it's high time I was teeing off,' he said, as he swung a phantom golf club and signalled to the impatient group.

Hugo held his hand out. 'A real pleasure meeting you, Sam. All the best to you.'

Daisy nodded, adding, 'and I hope you find what you're looking for, Sam.'

'If it's there, I'll find it. Nice meeting you folks, also. And if you want to look me up, Facebooks the place,' he said, as he made his way back to his friends. 'Oh and, cheers,' he shouted from the distance, laughing.

'Wow,' Hugo said, as the first image filled the screen. 'That's not us, is it?' He joked, as he squatted beside Daisy, angling the screen for a clearer view. Having few so-called 'proper' photos of both of them (most were selfies and casual snaps), thanks to their day in Howth, they were now spoilt for choice. And if there were few so-called 'proper' photos of them, there were none in existence where they both stood, together, on equal footing.

And like Hugo, Daisy almost didn't recognise the girl in the picture, standing tall as she was and leaning into him, arms cast loosely around his neck. Staring straight at the camera, she had a natural look only possible when turning quickly, or if suddenly startled. Her long blonde hair had taken flight, thanks to a timely gust of wind, and like a Bond girl in pose, she looked cool, confident and vaguely dangerous. The second photo was almost identical, but slightly less natural, being more staged with the element of surprise snatched from them. It had the feel of a promotional poster about it, as if all Hugo needed was a Walther PPK hanging by his side and a cast of characters listed below. Every single element in every single photograph appeared perfectly positioned and beautifully framed, with the exception of one or two, where the little lighthouse seemed to steal the foreground from its background position.

'These are great, aren't they?' Hugo said, hugely impressed. He scrolled back to the first picture, taking one long, satisfying look before closing the app and putting his phone away.

'By the way eh, sorry for, you know... dragging you to your feet there,' he said. 'It just seemed...'

Daisy smiled as she placed the warm palm of her hand on his cold, reddened cheek, playfully slapping it.

'You can drag me anywhere you like, Mr O'Neill. If I don't want to be dragged, I'll tell you. Ok?'

'Yeah, fair enough,' he said, as he stood up before pulling each trouser leg down with the sides of his shoes. 'It's just... well, for a moment there, the place seemed to demand we stand, you know? It was actually overwhelming.'

'Hugo, darling, you really don't have to explain

yourself. You'd have to be... I don't know, like a stone or something not to see how much this place means to you. I'm beginning to feel the same,' she said, looking over at the lighthouse and visualising a thoughtful, little Hugo taking a welcome breather on a rusty iron capstan as he gazed in wonder at the enormity of his surroundings.

Hugo smiled appreciatively as he looked back towards the village of Howth, ill-defined now with distance, the only recognisable landmark being its distinctive headland under which the bustling little town burrowed. To Hugo, it was a place like no other, being as he was, continually over-awed with the scale of its harbour and the monumental east wall. Forever compelled to traverse its full length, its indefatigable granite surface was magnetic to the foot. And though the vast structure ended half a mile out to sea, its reach seemed to extend beyond the horizon, creating the urge to visit time and again.

'I always felt this place had like, a duality about it, you know. If you sat, at the tip of the pier there and gazed seaward, you could journey anywhere, yet never actually leave. Strange feeling that. You were left fulfilled and unfulfilled. Think I was mostly unfulfilled.'

'And how do you feel now?'

'What, generally or... right this minute?' He joked.

Daisy shook her head dismissively. 'Come on,' she said, hand out. 'Let's go all the way to the end. See if it takes us anywhere.'

Chapter Eighteen

They made their way back down the ramp and continued past the sharp corner of the keepers' cottage, hugging tight to its perimeter. Even as they approached, the lighthouse remained paradoxically hidden from view until the point of revelation, where it suddenly lunged before them, much larger than expected and gleaming in the sun as it reached upwards.

'Oh wow,' Daisy said, clearly surprised with the scale of the building as she leaned back to view its full, skyward sweep. 'You are impressive, aren't you?' She added, slapping it affectionately. Carved to perfection from the lightest shade of impermeable granite, the lighthouse soared nearly fifty feet in height, towering above the keeper's house attached to the rear. Impressive anywhere else, but there, on the Head of Howth, facing all before it and proudly guarding the entrance to the harbour, it was magnificent.

Daisy peered upwards, following the granite blocks row by row and began to count them, but the piercing light and awkward angle she held her head at caused her to sneeze. Excusing herself, she held the tip of her nose as she made a second attempt at gazing up. After a few seconds, her face contorted yet again, as the tickly sensation of a second, more explosive sneeze overpowered her. Hugo turned away to conceal a huge grin. He could have sworn her last sneeze actually propelled her backwards. Unaware she was under observation, she abandoned her attempt to guess the height of the structure and made her way around the base of the building, moving out of sight. Moments later, Hugo followed her.

Within the area guarded by the lighthouse and the curved, terraced wall, the space was sheltered and unexpectedly calm.

'This is so cool!' Daisy exclaimed when she saw Hugo. 'It's like one of those provincial Roman amphitheatres, you know, the tiny ones scattered throughout the empire,' she said, remembering a family holiday in Majorca years ago, where they stumbled across a small, but significant set of Roman ruins. Complete with a micro amphitheatre carved from the living rock and crumbling columns, it also had what looked like a cleverly designed cooling area; a cave with a hole in the roof, somehow providing a shower of cool air for the roasted Roman. 'Listen to my voice,' she said, loudly. 'It's as if we're on stage. Comedy or tragedy, my lord?' She enounced, arms outstretched. 'Comedy, I think,' she suggested, frowning comically. 'Hugo, what an amazing space. It's so peaceful. No wind, not a sound.'

'Yeah, you'd never believe you were at the tip of a pier half a mile out to sea now, would you?' He said, grinning at her antics.

'Not from here, no,' she agreed. 'So what exactly was this wall for? And what a strange design,' she added, staring at the steep, terraced steps.

She moved closer to it, marvelling at the cut of stone and how the blocks curved perfectly together at the pedestaled end, the chiselled granite laid with such precision, a cigarette paper wouldn't fit between them. 'And what was this beautiful little thing crafted for?' She asked, as she ran her hands over the smooth surface of the pedestal. 'Not for a light, surely. That fellow wouldn't be at all amused,' she laughed, pointing to the lighthouse behind her. 'It wouldn't have held a cannon or something... would it?'

'Well deduced there, Holmes,' he said, laughing at her reasoning, the absurd threaded with pure logic. 'That's exactly what it was. A gun emplacement. In fact, the whole thing is basically a battlement.'

'Really? For a lighthouse?'

'Yeah. Britain was at war with France back then,' he said as he climbed, ladder like, to the top. 'This was the perfect spot to pick off enemy ships, fortified and reaching way out to sea,' he stated, pointing his arm, cannon like, over the waves. 'Hit them before they hit shore,' he shouted, as he negotiated the sweeping curve of the wall, arms out like a tightrope walker. Turning to make his way back, he noticed Daisy watching him longingly. He knew with absolute certainty, she would have joined him if she could, at first giggling, all pushy and playful, but soon competitive, clawing for supremacy. With heels and elbows flying, she wouldn't hold back at all, he thought, as he peered over the edge to the rocks below, imagining himself lying amongst them, vanquished by a victorious Daisy. He decided to walk down the steep, terraced blocks from where he stood to join her, rather than continue along the wall back to the pedestal. However, descending too quickly on the narrowing steps, he lost his footing and stumbled forward. Somehow managing to stop himself face-planting the granite slabs, he could only watch as his phone flew from his jacket pocket. Desperately, he palmed it up, first with his right hand, then with his left, before finally catching it with his right.

'Christ almighty, that was lucky,' he said, straightening up. 'Could've been a disaster that,' he said, wriggling his phone.

Daisy sat, hand over mouth, silent and fearful. But as he approached, she burst into laughter, bending over almost double.

'What on earth happened there?' She asked, tearfully amused.

'Dunno. That's what I get for cavorting about like a jack-ass, I suppose.'

'Aw, don't ever stop cavorting, my darling,' she replied, giggling as he squatted down beside her. 'And your phone! That was so funny. Quite the little juggler you are.'

'Never been called a little juggler before. Little bugger maybe,' he said, remembering that for a considerable period during his childhood, he actually thought his name was, 'you little bugger.' He made himself as comfortable as he could on the cold stone, before putting his phone away, this time buttoning his jacket pocket for extra safety.

'Like I said,' Daisy began, 'I know why this place means so much to you, Hugo. It's simply magical,' she added, as they both settled by the pedestal, the furthermost tip of the pier. 'I mean, I've only been here a short while, yet already I feel part of it. It's as if something of me will always be here. Like footprints on the moon.'

And it's magic seemed to extend beyond the beautifully crafted lighthouse and spectacular setting, reaching into the guarded core of who she was. Ruffling time, thought and memory, blending fact and fiction, past and present, it delivered a profound understanding of time itself, a deep, but fleeting notion it wasn't stalking her in terminal silence, inexorably driving her to the unthinkable end of being. Life wasn't, she realised, a continuous, unbroken journey, rather a series of free flowing moments, real or fanciful.

Moments she could hold still in time or revisit as she chose.

She dropped her skinny little legs over the edge of the pier and sat on her hands, first shuffling from cheek to cheek. She began to kick the smooth granite façade with her heels, marking a subconscious rhythm, as Hugo, with his muddied little face, frowned in concentration as he tried to pack as many scavenged stones and shells into the torn pocket of his bright red shorts.

They'd spent most of the morning by the pier, playing in the little rock pools nestling on the seaward side of the harbour, before chasing each other down the vast, empty promenade towards the lighthouse. With sticks for swords, they jostled for supremacy on the curved, terraced battlement, before agreeing a truce and jumping down, making their way cautiously to the very end of the great wall.

And side by side they sat, basking in the warm summer sun, with no sound but the relentless clap of waves. And on a sea as blue as the sky itself, not a care sailed past, nor a single trouble brewed.

And she would live each day as though her first, not her last. How absurd to spend a life in the shadow of death, continually waking to the prospect of oblivion, gorging oneself on all manner of activity before darkness descends.

And she would stretch each simple, joyful moment with her beautiful companion by her side and revel in what she now held. Because what she held now was now. And in now, she found herself immune to the passage of time.

Almost as if he heard the faint whisper of her thoughts, Hugo turned to look at her.

'What you thinking?'

She took his hand and pulled it down to her lap, rubbing it vigorously in both of hers. She couldn't begin to explain the profundity of her thoughts, nor describe how she felt. But there was one sentiment she could convey with ease... and satisfy Hugo's curiosity.

'How lucky I am, to be here, now, with you. And how amazingly special you are,' she added warmly.

'Funny. I was just thinking that about you.'

'Well, that's that then, isn't it?' She said decisively. 'We're both incredibly lucky and amazingly special.'

Shifting onto one knee, he leaned over the side of her chair and kissed her.

'Lucky yeah, but... you're much more amazingly special than me.'

Daisy smiled in disagreement and looked back out over the open water, slowly scanning the horizon. The sharp, blue sky pinned itself to the cold, grey sea and from that juncture of elements, that mystical divide, ships emerged, hazy and shimmering with distance, moving with the stillness of the hands of a clock. Her eyes drifted lazily back to harbour, meandering through the berths and moorings and the bright orange bobbing buoys, which for some reason brought a smile to her face. Things have concluded, she thought serenely as she looked at Hugo, himself staring outwards, deep within his own thoughts.

'Let's go back now.'

'What, now... you sure?'

'Yes. This moment was perfectly sculpted... just like this perfect place, and I don't want to linger any longer. It's time for a new moment. Anyway, there's probably a thousand people approaching, and I want to remember this... all this,' she said, looking around, 'exactly as it is.'

Hugo smiled and took one last look around. She was right. Perfect as it was, it was time to leave.

Chapter Nineteen

They paused for another view over the harbour and watched as the advancing tide elevated everything afloat almost to within touching distance. The wind too, had steadily increased, gusting more frequently as they made their way back from the lighthouse, and the vessels moored outside the sanctity of the marina responded accordingly, some rocking dramatically as the waves grew in force. The harbour gulls, masters of the skies that they were, faced the wind, searching while surfing with wings outstretched, expending little or no energy. Occasionally, one would dart to a crust and the rest would flock, squabbling and harassing each other.

'They're so annoying, aren't they?' Daisy said as she watched them.

'Yeah. I love the fact they annoy us. It's not like we don't deserve it, chucking food about and that. It's our lifestyle that's driving their behaviour, don't forget. But they *are* impressive, aren't they? I mean, look at the way they handle the wind,' he said, as a sudden, more powerful gust swept them skywards, where they paused, waiting for it to abate, before returning to the position they were in. Hugo whooped in admiration. 'Amazing.'

'They're still a menace,' she insisted. 'Skilful avionics and an eloquent defence won't convince me otherwise.'

Hugo was about to press home his point but was forced to wait as the constant, ever-present wind gusted again, buffeting his ears and muffling all but its own sound. He stood behind Daisy, arms around her, stoically deflecting the sudden fury of the elements. He looked back along the huge harbour wall, following its course as it reached out into the Irish Sea. Protective alcoves punctured the solid granite structure at regular intervals, offering sedentary relief for the weary walker and welcome respite from the harsh, coastal conditions. He leaned over Daisy, shouting they should make for the nearest one.

As they approached, Hugo slapped the cold, hard face of the wall, once again marvelling at the permanence of the entire structure. Two hundred years and they've not moved an inch, he thought, as he scanned the perfectly carved granite blocks, some decorated with decade's old graffiti, others with crude sexual images. He sat down and wrapped his arm around Daisy, pulling her closer, then took a quick selfie. Immediately, Daisy held her hand out.

'That's nice,' she said, granting approval to the picture as she leaned into him. 'Hmm, it's lovely in here, away from that wind.'

Hugo shuddered in agreement. It was a relief to be free from the relentless, deafening wind, but sitting still on a cold, stone bench wasn't much of an improvement. In saying that, Daisy was exuding joules of body warmth, and he pulled her tighter to harness it, smiling to himself as he realised what a pernicious little heat thief he'd become. He pulled back to smile suggestively at her.

'So, what's this about a train then?'

'I wondered when you'd get around to the train,' she retorted, elbowing him.

Daisy looked out at the bobbing yachts, their rhythmic movement offering buoyancy to some long submerged memories. As if she needed any such prompting, for in an instant, she visualised the entire carnal encounter she'd had in the toilet of a train on a blisteringly hot summer's day on a journey back from a school trip to Canterbury.

'I was seventeen, just. We were on 'your' train back from Canterbury,' she explained, a tad sarcastically. 'It was our last ever school trip, so it must've been May, two thousand and... seven? I'd been going out with this boy Mark for a few months. He was really sweet and so good looking. We met for the first time in the canteen at school. Well, that's when we first actually *spoke* to one another. I thought he fancied Katie and that he was hoping to meet her through me. You know how some guys operate. Turns out it was me he fancied, not Katie. What a surprise I got when he asked me out. So, we signed up for the school trip. Just a day trip, which was long enough, actually. It was so hot it was like being abroad, and there were loads of tourists about as well. Not like us. Proper ones,' she giggled. 'We were totally done in by the time we caught the train back. And what a journey. It was like an oven in the carriage.'

Daisy couldn't quite remember the point at which they decided to do what they did, but she remembered why. Almost as soon as they stepped aboard, they'd fallen victim to each other's subliminal, sexual predation, unwittingly coerced by the hot, sticky heat of the carriage and the constant, heaving motion of the train.

'I remember whispering something about the toilet and needing to cool down as I pulled at my top. He knew what I meant of course, and a few seconds later, he followed me out. We went a few carriages down, just to be safe, and with no one looking, we snuck into the nearest toilet. I pulled my skirt up past my waist. He got such a shock when he saw I'd no pants on. I took them off earlier in a restaurant, you see. And before you ask, it was because the ticket was really annoying me.'

Hugo considered moving out of range of Daisy's elbow, expecting yet another sharp poke in the ribs. But she'd already decided she couldn't justify elbowing him. This time he'd actually *said* nothing. Thoughts didn't count.

'I didn't have a bra on either. Didn't need one then,'

she laughed. 'So when I took my top off, I was practically naked.'

Daisy went on to describe, in exquisite detail, what happened in the carriage as it sped through the scorched English countryside, the cramped, airless space of the cubicle somehow heightening their excitement and forcing them hungrily upon each other. Privately, and through a deep intake of breath, she recalled her (fairly rapid) energy sapping flood of fulfilment and their fusing together in astonished silence in the stifling, noisy aftermath.

It was Daisy's moment of quietude that spoke volumes to Hugo, for within the story's electrifying, mute conclusion, he imagined himself both voyeur and lover, each satisfying in their own unique way. And if he were to select one, it would be the former. He had no right to invade her memories by choosing the latter.

'It was so amazing,' she whispered. 'I'd never felt anything like it, and we didn't even make love,' she added, as she squeezed her hands tightly between her thighs. 'Then he said it was too painful and he had to... get more comfortable? I so knew what he wanted of course, so I slid off and knelt in front of him. He lifted himself up so I could pull his shorts down just far enough for him to spring free. It actually pinged onto his stomach.'

'His stomach! You're kidding.'

'No! He was huge. It was like grabbing a cucumber or something,' she said, giggling. 'And then... well I'm saying no more,' she said as she slapped his arm, 'other than I couldn't say a word if I tried. I was literally speechless,' she laughed, embarrassed, yet highly excited with her admission. 'So, I got myself together and snuck out as inconspicuously as I snuck in, leaving him to... tidy up, shall we say.'

The last element of Daisy's story crowned for Hugo, what was already an extremely erotic tale.

'I need to get a bit more comfortable after that,' he joked. 'Pity there's no toilets on the DART. Would've been a right old journey back to the hotel.'

'So, Mr O'Neill, don't tell me you haven't a story or two to tell. There must be dozens of women who've succumbed to your charms and manipulations over the years.'

'Eh, dozens no, and what exactly do you mean by manipulation?'

'Oh there's nothing wrong with a bit of manipulation, Hugo,' she replied. 'Think of it as encouragement. Come on, she said,' wriggling with enthusiasm. 'You must have an erotic story tucked away somewhere.'

'You're something else, you know that.'

'Well?' She demanded, this time wriggling impatiently.

Hugo smiled to himself as he realised he could now identify her moods, be they good, bad or indifferent, just by her distinctive wriggles alone.

'Well, there was this 'incident', years ago,' he began. 'Think I was about your age as well, funnily enough.'

Hugo then described how, one morning, he found himself at the table in the kitchen of his brother's best friend's house. He couldn't remember why he was there, only that he *was* there. He recalled the time however, as being just short of eleven o'clock – and pretty much everything that happened thereafter. A girl, drowsy as though just awake, glides into the kitchen looking entirely as if she owns the place. With a long, white nightgown billowing behind her, she reminds him of Rose 'what's her name', running through the bowels of the Titanic (somehow managing to avoid the showers of sparks and clouds of coaldust). Judging by how tightly she grips the white, silky lapels, he concludes she's got nothing on underneath. He's surprised she's not bothered there's a strange young lad sitting at the table, and he watches in amusement as she falls heavily to a chair, moaning about sleeping in. Curious as to the nature of her job, he wonders what she means by several important hearings missed, some still to attend? Eventually, she involves him in her conversation and they chat away quite happily, trading places to go at night, who they knew and didn't know, laughing at things they probably shouldn't be laughing at. She even gets up to make him a cup of tea. Milk, sugar... both? As she plonks herself down again, he notices she's not gripping her dressing gown quite so tightly (it's now hanging either side of her chest like a pair of partially drawn curtains). He entertains the notion that maybe she'll sweep them aside, or perhaps they'll simply fall from her shoulders? He quickly dismisses it. Things like that don't just 'happen'. You're reading it all wrong, he tells himself. But then, just as he lays his cup down, she suddenly jumps up. Opening her gown like a flowering orchid, she drops onto his lap, throwing her legs either side of him. Undoing his belt, she tugs at the zip, frustrated as it sticks before finally drawing it down. Pulling him free, she assumes position and settles down heavily upon him. She sets to work, grinding away vigorously as she continues to gorge herself noisily on his face. Already, he feels consumed. It's only ten past eleven. His tea is still hot.

Daisy was astonished.

'What? She didn't waste any time, did she? At least we had a romantic day out and a slow, steamy build up.'

'Well, we did have a cup of tea,' he reminded her. 'Anyway, I wasn't sure if I was enjoying it or not. She was pawing and gnawing at me like I was a piece of meat or a butchers bone. She had me for breakfast, for Christ sake!'

'Now you know how we feel.'

'Fair point, that,' he said, nodding. 'But I still went along with it. No surprises there. Didn't last long, though. Probably... what, a minute or two? Think she was a bit shocked it happened so fast. She kept kissing me and going at it, hoping something else would develop. Not a chance,' he said, absolutely. 'That particular horse had bolted,' he added. 'The tank was empty, and whatever way you want to look at it, the focus had switched to self-preservation. It's an instant, chemical thing with us,' he explained, 'we generally have to leave in a hurry, or fall asleep after sex. Anyway, I mumbled something about going to the toilet. She wasn't too happy. Not at all impressed when I stood up quite forcefully. She was still hanging around my neck, even.'

'Hugo! That was mean of you.'

'It was a bit,' he conceded. 'It didn't help that I was in the toilet for ages as well, like I was hiding or something. But it's impossible to pee when you're 'on parade', as they say. Mind you, I was quite happy she wasn't there when I got back. She must've gone for a shower or something. So, I grabbed my jacket, a black leather one I bought in the Irish Life mall the day before and... in fact, that was the building we passed on the DART before we got to the train station yesterday, remember? I pointed it out to you. The big, copper looking thing.'

'Yes I do,' Daisy said, recalling how unusual the building looked, its windows shining like polished copper in the morning sun. She'd watched, mesmerised, as their reflection tracked them pane by pane as they trundled past before crossing the river, which fractured the hazy, sweeping vista of central Dublin. 'That's strange, isn't it?

I witnessed part of a story you hadn't yet told.'

'Yeah, that's a bit weird, alright.'

'So, you got your jacket, then what?'

'So, I got my jacket and crept out. I didn't want to announce my departure, have her chase me down the street. Anyway, for all I knew, she could've been on the phone to big bro and his hurling mates. I could hardly hang about now, could I?'

'So you didn't feel guilty then.'

'Guilty! For what?'

'Denying her affection, Hugo. That's a serious criminal offence, in any woman's eyes.'

Hugo laughed. 'She wasn't after affection, I can assure you. The funny thing is, I almost ran into her a couple of days later, would you believe it. Luckily, I saw her first and ducked into a doorway. She walked right past me. Never saw her again.'

'Hmm, overall, I would categorise that as erotic, but in a rather... clinical way.'

'Yeah, I suppose it was,' he agreed. 'A short burst of random sexual activity. Short being the operative word,' he added. 'Typical teenager. Like a coiled spring I was. One touch and boing, off I popped,' he laughed.

'Boing and pop,' Daisy repeated, giggling at Hugo's description. 'That's funny,' she added, imagining a world populated by teenage boys in a constant state of sexual tension. 'What if they made a popping noise as well... when they popped?' she said, laughing out loud.

'God now, could you imagine that? All that popping coming from everywhere. Parked cars, toilets, your mum and dad's bedroom.'

'Too far, Hugo.'

'And how would you know, if you were in a restaurant for example, that the waiter popped a cork and not something else? How could you tell?'

'Hugo! That's beyond rude. I'll have to think twice before I order a bottle of wine in a restaurant again,' she said, wriggling now with disgust. 'So, did you ever find out who this... girl was and what she was doing there that morning?'

'Yeah, I did. She was my brother's best friend's *wife's* younger sister,' he replied. 'There's got to be an easier way of describing that relationship, surely to hell.'

'You could've just asked her name.'

'I could've alright. But that might have encouraged her. Anyway, I was off out that night with a couple of mates and, well, you know...'

'Hugo! Don't tell me that was on your mind after all that happened. Honestly.'

'Yep. Fraid so. We could be trapped in a burning building, twenty stories up, and we'd still think about it.'

'That is so weird,' Daisy said, emphasising each word slowly and deliberately, as she pushed herself away from Hugo. 'I would be desperately trying to get out.'

'What, and you think we wouldn't? I said we *think* about it at inopportune moments, not that we'd go looking for it.'

'Yes,' she agreed, 'but the *thought* itself is pointless, isn't it?'

'No. It's the *act* that's pointless. The thought isn't something you can switch on or off. It's just... there. We have genes to impart before we depart. That's the rule of nature.'

'Hmm,' Daisy murmured, accepting Hugo had indeed made a relevant point. 'I do know what you mean, though' she said. 'Mark didn't need any encouragement either. Not that it was a regular occurrence. We actually only made love a couple of times. And there was only *one* train incident, I can assure you,' she said.

'Nothing to do with me. It's your past, not mine.'

'But I wasn't like that,' she insisted.

'I know you weren't. I wasn't either,' he said, as he pushed her hair behind her ear, then tugged gently on her earlobe, which hung, cold as ice, outside the warm protection of her hat. He tightened his hold on her and settled back, as comfortably as he could, against the hard, granite rear of the alcove.

It was now early afternoon and the harbour, sparkling under the piercing mid-day sun, suddenly seemed to brim with activity, with more and more people strolling past, some smiling warmly at them. A striking, chocolate brown Labrador bolted over for a friendly nose, its silky ears irresistible to the touch, and a tiny, two year old girl stopped and stared before being hauled away by her parents. The triplets reappeared, each now clutching a strawberry flavoured ice-pop that dripped blood red juice onto their matching Disney bibs, and some kids were being yelled at to stay away from the wharf's edge. Then, from the depths, a frogman appeared at the top of a rusty metal ladder and flopped obesely onto the pier, heavy as a walrus and spilling seawater from the creases of his rubber suit. He playfully made for the children, arms out with menace, and they squealed back to the safety of their mother.

'That's funny,' Hugo said, as he watched the events around them unfold. 'I remember a scuba diver coming up that very ladder when I was a little boy... just like that fella there,' he added. 'What a shock I got, seeing one for the first time. This big, black greasy thing appearing from nowhere. Didn't look anything like in the Bond movies either. And there was always a dog running about the place as well, kids messing around, parents giving out to them.' He smiled. 'Dad took us here loads of times. Mainly me and Kathleen... and the odd friend or two. Very odd they were,' he said, grinning. 'I think he loved the place more than we did. He'd be busy telling us all sorts of facts and things, and we'd be just as busy ignoring him. I used to sit at the end of the pier there, just like we did today, and gaze into the distance. There was this one day in particular. Absolutely roasting it was. In fact, it was that hot, the tar on the road was starting to melt. Even the seagulls couldn't be bothered flying. There was hardly anyone at the end of the pier as well. Too far to walk, I suppose. I remember Kathleen coming over and dropping herself down beside me. We never said a word to each other. We just sat in the sun and stared at the horizon. Two tiny bookends sitting there, knees up, arms around our legs. I'm sure she must've felt like I did, wondering what on Earth was out there. Whatever it was, we knew it was huge. Way bigger than our own little world. I would've given anything to skip across the waves and see what was going on for myself,' he added. 'And here I am, back at the same spot, and I'm thinking, you don't have to travel far to find a new world now, do you? I mean, look what could be sitting on your own doorstep. All you have to do is to open the door. Remember?' He said, gently elbowing her. 'So yeah, great journeys have to be undertaken. It's our duty as humans, I think. But the thing is, you can journey anywhere,' he said. 'Even in here,' he declared, slapping his chest. 'All you need is curiosity and imagination. And I had plenty of that back then. Spades of it, in fact.'

'You haven't changed at all,' Daisy whispered. 'You're still a curious, little explorer at heart, aren't you?'

'Not sure about that now.'

'Well I think you are,' she said emphatically, as she recalled her own precious moment at the pier's edge, watching as mysterious vessels plied their ancient routes, some setting course for shore, others slipping lazily from view. Like silent time travellers trading in knowledge, they ferried wonder and enlightenment to mind. 'We did travel somewhere today, Hugo. And we were rewarded with something special. It's as if our souls touched and we traded secrets. More than secrets, actually,' she added, as she wriggled lovingly into him.

Hugo nodded and leaned down to kiss the top of her head. She was right, something magical occurred and somehow he knew it, his affirmation coming from a place he didn't fully understand. He felt as if they *had* tunnelled through time and tide into each other's guarded realms, their journey driven by the magnificence of the surroundings and sudden, powerful bursts of nostalgia. And though doubt persisted, he was happy to have witnessed something wondrous and just... marvel at it. He was tired of analysing his life and searching for answers to the point of yearning for the comfort uncertainty brought, to be enveloped in the wonder of imagination and make-believe, to be once again like the little boy that sat at the end of the pier, knees up and awestruck, all those years ago.

Suddenly, he lifted his arm from Daisy and searched for his keys, selecting a screwdriver from the attached mini toolkit.

'I know I shouldn't really,' he said, as he began to etch some tiny words in the top corner of the alcove, 'but this moment's crying out for it.'

'Hugo, you can't do that,' she whispered, looking around. 'Someone might see you, a warden or somebody.'

'Sure there's no-one about. Anyway, they couldn't prove anything, could they?'

'Well, they could just ask our names.'

'Hadn't thought about that now,' he replied, stopping briefly before deciding to continue. After several passes, each time etching a little deeper, he finished.

'That should do it,' he said with satisfaction, as he blew the dust away. Looking at his crudely etched efforts, they both read the words, Daisy & Hugo Forever 14-2-16.

'Aw, that's so sweet, Hugo. Do you think it *will* last forever?'

'Don't see why not,' he said, looking at the rest of the graffiti, a mix of graphics and messages, some barely visible, others easily legible. 'There's one from nineteen forty seven,' he pointed out, 'so maybe,' he added. 'Tell you what, we'll touch it up when we're back one day. Dig a little deeper, yeah?'

Chapter Twenty

'Here, you fancy a cone?' He said, as he looked back at the entrance to the promenade. The 'out of season' ice cream van had suddenly sprung to life, broadcasting its distinctive, chiming melody across the harbour. 'I know it's a bit cold and all that but, we are by the seaside. Well, almost,' he said, looking around.

'Oh, I'd love one.'

'Be right back,' he said, kissing her forehead before sprinting towards the van.

Breathing heavily, Hugo stood at the open window of the ice cream van, amused but slightly embarrassed he was immature enough to have raced a group of school children to the vehicle.

'Two ninety-nine cones, please,' he asked, wondering how many years had passed since he last uttered such words.

'Certainly, sir. Would you like strawberry sauce, sprinkles or better still, both on dem?' The vendor asked, in an accent more suited to the confined, bustling markets of Moore Street, than the grand, sweeping promenade of Howth Harbour.

'Eh, no thanks, just the flakes.'

As he waited for his cones, the children, (primary school age, but street-wise), began grappling and elbowing each other in a hierarchal struggle for pole position behind him. One of them, a small, ginger lad who found himself forced to the back of the queue, started kicking the rear wheel of the van in frustration. Muttering what the feck, the vendor leaned out the window.

'Would ye stop that at once. How would ye feel if I went over and kicked your car, ye little bugger. Stop it, or der'll be no cones for you.'

Being distracted, he overfilled the second cone, the ice-cream expanding exponentially, like a shaken Cola bottle. Cursing, he scooped some of the excess off, before sticking the flake in.

'Sorry about dat,' he said, as he handed Hugo the second one. 'You got more than I bargained for there. But it's your lucky day, so it is. No extra charge for the big one,' he laughed. 'That'll be four Euro, please.'

'Four Euro it is,' Hugo said, as he handed over the cash before carefully backing away from the window, eyes fixed on the cones. Negotiating his way backwards through a bunch of feral children with a couple of ice-creams proved more difficult than he anticipated, and as if events were scripted by the hand of a divine retributionist, the top heavy ice-cream achieved what all top heavy ice-creams aspire to achieve, and toppled from its base. Hitting his jacket with a greasy, glancing blow, it slid to the ground, where he just managed to pull his foot away. The kids all erupted with foul-mouthed squeals of delight.

'Did ye see dat?' One cried with laughter.

'He bloody deserved dat,' another one said.

Then they started chanting, 'back of the queue, back of the queue, back of the queue for you-who,' as if queuing for school dinners and haranguing some unfortunate kid whose sausages rolled off the plate.

Hands out in disbelief, Hugo looked over to where Daisy was sitting, and could see she was contorted with laughter, slapping her thighs with delight. Being a highly perceptive bunch, one of the kids tracked his stare up the promenade, and seeing Daisy, shouted to his pals.

'Look! Even his bird tinks he's a prick.'

More raucous laughter followed, and all Hugo could do was smile and move to the back of the queue, but not before he fished the flake out from the pool of ice cream on the ground, sticking it into what he decided would be Daisy's cone.

'Well,' he said to his tiny audience, 'what she doesn't know won't hurt her.'

'Hey mister, that's disgusting, that is,' one said.

'Yeah, we're telling on you,' another yelled, genuinely horrified, but visibly impressed an *adult* would consider such a wicked act.

Hugo felt himself rise in their estimations, but was again, amused and embarrassed that *this* time, he felt it necessary to impress them.

'Tell you what,' he said, 'not a word to her over there and I'll buy you all a cone each. Deal?' He asked.

'You bribing, us mister?'

'Yeah, why?' Hugo replied.

'Nuthin. At least you're honest, so you are.'

'Fair play to him,' his ginger friend added.

'Yeah, he's alright, so he is,' said a third.

Hugo was happy.

Approaching Daisy, he could see the after-effects of her unrestrained burst of laughter as she sat, smiling as though in pain and patting her eyes dry with her fingertips. He smiled to himself, thinking what a thin line existed between grief and humour and how the two blended on occasion, dipping into one another, leaving the tearful victim short of breath and sobbing with joy.

'Oh thank you,' she almost squealed, as he handed her the ice cream. 'I can't remember when I last had a cone. And not one, but *two* flakes,' she said, wriggling with delight.

Hugo sat down beside her, vaguely guilty but saying nothing. He began licking the soft, creamy topping before removing the flake and nibbling on the cold, submerged section, savouring the sweet, brittle nature.

'Oh you're so cruel,' she eventually snapped. 'Why are you saying nothing?' She demanded, slapping his shoulder. 'Aw come on, talk to me, please,' she begged, now trying a different route, pulling his sleeve like a spoilt child.

'What's there to say? You saw everything that happened.'

Daisy grinned victoriously. '*That* was the funniest thing ever,' she said, as she started to giggle, before shaking with laughter. 'You were like a big bully, pushing in front of those little children like that. No wonder they were so mad at you. And then dropping the ice cream,' she just managed to say. 'I could see your face from here. You were so... furious, and they...'

'I wasn't actually furious,' he retorted. 'And less of the bully, by the way.'

But despite Hugo's protestations, Daisy continued to giggle intermittently, stopping and starting, like an engine on the cusp of roaring to life.

'Well I'm glad you all enjoyed yourselves at my expense. Even the ice cream man said it was a good afternoon for him. Make sure you come back tomorrow, he said. No, I don't think so, I thought. By the way, you know what one of them shouted?'

'No, what?'

'Look over there, even his bird tinks he's a prick. Can you believe it? Ten years old, if that,' he said looking at Daisy.

'Oh, that's so rude,' she whispered, caught between a smile and a frown.

'And it cost me fourteen Euro.'

'Fourteen Euro! What, for two, no... three cones?'

'Well, I treated them all one each. That was another eight Euro.'

'Aw, Hugo. That was so kind of you. You're so sweet… and calamitous,' she giggled.

Hugo threw his head back and began to laugh himself.

'Sweet and calamitous. That's me alright. It's a wonder I didn't slip and end up on my arse. Cheers,' he said, as he pressed his cone against Daisy's.

'There's a B&B up there,' she suddenly said, nodding towards a large town-house, perched on the hill, high above the streets. Clad in a thick coat of ivy, it blended perfectly with the trees and foliage it sat amongst, only its grey, slated roof and sparkling windows catching the eye. She studied it for a little while before looking back out over the harbour, allowing her gaze to sweep the full length of the pier. By the time her eyes returned to Hugo's, her mind had been set, reinforced by the spectacle before her and their evocative afternoon's journey.

'This place is ours now, Hugo,' she said decisively, 'every last stone of it,' she added. 'And I want to be with you... here... tonight. It must be here and it must be tonight,' she insisted. She pointed to the B&B. 'Look, they've even got vacancies.'

Saying nothing, Hugo followed her gesture, then lowered his cone, slowly and deliberately, all of a sudden disinterested in its icy cold sweetness. With satisfying precision, he threw it, dead centre, to a nearby bin.

'Let me get this right,' he began. 'I spend the night with you, my favourite ever person, here in Howth, my favourite ever place, *and* I get to keep you for the rest of my life?'

Smiling, Daisy nodded and handed Hugo her cone, where he took aim once again.

As soon as Hugo peered around the door and saw the

super-king bed, he rushed over and fell onto it, heavily, as though caught squarely on the jaw.

'Now we're talking,' he said, bouncing about, as if stress testing the frame. Settling into the starfish position, he digitally beckoned her over.

Daisy shook her head, as she began to fully inspect the premises, checking first the drawers, the cleanliness of the cups and spoons, a critical scan of the toilet and, for some reason, the shelves and tops of the skirting boards. Only when satisfied with the upkeep of the suite, did she decide to shower. Before closing the door, she smiled over at Hugo, still fully jacketed and holding everything but fatigue at bay.

For the first time in her life, she felt truly as one with another person, without knowing how or why. It was as if their bodies had secretly brokered a deal and cracked an ancient code, somehow managing to communicate with each other on a level beyond reason. She'd watched, rigid in amazement as his wanton, desperate lust slowly consumed and transformed him, his heaving masculine intent rampant and penetrative. Grabbing his arms, she felt the unbridled power in his biceps and shoulders, realising with heart stopping excitement that something had started that couldn't be stopped. And under his weight and driving presence, she shuddered with insane gratification, a sweeping pleasure that left every nerve ending sparking and crackling like frayed, overloaded circuits.

He'd watched as she closed her eyes, passive and fulfilled, unaware he'd become utterly unrecognisable as he reached a furious, exhaustive pace, straining as though horsewhipped and beaten to frenzy. And then, tickling like a host of feathers gathered and drawn, came reward for his frantic efforts, irresistibly overpowering, surging with bewildering sensitivity.

She'd kept her arms locked around him, blocking his retreat, as if to allow it would disrupt something divine happening within her. Loosening her grip allowed him to shift to his elbows.

God Almighty, that was... amazing, she heard him say.

It was.

That's us then, isn't it? she heard him propose.

Forever.

Well... here's to forever, she heard him pledge, as he kissed her lightly before rolling off and settling alongside his spiritual bride.

'That first night... in your apartment,' she reminded him, 'that was so wonderful. I can still remember trembling as you moved closer. I could feel you, even before we touched, this... strange sensation on my forehead when I closed my eyes,' she recalled. 'I was just... buzzing. So I knew then,' she admitted, as she continued to caress his stomach, moving slowly in decreasing circles, where she found his belly button and gently pushed her finger in. Hugo reacted immediately by pushing her hand away, almost apologetically.

'Sorry,' he laughed. 'Too tickly there.'

'Where?' She asked mischievously, 'in there?' She said, poking him again.

He yelped and retaliated by tickling the back of her neck, then under her arms.

'Stop it,' she squealed, before nipping him sharply below the waist as she wriggled and squirmed on top of him.

'Ow! That was really sore,' he said, looking down at the mark. 'What you do that for?'

'Armpits are a total no-no,' she instructed. 'It's funny, I don't agree with physical violence of any kind, yet I've found myself slapping and elbowing you quite a lot lately. And now this pinch, which is really just an escalation of hostilities,' she said, authoritatively, like a newsreader. 'I'm scared as to what level I'll ascend to next,' she giggled, as she shifted down and gently kissed where she nipped him. 'Though you do make me want to eat you,' she added, as she slid her tongue slowly around the bright red mark, leaving behind a salacious, silvery trail. Shifting onto her elbow, she caressed his lower abdomen with the tips of her fingers, then used her long, painted nails to lightly scratch, resisting the urge to scour a little harder. It made her wonder if she could tear him open and climb inside, feel what he felt, see what he saw, hear what he heard, as she donned her coat made from Hugo. She paused to smile, before continuing.

Working her way down to his groin, she began to tug scurrilously at the thick mass of dark, wiry hair, before burrowing between his thighs. Struggling to contain his excitement, Hugo lay still and rigid as a board, taking short, shallow breaths. But predictably, he capitulated. Opening his legs, he sprung skyward, like a medieval trebuchet.

'Oh, you naughty thing,' she squealed triumphantly, marvelling at the speed with which it readied itself. 'And so angry too,' she added, wrapping her fingers around it. Sensing his rising excitement, she moved closer and positioned herself above him. 'Like I say, you make me want to eat you,' she whispered, as Hugo, excited now to the point of panic, looked on.

Shivering under Daisy's warm, carnivorous touch, he settled back, arms out and legs apart, as though sacrificially splayed and inescapably bound. And soon, nature would succumb to Daisy's wicked encouragement, coaxed into delivering its searing, silvery package with outrageous tingly pleasure.

'Such a big boy too, aren't you?' She said, poking him as he slowly deflated, lying like some glistening sea creature, washed up and beached against his left thigh. 'You won't be getting much sleep tonight,' she threatened, as she rested on his chest once again.

'Now who would come to a place like this with a girl like you to sleep?' He replied, as he ran his hand lightly along her arm before moving to massage her neck, kneading her hot, tired muscles.

'Hmm, that's really nice,' she murmured, as she leaned her head forward, encouraging him to continue. 'Ooh, right there,' she purred, laying perfectly still, as if movement of any kind would cause him to stop. Grinning, he brought his other hand over and set to work on her shoulders, before drawing his nails up through her scalp – something he knew she loved. When one of his hands came within reach, she suddenly grabbed it and pulled it tight to her chest. 'I'm yours now, Hugo, and you're mine,' she declared. 'And no minister on earth, no elaborate ceremony could ever bring us closer than we are now. It's official,' she whispered.

Daisy watched as he walked to the shower room, smiling at him as he turned to look back at her.

'Cover your ears… and your eyes,' he joked, as he switched the fan light on.

His warning came with good reason as the blades kick-started like an old scooter, rattling noisily within their white plastic housing as they gathered speed. The fluorescent completed the assault on the senses, blinking erratically until it eventually sprayed its unnatural white light outwards. Hugo closed the door after him, more to spare Daisy the noise, than for his own privacy. She threw the covers off and lay on her back, looking up at the ceiling and smiling at the sound Hugo made as he relieved himself. After the flush, she heard the squeal of taps as Hugo twisted them, followed by a sudden thud of water on the shower tray. They couldn't have chosen a better place, she thought happily, as she listened to the mundane yet joyous sounds of everyday life. She recalled approaching the Georgian frontage like a couple of eloping teenagers, then signing the register as though married. Mr and Mrs O'Neill. From up north. Recently married. (She'd placed her gran's eternity ring on her wedding finger, turning the precious stones inward.) And when Hugo questioned the accessibility of the upper rooms, they were cordially awarded the premier ground floor apartment, complete with a wondrous view of the magnificent pier, which by then was disappearing into the creeping darkness of late afternoon.

Following her shower, she'd unintentionally fallen asleep beside Hugo, and she recalled how they'd both woken in a panic, with Hugo hurriedly checking his phone thinking it midnight. In reality, they'd only slept for two hours or so, and once free from the confusion of sleep they soon realised where they were. She remembered tingling with excitement as Hugo threw his coat to the floor and began to slowly undress in front of her, saying nothing, not asking for permission, not even if she were willing or prepared. And that's what she wanted, how she planned it. She wanted him to take from her what she so desperately wanted to give. And he understood. She knew she would never forget the moment he began to silently unwrap her, as if peeling a forbidden fruit, before running his warm, trembling hands over the soft contours of her body. She could feel his slow, purposeful intent as he moved closer, breathing heavily as he positioned himself above, pushing her legs apart. Her heart raced with the notion of what followed as his full, weighty presence, his powerful locomotion, his despicable, sexual thievery called upon her once again.

A sudden clatter from the en-suite caught her attention, and startled, she glanced quickly at the toilet door, before recognising the noise as the soap bouncing off the shower tray. Sitting up, she shifted to the edge of the bed, and after a moments preparation, stood. Like Hugo, she stretched her arms up to the ceiling, then shuffled cautiously to the shower room. Knocking on the door, she asked, 'room for one more?'

Chapter Twenty-One

'Oh, what a lovely pub!' Daisy said, as Kathleen, Hugo's younger sister, held the doors open for her. She'd picked them up from the B&B earlier that morning, taking them back to the farm, where Daisy met Margaret, Hugo's mother. It wasn't long after a cup of her finest Irish breakfast tea that Kathleen decided they hit the local pub, whisking Daisy away before she knew what was happening. (Hugo would want some time alone with his mother, was the official reason.) And though initially concerned at what was effectively her abduction, she quickly warmed to Kathleen. For a start, she loved her character: cheeky, direct, and seriously funny. In an unrestrained manner, it has to be said, her sense of humour comparable to Hugo's, but without any of his checks and measures. And she had a quirky, off-road approach to life, evidenced by her choosing a route to the pub littered with several 'cultural' landmarks along the way. Not least the burnt out shell of the 'Bull and Barn' and 'Billygoat hill', which wasn't much of a hill, and was completely devoid of goats.

As the doors closed behind her, she was immediately struck by the authenticity of O' Grady's. This was the real deal. A genuine Irish pub, with genuine Irish people, with genuine Irish craic – unlike the sun, sea and Sangria type populating the Costas. The highly polished counter ran along the back wall, where it curved round to the access hatch, next to the toilet door. To the right was the main seating area with several assorted tables and chairs, few of which matched, as if donated at different times by different people, further accentuating the character of the place. Cast iron fireplaces sat at either end, one with a bevelled mirror above, the other, a dramatic Irish coastal scene, and apart from the usual array of Guinness plaques and pictured mirrors, the walls were busy with dozens of photographs – at least two of which were signed prints of both Clinton and Obama, under which someone scrawled, *O'Bama*. On the other side of the toilet door was a small, wooden stage, presenting itself as the perfect little arena for showcasing the local musical talent. Microphones waited silently in their stands for dusk when the night shoppers would arrive, purchasing their one and only item, again and again until robbed of inhibition and prepared to listen to anything thrown at them. Across the room, light streamed in from the twin Georgian windows on either side of the main entrance, and although it was only three o' clock, there were at least a dozen other people in the bar.

Looking for somewhere to sit, they choose a small, round table between the door and one of the windows.

'Right, what you for?' Kathleen asked, as she flung her jacket on the back of a chair.

'Hmm... half a lager?' Daisy said, amused at the casual way Kathleen made herself at home.

'Half a lager? Sure what's wrong with a full one?'

'I've got the bladder of a small mammal,' she lamented.

'Half it is then.'

Kathleen returned to their table with two bottles of lager and a huge grin on her face, having left behind howls of laughter at the bar.

'You don't wanna know,' was all she would say.

Sitting down, she pulled her chair in and dropped her handbag to the floor. She stared out the window for a few moments before looking at Daisy.

'It's nice to meet the one and only Daisy,' she finally said. 'Heard loads about you.'

'Oh?' Daisy said, feigning surprise. 'Not from me, you

haven't.'

Kathleen grinned and knocked their bottles together. 'Me and you are gonna get on just fine,' she replied. 'So, the pair of you went to Howth yesterday?'

'We did. It's an amazing place, Kathleen. I could go back tomorrow, really. We got some fab photos too,' she added, as she opened the folder before handing Kathleen her phone.

She'd been charmed from the moment she arrived at Howth's tiny train station, which looked more like a traditional Irish pub than a provincial railway terminus. And her first view of the promenade, with the lighthouse barely visible at its tip, was one she would never forget either. Kathleen, more than anyone, understood how Howth eased its way into Daisy's affection. It was a place like no other. Stunningly set, historic, bustling, it seemed to draw the best from people and the best of people to it. Everybody who explored the seafront and strolled it's harbour walls felt they owned it, that it was created just for them. It was more than a holiday destination. It was a profound emotional experience, one that would persist for years and tempt the visitor back, time and again. Kathleen continued flicking through the photographs, until one in particular caught her attention. It took a moment before she recognised the girl standing with Hugo in one of the most striking images she'd seen in a long time.

'Jesus. Is that your twin or something?' She asked, looking at Daisy, then at the photo.

'Oh yes, I *can* actually walk... with a little difficulty.'

'I didn't know, I...'

'That's ok. I just find it quicker and easier using a wheelchair... except for doorsteps and pavements,' she added, straining for a better view of what Kathleen was seeing.

'God, that one's absolutely beautiful,' she said, scrolling to the next one. 'You're like a model, so you are.'

'Hardly,' Daisy replied.

Kathleen flicked through the rest of the photographs, pausing at one with the rusted metal sign advertising trips to the tiny island of Ireland's eye. Sitting beyond the mouth to the harbour, it's terrain rose sharply before dipping gently towards the squat Martello tower at the tip.

'God Almighty! I remember that sign, and those slimy steps leading down to the boat. I was terrified of them, disappearing into the dirty, green water like that. Ugh,' she shuddered, as she quickly scrolled to the next one; a grand, sweeping view of the harbour wall, reaching out to Wales itself (as her father would say to tiny, impressionable ears). 'It was great being on the pier, going all the way up and coming all the way back again. It was just such a simple, joyful thing to do, you know? Mind you, we especially loved the ice cream... our treat at the end,' she said, grinning. 'Funny, isn't it? What's your favourite memory of Howth we'd all be asked? The ice cream, we'd all shout. Dad would always pretend he'd no money, even to the point of pulling his pockets out. We believed him every time.'

'Aw, that sounds lovely, Kathleen. Hugo bought me an ice cream too. Just like your dad would have. It turned into a right old farce, though. He decided to act his shoe size and not his age by racing some school kids to the van. It was so funny. And then, just as he...'

Wondering why there was little or no reaction from Kathleen, Daisy looked up to find her staring at the photograph, hand over mouth. Realising it wasn't such a good idea to talk about ice cream and having fun on the pier, she began to apologise, wishing she could somehow gather the words up and rearrange them in a more sensitive case. Kathleen however, brushed her concerns aside with a sweep of her hand.

'Don't worry about it. It's just that me and Hugh agreed we couldn't go back to Howth, that's all. Too... well, it's our deal, you know?'

Both girls smiled at each other before Kathleen resumed scrolling through the remaining pictures. The last image captured a view of the pier stretching back to Howth itself, and like Hugo, she suddenly recalled a fleeting memory of running its length, head down and oblivious. She could almost hear her tiny, sandaled feet slapping the smooth, warm surface, the sound reverberating all around her. Putting the phone down, she slid it across the table to Daisy.

She couldn't go back to Howth, she'd said. Part of her never left, she realised.

Following their emotional ice-breaker and another couple of beers, both girls traded their background stories, with the detail of Daisy's accident causing Kathleen to wriggle and squirm, as if she'd experienced it herself. Daisy had never heard as many religiously inspired expletives uttered in one sentence before. And though some were familiar, others weren't. And from the 'weren't' selection, she would hijack one or two, she decided, and use them for herself. If and when an appropriate moment arose. Certain company dependent, of course.

And for *her* life story, Kathleen started at the end, believing where she was now to be far more interesting than how she got there.

'You see, there's two important establishments in any Irish town,' she explained. 'The pub and the bookies. One robs you of your senses, the other of your money. Most of them are in here as well,' she added, hiding her face.

'I know nothing about gambling,' Daisy admitted. 'I've never even placed a bet! How much do people spend on something like the horses, or a football match?'

'That depends.'

'On what?'

'How long they stay in this place,' she said, grinning. 'Sure the bookies will be gone soon enough, anyway. It's all online now. And it's even easier to rob people that way.'

Daisy laughed. 'You're wicked, Kathleen. So, how long have you been in the bookies?'

'Just over a year now. After uni, I came home for a while, helping out with the lettings and stuff. I was passing the bookies one day, and I saw they were looking for a manager of all things. I know Billy well, so I went in for a chat and got the job there and then. Billy moved on and I moved in... literally. I rent the flat above.'

'Sure he's a lucky man, finding someone like you, for all his faults... and there are loads of those,' she laughed.

Daisy smiled at Kathleen's good-natured roasting.

'Seriously, you're just what he needed. You're no pushover, yet you're that sweet and innocent you make the Corrs look like a bunch of bitches. Smart too, I hear.'

'I do have my bad points, you know.'

'Don't we all?'

'I pick on him... quite a lot, actually.'

'Sure so did we.'

'And I slap him, occasionally,' she admitted, giggling.

'Jesus, that was one of our favourite hobbies.'

'And I, well... let him run after me.'

'*That,* he doesn't mind. You're doing him a favour there, Daisy. He's got the soul of a slave, so he has. He always followed orders with very little fuss. Get that for me Hugh, and he'd get it. I used to drop things deliberately for him. I think it made him feel good to pick them up, like he was contributing, you know. So yeah, it was therapy,' she justified to herself, as she reminisced. Leaning over the table, she added, 'seen as we have so much in common, we're now officially the best of pals. Deal?' She asked, pretending to spit on her hand.

'Deal,' Daisy replied, as she grabbed it.

'Right, we'll drink to that, so hurry up,' Kathleen ordered, as she grabbed her bag and noisily pushed her chair back. 'I'll get us a couple of Guinness's to celebrate.'

'No, it's my round, Kathleen. I'm getting this.'

'Sit where you are,' she barked, as she stood. 'I'm fairly certain you've not had a *proper* Guinness yet so, as your host, the honour has fallen upon me to introduce you to it.'

'Hmm. This is actually quite nice,' Daisy said, sipping a Guinness for the first time. 'Really creamy too,' she added, as she licked the trademark evidence from her top lip.

'We're the only ones who can pour it properly,' Kathleen stated proudly, as she nodded towards the bar. On the counter stood several, solitary half-filled pints of Guinness. The equivalent of a ghost town, it was as if the owners had quietly slipped away or were collectively sacked. 'That only happens in Ireland. The regulars will be here shortly, and Cian there will just top them up. Best way to pour Guinness,' she said. 'Sorry,' she added, leaning forward, 'the *only* way,'

That wouldn't happen back home, Daisy thought. Someone would be off with them before you knew it. Health and safety would probably prevent it anyway, she figured. As she looked around the bar, she noticed more people had arrived, rubbing their hands and stamping their feet against the cold they left behind. Cian had lit the fires at both ends of the pub, and soon the warmth, along with the pungent smell of peat, swept over her, blending with the alcohol to gently nudge her towards a state of ease and relaxation. She felt herself smile at the silliest of notions, not really knowing why, until she remembered she'd eaten nothing in hours. This is just going straight to my head, she thought, smile broadening.

'Penny for them?'

Startled, Daisy looked up to see Kathleen studying her, with her now familiar, dark Irish gaze.

'I was just thinking, well... I feel sort of... actually, I don't really know how I feel,' she answered. 'I don't even know what to think,' she added, lifting her hand quickly to supress a burp.

'Ah, the unbridled power of the Irish pub. You leave your shit at the door and collect it on the way home.'

'I'd rather leave it at the door. It's far too heavy to carry.'

Kathleen grinned. 'You see now, you're not even Irish, yet you get it. You've come home, so you have. Doesn't matter if you weren't born here. You're ours now,' she declared.

Daisy raised her glass. 'Well then, to *us*,' she giggled, as she downed the remainder of her drink in one go, before slamming her glass on the table. 'So, what you for?' She asked, with all the authority of a seasoned regular.

'Same again... and a Paddy's.'

'Paddy's?'

'Yeah, Paddy's. Irish whiskey. You're in Ireland. Or have you forgotten?'

'Hmm, not so sure about mixing drinks.'

'It's not mixing. Everybody drinks Guinness and

whiskey. Even the Pope. Dash of water for the whiskeys,'
she called after Daisy, as she made her way to the bar.

Chapter Twenty-Two

Daisy waited patiently at the busy counter, scanning first the glass shelves, then the optics for the distinctive bottle of Paddy's. A man in his late sixties, dressed in a suit jacket and jeans with the ubiquitous pint of Guinness and whiskey to hand, turned to her and smiled.

'That barman's a very silly fellow,' he confided in her. 'I'd be serving you, long before I'd serve that rascal there,' he said in a soft, Irish accent.

'Maybe he prefers rascals,' Daisy said.

On hearing Daisy's swift reply, the man laughed so hard he began to cough, a rasping cough, like that of a seriously heavy smoker. When his fit of laughter subsided and he steadied himself on the barstool, he shouted at the barman.

'Cian! Cian! For feck sake, there's a lady here waiting to be served, ya big eejit,' he said, muttering the last few words and winking at Daisy. 'That would be about the funniest thing I've heard all day. James Connolly,' he said, reaching his hand out.

'Daisy Jane Harris.'

'Harris. That would be a Scottish name, wouldn't it?' He enquired, rubbing his chin.

Daisy noticed the dark brown staining on his fingers as they moved around his face.

'It is. My dad's Scottish. He's not actually from Harris... the Island, which would've been amusing. He's from a small town called *Oban* on the west coast, not far from Glasgow?'

'Ah, Oban,' he repeated, clearly with little geographical sense of the location. 'I've been to Scotland many times. Murrayfield… for the rugby, you understand. Lovely city, Edinburgh. The Scots are a fine lot, so they are. Even in defeat, and that's a fairly regular occurrence,' he added as he laughed. 'And what part of England are you from, my dear?'

'London.'

'Ah now, the finest of cities. I worked there for many a year. But,' he added, leaning closer, 'I wouldn't miss her if I never saw her again. Not one tiny, tiny bit.'

'Connolly,' the barman yelled, 'leave the young lady alone, will ya?'

Jumping in fright, the man angrily snapped, 'Jesus wept, your job is to serve us, not bloody well frighten the life from us.' Turning to Daisy, he calmly invited her to place her order, 'on you go my dear.'

'What'll it be, Daisy?' the barman asked.

'Two halves of Guinness and two large Paddy's please.'

'Large ones! You sure now?' He asked, as he flicked the tap.

'Yes, thank you.' She decided on large ones, as the last time she bought a single measure, a gin for Katie, she noticed it barely covered the bottom of the glass. But, unknown to her, if measures in city bars barely wet your lips, those in Irish country pubs filled your mouth. 'And with water, please,' she added.

'Would that be solid form or liquid?' The barman joked.

'Ah would you listen to that gobshite,' the man said. 'Excuse my French,' he apologised to Daisy. 'That barman brings out the very worst in me. Sure I never swear in anybody else's company.'

'Be quiet you,' the barman hissed. 'And any more of that cursing in front of ladies and you'll be barred, I tell ya.' Quickly pouring the half pints, he let them settle as he reached for the optics, both glasses in one hand. In no time at all, he had the whiskies poured, each with a dash of water, the Guinness's topped off, and all duly lined up in front of her.

'There you go, that'll be 22 Euro please.'

'Very efficient,' she said, glowing with admiration.

He grinned. 'I'm actually a machine.'

'In that case then, I wish somebody would bloody well unplug ya,' Connolly rasped.

'Wouldn't work that. I'm solar powered.'

'Well, here's to the night,' he shot back, as he emptied his glass.

Daisy smiled as impartially as she could at the heated, incisive banter taking place, literally, over her head. About to pay the exact amount, she stopped and looked at Mr Connolly, arms now folded across his chest, eyes barely open under his large, bushy brows.

'Would you like a Paddy's too?'

'Of course he would,' the barman said, already filling the glass, water added but no ice. 'Wouldn't ya?' He laughed.

'Don't mind that ignoramus,' he said, glaring at the barman. 'Thank you very much, my dear,' the man said, genuinely appreciative.

'You're very welcome.'

'Eh, that'll be twenty four Euro then, Daisy.'

Daisy handed over twenty five Euro and left the change as a tip before turning to Kathleen. 'Could you help me bring them back?'

'Jesus, can you not balance them on your head or something?' She asked. 'Here,' she said, getting up, 'give them over.'

'I see you met old Connolly there,' Kathleen said, smirking.

'Yes, I did. What a nice man.'

'Yeah, very nice. Cute too. Gets at least one drink from everyone he doesn't know.'

'Oh what's the harm in that?'

'No harm at all, if you're not a raging alcoholic, that is.'

Daisy gasped. 'Oh my God. He's not, is he? Kathleen, I shouldn't have...'

'Ah don't worry about it. Sure nobody dragged him here.'

'Maybe so, but I still feel terrible,' she said, as she glanced over at Mr Connolly, watching regretfully as he supped his 'poison' from the very glass she paid for. 'He seems such a lovely man too. Very eloquent and clever. Where did he work, do you know?'

'Clever alright. He was a history teacher... until the drink got a hold of him. Hit the bottle hard, years ago. Then it hit him back, harder. That's the thing with drink. All pally at first, then it turns on you,' she said, soberly. 'And before you say it, I get the whole addiction thing. Just... some of us take the wrong route, you know. Slainte,' she finished, as she stared ironically at her whiskey glass. With no response from Daisy, she looked up. 'That means cheers... to you lot.'

'Cheers,' Daisy replied, somewhat distantly. 'That means to your health... to you lot,' she added, as she raised her glass. 'Ugh,' she uttered, her body shuddering instinctively, as if trying to prevent the noxious liquid's journey south. 'That's somewhat harsh,' she said, her face contorting. 'What did the Indians call this stuff again?'

'Fire water.'

'How appropriate. I've no idea what Hugo sees in it. Actually, it's time I got used to calling him Hugh, don't you think? I mean, for your mum's benefit.'

'Whatever floats your boat, Daisy. Mam wouldn't mind a bit. Sure she'd forgive you murder, so she would.'

'Well, I think I should try, nevertheless. I can see me

slipping up, though.'

'Look, as soon as I think you're about to say Hugo, I'll cough or something… just to remind you.'

'You'll be coughing all night, then.'

'Possibly,' Kathleen agreed. 'Maybe we should invite old Connolly there and he can do the coughing for us.'

They both laughed at the notion of arriving home, the worse for wear, with old Mr Connolly in tow, drowning the conversation with his rasping cough.

'But how would you know I'd be about to say the wrong name?'

'I can tell what you're thinking, just by looking at you.'

'That's what Hugo says... and you didn't cough there now, did you?'

'Eh, give me a minute to psyche myself up. You can't just... launch into it.'

Daisy waited several seconds before leaning forward.

'Well then, smarty pants, what am I thinking?'

Placing her fingertips against her temples, Kathleen looked hypnotically at Daisy, narrowing her eyes and staring straight into hers. For a moment, she imagined feeling as Hugo must have felt, understanding in an instant how he fell for her, captured as he must have been by her enticing, asymmetric smile before falling into the dark, swirling pools of her gorgeous brown eyes.

'Well?' Daisy asked.

'Sorry,' Kathleen said. 'I left the planet for a minute there. Right then,' she began slowly, 'you are thinking at this very second… what a load of shite she's talking.'

'That's exactly right! Though I wouldn't normally use the word shite.'

'Well now, that's the side effect of spending too much time in here.'

Just as she finished her Guinness and lowered her

glass, the doors swung open, ushering in a blast of cold, sterile air, along with a tall, slender lady in her sixties. Fully laden with shopping bags, she backed her way into the pub, moaning and cursing under her breath with the effort.

'This'll be fun,' Kathleen whispered, as she nodded towards the door. 'I'll give him five minutes before he's hauled out by the lugs.'

Daisy looked at the woman, then back at Kathleen.

'Mrs Connolly,' Kathleen explained, 'and he,' she continued, looking at Mr Connolly, 'will be lucky to finish his pint.'

'Howya Mrs Connolly,' shouted Cian mischievously, as he caught Kathleen's look and winked at her.

Jumping with fright at the sound of her name, Mr Connolly turned to look over his shoulder. Fearfully acknowledging his wife, he swivelled back, before rounding on the barman.

'Sure you've dropped me in it... again.'

'He did no such thing,' Mrs Connolly barked, as she turned on her husband. 'Can you not leave the place alone for one single day.'

All set to 'haul' him home, the conciliatory offer of a hot cup of tea from Cian persuaded her otherwise, and she decided to stay long enough for him to finish his pint. Taking his newspaper off the seat next to him, Mr Connolly cautiously beckoned his wife towards it. Dropping her bags beside the chair, she sat down and shifted closer to the bar, in the process knocking her shopping over. A turnip broke free and rolled haphazardly across the floor, where someone skilfully trapped it and passed it back, bowing to a roar of approval. The silliness of the incident, along with the tea and a welcome seat, somehow infused Mrs Connolly with an even deeper sense of empathy for her husband, and the

232

latest addition to the pub was soon absorbed into the warm, friendly atmosphere. With the doors sealed against the cold, outside environment and the fires roaring in response, the space reverted to kind indifference, its occupants turning away from the drama and settling back to their tables and tales.

'I told you,' Daisy grumbled, as she tugged at the strap of her handbag which was caught under the front wheel of her chair, 'I really do have the bladder of a small mammal.' But before Kathleen could respond with a suitably cutting riposte, the sound of a cough and a wheezy, laboured breathing from behind caught their attention.

'Pardon me for interrupting, ladies,' Mr Connolly began, as he stood, swaying slightly, his silvery, bushy brows raised, eyes tightly closed. 'I'll be off now... under duress as you may gather,' he added, under his breath. 'But I couldn't leave without bidding farewell to thee,' he said, as he squinted at Daisy. 'It was a pleasure meeting you, my dear.'

'And you,' Daisy said. 'And I hope you enjoy the next rugby game... whenever it is.'

'That I will dear, that I will.'

'What are you up to later?' Kathleen asked.

'What am I up to later?' He repeated, looking bewildered. 'Sure I'd tell you if I knew myself,' he said, before issuing a long, rasping cough. 'Good night to you, ladies.'

Mrs Connolly smiled her goodbyes before squeezing past her husband, who only just managed to hold one of the heavily sprung doors open for her. Kathleen watched as they left, clearly caught in two minds, as she followed their receding outlines through the translucent glass doors. As they shuffled from view, she stood suddenly before grabbing her coat and reaching for her bag under the table.

'I'm gonna help them up the road with their messages. It's not too far, so I won't be long,' she said, filling the sleeves of her coat. 'You be ok?'

'Of course,' Daisy replied, 'see you whenever.'

Once Kathleen had left, Daisy sat back, happy to do nothing other than wallow in the soft, mellow ambience of O' Grady's. The warm, yellow hue from the electric lamps swapped places with the fading, natural light of the day, and the once roaring fires had settled to a glowing, crumbling pile of red hot cobbles. She felt as though she were on a journey, trundling through the cold, dark night in some imaginary vehicle, stopping occasionally as a bus, beckoning people aboard to visit warmth and relaxation upon them.

Reaching for her glass, she found it to be empty. Looking up, she caught Cian's stare, which broke quickly to a smile.

'What'll it be, Daisy?' Cian asked.

'Hmm,' was all she could say when faced with the huge array of spirits on the gleaming gantry, not to mention the dozen or so stouts and ales to choose from.

'I'll have you know, I'm supremely talented at everything... *except* mind reading,' he laughed.

Daisy smiled. 'Two pints of Guinness, then.'

'Two! Is one not enough for you?'

Daisy watched as he skilfully executed her request, laying the first pint down on a beer towel of the same brand, before reaching for the second glass. He smiled at her as he topped the first one up, working the glass to create the distinctive creamy head. Smiling back, she wondered how old he actually was. Early twenties, perhaps? She found herself almost obliged to take a closer look at his attributes. He was (notwithstanding the effects of an afternoon session) insanely attractive, having a gorgeously wicked smile, the most perfect of features and a full head of thick, black hair. He wore a white fitted shirt, the sleeves of which were rolled up to his elbows, and with a stylish watch on his right wrist, she concluded he must be left-handed! With a heavy sigh and much reluctance she tore her eyes away, where they fell upon the large open fire at the opposite end of the bar, smouldering now with astonishing warmth as it greedily consumed the last of its cobbles. Soft leather armchairs sat either side, crouching like vintage racing cars, growling their comfort and exuding an irresistible ergonomic pleasure. Should she mark them as hers with a jacket or not?

It was within that brief moment of indecision that Cian lay the second pint down, interrupting her cosy, meandering thoughts.

'That'll be eight Euro, Daisy.'

'I'm sorry?'

'Eh, eight Euro, thanks,' he said again.

'Oh, of course, forgive me,' she replied, as she searched for her purse. 'Could you bring them over to the table for me... if you wouldn't mind?'

'Sure I wouldn't mind at all,' he said, as he dived under the access hatch and carried her drinks the short distance to the table.

'So, you going out with Hugh, then?' He said, as he stacked the empty glasses.

'I am,' Daisy replied. 'We met last Christmas.'

'Really. Were you all nicely gift wrapped?'

'No, actually. I had a pair of cider stained jeans on.'

'Did you now? That's an interesting look.'

'Do you think?'

'Yeah. Sure girls and jeans were made for each other,'

he laughed.

'And what about the cider?'

'Not sure about that now. You don't strike me as being a cider drinker.'

'I'm not. A friend spilt a pint over me. Well not a full pint, but enough.'

'Enough for what?'

'To soak my legs.'

'No way. Was that before or after the ladies?'

'Before… luckily.'

'Just as well, then.'

'Yes. After would have been difficult to explain.'

'You'd have come up with something, I'm sure. Anyway,' he said, noticing two more customers waiting at the counter, 'back to work.'

'Oh, so this isn't work?'

'No, this is pleasure.'

'Aw, well thank you so much,' Daisy said, as she raised her drink.

'You're more than welcome,' he said, as he hurried back to the bar.

Suddenly, the main doors sprung open, through them bursting Kathleen, red faced and apologetic.

'Sorry Daisy,' she said as she sat down. 'Gran would've beaten that fellow home... and she's been dead for ten years.' Looking at the pints on the table she asked, 'here, what have you been up to? Honest, I can't leave you alone for a minute.'

'Hey! It was way more than a minute,' she retorted. 'One for the road, I thought. We'll have to hit it soon enough... before Hugo sends out a search party.'

'Hugh! Sure he couldn't find his way out of a lift.' Looking at her phone she added, 'so long as we're back for half six, we'll survive.'

Daisy laughed. 'You're so funny, Kathleen, honestly.

What a way with words you have. I love listening to you.' Leaning forward, she added, 'and looking at you. You're simply gorgeous.'

'Stop that nonsense now.'

'Why?' Daisy demanded. 'I recall you paying me similar compliments earlier. What's good for the goose is good for the gander, is it not?'

'Not in our case. We're two geese.'

'Well, is there a gander in your life then?'

'Only at Christmas dinner.'

'Aw, Kathleen, that's horrible. Poor little goosey. I meant, are you seeing anyone.'

'Seeing anyone. A man?'

'Obviously.'

'From around here?'

'Where else?'

'Jesus no.'

'What about Cian?'

'Cian? Sure he's lovely, but he's just a boy,' she said, looking over at him.

'So,' Daisy persisted, deciding not to argue over the masculinity of Cian, charismatic and brooding as he was, 'when were you last on a date?'

'A date. Are you serious?'

'Yes, I'm serious.'

'Can't remember.'

'Oh you must.'

'No, honest, I can't.'

'Ok then.' Trying a different tack, she asked, 'who were you last with, what happened and why?'

'What? Listen here, I'm only putting up with this crap cos it's you and no one else.'

'Oh, I'm so not worthy.'

Kathleen's response was to cast an angrier than usual look, and in spite of their burgeoning 'special' relationship, Daisy instinctively backed off.

'I'm sorry. I just find it hard to believe there isn't someone special in your life. I know if I were a man, I'd love your company.'

'If you were a man, you'd be on your arse by now.'

Daisy looked at her, aghast, then burst into laughter. Proper, belly laughter. As such, it wasn't long before Kathleen began to laugh herself, without really knowing why. Daisy was infectious. No matter how hard she tried, she couldn't resist her innocent manner, warmth and affection. Talk about a charm offensive, she thought. This one's written the bloody book on it.

'The last fella I was with? Yeah, he was ok. Good looking... mature,' she emphasised grinning. 'He eh, well let's put it this way, he wasn't happy with certain aspects of my life. Far as I'm concerned, if you can't have me as I am, you can't have me at all.'

'So, what happened? Was he like... horrible to you?'

'Ha, if he was he'd be planted by now. No. He just didn't like the fact I ran the bookies. Thought I should make more of my degree, move to the city, find a big financial institution to work for, then on to the US or Hong Kong or somewhere. Basically, he was telling me how to... *now* what are you smiling at?' She snapped again.

Daisy continued to smile, saying nothing.

'For God sake,' Kathleen said, smiling herself. 'What are you doing to me?'

'I'm doing nothing to you,' Daisy protested. 'I was just thinking how wonderful you are. You're so strong and determined. Your character will take you anywhere, Kathleen. Anywhere in the whole world. And who in their right mind wouldn't enjoy your company.'

'And?'

'And... maybe that strength is your weakness. Maybe

he saw this… this huge potential in you, and I mean huge, but he didn't play it right?'

Kathleen stared at Daisy, listening intently. She brought both hands to her face, fingers covering her mouth as though to prevent a retaliatory outburst.

'You suggesting I have a problem with authority?'

'And do you?' Daisy asked.

'Maybe, but I don't somehow think that's your point.'

'I don't really have a point, Kathleen,' Daisy said honestly. 'I just get the feeling you'll always meet force with force, like you won't ever explore a different route.'

Looking down at her pint, Kathleen pushed it away, as if irritated with the role it played in loosening the grip on her inhibitions – a loosening driven by Daisy's approach: relentless and gentle, dismantling her defences brick by brick, rather than smashing through them. And then, taking Daisy completely by surprise, she started to cry, solitary little tears at first, then enough to hide her face behind her hands.

'Kathleen! Oh my God,' Daisy said in a hushed voice, looking around. 'I'm so sorry. I didn't mean to upset you.'

'You've not upset me, Daisy,' she said calmly, having stopped her tears almost as quickly as they started. Wiping both eyes with her fingertips, she dried them on her top and continued. 'The thing is, I always sort of knew I was moving backwards, but hey, nothing like being slapped in the face with it,' she laughed. 'And that's not a dig at you, by the way. No, kiddo, this one's on me. You want to hear my life story? Let's see now. Hmm... she flew the nest years ago, only to fly right back to it. Now look at her, stuck in a stupid flat above a stupid bookies in a stupid little town. You shouldn't grow old in the town of your birth, Daisy. Looks like you've gone nowhere, done nothing, you know. Then I think, Jesus wept, I'm only fecking thirty! Life can't be over yet, surely,' she said. 'So you were spot on there, Daisy. I blew it, big time... every time,' she added. 'Soon as something or someone worthwhile approached, I pushed them away. And I didn't even know it half the time. I used to think it was bad luck, but no, it was me, Miss antithesis to good fortune,' she declared, smiling as though pleased to have found the most befitting of self-titles.

Daisy sat and listened, stunned by the short, but ferocious nature of Kathleen's emotional admission, coupled with the fact she was probably the first person in all eternity to witness such an event.

'Hey,' she said, grabbing her forearms and pulling them down to seize her hands, 'nothing is set in stone, Kathleen, nothing. Things can change even if you can't. I mean, I've only just turned a corner myself,' she said, 'and it just... happened. Meeting Hugo was totally out of the blue. Turns out it was the best thing that's ever happened to me. And not only that, I've gone and met you. Now you're part of that best thing too.'

'At last! I've done something good and I didn't even know it.'

'You shouldn't feel like that, Kathleen. Like I said, you...'

Kathleen shook her head. 'Actually, I'm feeling grand... other than the fact I've never told anybody stuff like that before. And before you ask, I don't make a habit of crying in front of people either.'

'Well, you don't have to worry, Kathleen. I would never say anything to anybody.'

'That's not what I was intimating at all, Daisy. I know you wouldn't. What I meant was, the only person who knows that about me, is me. Until today that is. Sometimes it feels like I'm talking to myself when I'm talking to you, you know? I sort of trust you with stuff I would only ever trust myself with.'

Daisy smiled. 'That's so strange. Hugo said the same thing to me too. Not long after we met, actually.'

'There you go then, Daisy. There's something about you alright.'

'Something about you and Hugo, more like. What is it with you two?'

'What indeed? Being in each other's pockets for years, I suppose. Sean and Michael were much older, and there weren't many other kids to play with. So, we created a world for ourselves, you know? We just let our imaginations run wild. The back woods were a huge rainforest, full of dangerous beasts and cannibals with poison darts. The place is tiny now when you see it. And the stone circle! That was our round table,' she laughed. 'We used to see who could jump from stone to stone without breaking a leg. The old beech tree had little aliens living on every branch. You couldn't see them though. They were invisible. Mad isn't it?'

'Oh no, it's not mad. It's magical,' Daisy argued. 'It sounds wonderful,' she whispered, for a painful moment wishing she could've joined them, running and hiding, jumping from stone to stone, avoiding poison darts and climbing the trees of Ireland's very own tropical rainforest.

'In a way, we've always been together. Even now, there's sort of a shared crisis thing going on... particularly with relationships. So when I heard he met you, I was a bit jealous,' she admitted. 'I didn't know much about you, if it would last or not, but I thought third time lucky for him. There's a chance it would work, the laws of average say so. Then it would just be me, on my own again, going nowhere. I know that's really selfish of me, but that's how I felt.'

'That's really honest of you to say,' Daisy said.

'Call it whatever you like, it's still pretty destructive, so it is.'

Daisy was about to challenge her negative view, but Kathleen motioned her to stop.

'Look, meeting you *has* actually changed everything here. You and Hugh belong together. That's patently obvious. Even old Connolly would pick up on that. It would take a mean spirited, twisted person to think otherwise and... well, I think you know what I'm saying.'

Daisy reached again for Kathleen's hands, and squeezed them tightly.

'And neither will you go away thinking you've been under scrutiny all evening, because you weren't. I knew within minutes you were the real deal, Daisy. So the craic's all been genuine. In fact, this afternoon's been brilliant, so it has.'

Looking over at Cian, she added, 'he is cute, isn't he? Maybe I should broaden the old horizons after all.'

Several weeks later, in a tiny flat above the bookies, Cian, breathing heavily and soaked in sweat, slowly pulled away and rolled on to his side. He looked adoringly at Kathleen.

'God, I never thought in a million years that would happen.'

'Why not?' Kathleen asked, more with curiosity than confrontation.

'Always thought you were out of my league.'

'Always?'

Cian smiled. 'Sure I've always fancied you, Kathleen O'Neill. There's no-one anywhere in the world quite like you.'

Chapter Twenty-Three

Heading up the long, gradual incline of Billy Goat hill, Kathleen offered to push Daisy, just as they neared the tiny wooden bridge that crossed the stream. Though fatigued, Daisy strongly objected, reminding Kathleen that she was, in fact, more than capable.

'Yeah, we all know that,' Kathleen snapped back, out of breath herself. 'That's not in any doubt, Daisy. It's just that I'd like to get home before midnight, you know?'

'I'm not that slow… am I?'

'Not at all. Sure I can hardly keep up with you,' she said, as she seized the handles.

'Hmm, that bridge doesn't look very safe,' Daisy calculated, as they approached it. Squinting in the light of a distant street-lamp, she added, 'some of those slats are missing, too.'

'None of them are missing. It just looks like it, that's all. Sure that thing can take the weight of a Landover. Come on, let's go for it,' she said, as she gathered enough speed to force their way over the threshold and on to rickety looking structure.

As they crossed the slatted walkway, the bone-shaking vibrations reminded Daisy of the previous day at Howth, where Hugo dragged her along an uneven stretch of pier, and she resisted the urge to utter a low, mumbling sound as she did then. She noticed a solitary glove clinging to a splintered section of handrail and was about to pass comment, when one of her front wheels lodged itself in a particularly wide gap between the slats. Bringing her to a sudden stop, she was convinced, for a terrifying moment, the bridge gave way. Kathleen, unable to stop herself, flew into the back of her, adding to the force of impact. After a stunned, frozen silence, both girls burst into laughter, briefly shattering the eerie calmness before their voices were swallowed by the huge, black sky.

'For God sake, you're giving women drivers a bad name,' Kathleen roared dramatically.

'Me? You were the one speeding, I'll have you know.'

'Speeding my arse,' Kathleen retorted, as she pulled the chair free by shifting weight to the rear wheels before powering forward to clear the gap. Once off the bridge, it took all her efforts to stop Daisy free-wheeling down the steep access ramp. Coming to a stop and looking back, both out of breath through exertion and fear for their lives, they started to laugh again.

'We're getting a bleedin taxi next time,' Kathleen said, gasping.

'Yes, definitely,' Daisy agreed. 'What if that bridge gave way and I fell into the stream?' She asked, genuinely horrified, as she imagined herself gripped by the boiling current and pulled under the cold, black surface.

'Well, you'd be pushing up Daisies, so you would. Just like I've been doing for the last ten minutes,' she snapped.

'Oh, you're so evil,' Daisy laughed.

'Not far to go now,' Kathleen declared, as they reached a level section of path, allowing Daisy charge of her own traction. The light from the solitary street-lamp vanished as they passed the huge, dark outline of one of the farm buildings, the gabled façade resembling the face of the great pyramid, with a smaller structure mimicking the Sphinx. Daisy's imagination swapped places with reason, and for an anxious moment in the complete darkness, she thought she heard the breath of something large and menacing. Something powerful and otherworldly. Something alarmingly close. Moving as silently as she could, she heard it again, this time followed by a prolonged snort and some deep, heavy thuds on earth.

'Kathleen,' she hissed. Unsure how far ahead she was, she called out again, this time as loud as she dared. 'Kathleen!'

'What now?'

'I think there's something watching us.'

'What do you mean, watching us?' She asked, as she walked back to Daisy.

'Shush,' Daisy said, 'listen.' On hearing the sound again, she said, 'there, did you hear that?'

'Yeah I did, why?'

'Well, what is it?'

'Not sure,' she answered. 'Ah, wait now. That must be Finnegan's old bull.'

'A bull?' Daisy shrieked. 'Kathleen, I'm terrified of farm animals… especially bulls. Where is he? We're not in his field, are we? Don't say we've strayed onto his patch.'

'I don't think we have,' Kathleen replied. 'Anyway don't worry. You'll know all about it when he charges. The ground shakes, so it does. And he makes a growl as well. Funny that, being a bull.'

'Kathleen, I'm not joking, please, I'm starting to hyperventilate.'

Kathleen began to laugh, so much so, that she grabbed Daisy's hand-rests to steady herself. 'You're alright. He's in the barn there.'

Staring into the blackness and with her eyes slowly adjusting to the low, almost absent light, Daisy could indeed see that the great pyramid was, actually, a huge barn, fronted by a long railed gate, behind which stood the bemused bull.

'I say barn,' Kathleen continued, 'it's actually his bachelor's pad.'

'What do you mean?'

'He's a stud, so he is,' she explained. 'Here, maybe he fancies you.'

'Kathleen, that is beyond disgusting,' she said, as she began to laugh herself, partly with relief and partly with the situation she found herself in. 'You know, if someone had told me just a few months ago that I'd be drunk and incapable, meandering across the open Irish countryside, nearly drowned in a stream and accosted by a bull, I'd have laughed in their faces. And yet here I am,' she said loudly to the stars, bewildered and ecstatic in equal measure.

With the farmhouse just visible in the distance, Daisy could already smell the unmistakeable scent of seriously good cooking, the aroma bypassing words and logic as it painted an edible picture of something baked, with a contradictory savoury sweetness.

'That smells wonderful,' Daisy yelled. 'I'm so hungry I could eat that old bull.'

'I didn't think you ate meat,' Kathleen shouted back. 'Hugh said you were borderline vegetarian, or was that borderline something else?'

'Well, I am,' she admitted, 'but I wouldn't *not* eat meat at a party or...'

'Well, don't worry. Mam's made her speciality... just for you.'

'Really? Oh that's so nice of her. What is it? It's something baked isn't it.'

'Not saying. It's a surprise.'

'Oh no, you have to tell me.'

'Eh, no I don't.'

Daisy persisted.

'Ah, for crying out loud, ok.'

The family had decided it wouldn't have been particularly clever to expose an entirely unprepared, almost vegetarian Daisy to the sight of a full rack of lamb, its blackened ribs prominently displayed, nor that of a young pig stuffed and cooked, sitting morosely amidst a selection of oven baked fruit and vegetables. Hence the choice of the meat free dish. Not fish free. A step too far that, for the carnivorous O' Neill clan.

'It's mam's fish pie... though the name doesn't do it justice,' she added. 'Freshly caught, wild Irish salmon, and I mean, really, really angry,' she joked, 'served with char-grilled vegetables and wrapped in a warm, puff pastry blanket. And of course, served with our very own Irish potatoes, coated with thick Irish butter and dressed in forests of parsley, sage, rosemary and thyme,' she recited.

'Oh stop it,' Daisy said, as she joined Kathleen on the porch. 'I'm drooling all over myself.'

'Would you listen to you,' Kathleen laughed, as she reached for the door handle.

Chapter Twenty-Four

Margaret hurried back to the cooker. 'That was your aunt Molly,' she said of her sister. 'They're still in O'Grady's,' she added, looking up at the clock as she stirred the soup. 'Sure what are they doing there till this time?'

'Molly, was it?' Hugo asked. 'How did she know where they were?'

'She said she passed Kathleen on the road. She was helping the Connolly's home with their messages.'

'Kathleen? Walking the Connolly's home?' Where the hell was Daisy then? He thought.

Shaking his head, he finished setting the table, then helped himself to a can of Guinness, the non-explosive type. He didn't care for the scientific approach to recreating the smooth taste of a pint at home. If you wanted a perfectly poured pint of Guinness, you went down your local. With his mother standing guard at the stove, he looked at her as she worked away with her back to him, the image as familiar as that of his own name. It was a scene from one of many over the years tagged directly to the kitchen, still a powerfully evocative space for him. Looking down, he remembered the times he'd washed the floor for extra pocket money, almost hearing the sound of the heavy, wet mop slapping against the tiles. Scanning the ceiling above, he found the roughly plastered attempt he made at filling a large hole brought on by a water leak one Easter, the last before the millennium. He saw the corner where he held poor Sunny in his dying moments, and the table he sat at, was the same one he hid beneath whenever threatened with physical discipline. But his recollections felt, for the first time, ancient and static, almost irrelevant. Far from deriving comfort and a sense of belonging, he felt stifled.

Meeting Daisy was truly a breath of fresh air that fundamentally shifted his view of everything. And like her, he felt he'd outgrown his formative space. The place he viewed now was simply his point of origin, with room only for memories.

'You want me to nip to O'Grady's, haul them home?' He asked his mother.

Turning from the stove, hand on hip, she looked at the clock again.

'Ah no. Sure what if they've left already?'

'Fair enough. I'll switch the porch light on for them.'

'Sure I did that earlier,' Margaret said, as she checked the state of her salmon pie, now golden brown and billowing aromatic steam from tiny air vents cut into the pastry.

'I think that's them now,' Hugo said as he stood, wondering what condition they'd be in, particularly Daisy. Four or five long hours in a pub in the afternoon offered considerable opportunity to take complete leave of the senses, and being with Kathleen, there was every chance Daisy would arrive back without them. Before he went to the door, he put his arm around his mother's shoulder.

'Thanks mam… for having us, and for doing all this.'

'Go way,' she said, shaking his arm off.

Smiling mischievously, he grabbed her around the waist with both arms, hugging her firmly.

'No I won't go away at all.'

'Go and get the door,' she ordered, slightly flustered but smiling.

Kissing the back of her head, he complied.

Hugo reached the door just as Kathleen burst through it.

'Jesus, what a fright you gave us,' she said, as she staggered past him into the foyer, followed by Daisy.

Cheerful and muddied, her hands and forehead brown with soil from the wheels, she brushed her hair to one side, unwittingly demonstrating how the mud got everywhere.

'Hi Hugo,' she said. 'Sorry, I think we're a little late.'

'Late? It's practically tomorrow, so it is. You not think of getting a taxi?' He asked, turning to Kathleen, who was busy trying to prise one of her shoes off.

'No. Sure it was just as quick going over the stream and across old Finnegan's farm,' she replied. 'I tried to do away with her, but she kept bobbing to the surface. Even the old bull wouldn't go near her.'

'I thought you said that bull was locked in the barn!'

'I didn't, did I?'

'Come on you two,' Hugo said, as he spun Daisy around and pushed past Kathleen, by now bent double and cursing at the other shoe. Trying to avoid her builders cleavage, he joked, 'very flattering,' before moving swiftly out of firing range.

'Daisy! You poor thing,' Margaret said, as she dried her hands on the dish cloth before rushing over. Grabbing her face, she pinched and rubbed her cold cheeks as though she were a little girl. 'Ah would you look at you now,' she said, as she flicked some of the mud from her hair. Daisy sat patiently, eyes tightly closed and smiling, happy to be concerned about and pampered in such a caring, maternal manner.

'You'll want to go and tidy yourself before dinner, won't you?' She asked. 'Hugh, show her where the bathroom is, will you?'

By the time they came back, Kathleen was already dishing out the starter: Margaret's inimitable thick vegetable broth, served with freshly baked Irish soda bread, still hot from the oven. Seated at the table were Sean, Hugo's next oldest brother and his girlfriend, Michelle. They both stood up, with Sean making room for Daisy to take her place, before trading pleasantries (most of which centred on Daisy's 'abduction').

'Never mind them now, Daisy,' Margaret said protectively, as she pulled one of the heavy pine chairs to one side. 'In you come here, love.'

'Oh no, I'm fine, thank you. I'd prefer to sit on one of those,' she said, as she fixed her wheelchair in place next to the wooden chair, before swapping seats. As soon as she was seated, Hugo dragged her wheelchair to the wall, initially baffled with its stubborn resistance, until he realised the brakes were on.

'That's me,' she said, smiling around the table, as they all stared back.

'Just look at you lot,' Kathleen laughed. 'It's a bleedin miracle, you're all saying. Suppose it is. Saint Paddy's and Brother Guinness. That right, Daisy?'

'Paddy's *and* Guinness?' Hugo asked.

'Sean dear, will you say grace?'

'I will indeed mam,' he said, as he clasped his hands and closed his eyes. 'Dear Lord, we are blessed to have a special guest here at our table this evening, and we ask that you look kindly upon her. And for what we are about to receive, may we all be truly thankful.'

'Thank you,' Daisy whispered.

Sean smiled. 'No worries there. Hope the big fella's listening,' he laughed. 'Right then,' he said, 'let's tuck in before it gets cold.'

'Hmm, this is exactly what I needed,' Daisy said, almost as the spoon left her mouth.

'Here, you're supposed to have it *before* you go on the lash,' Sean joked.

'The lash, as you put it, occurred spontaneously,' Kathleen retorted.

'Sure they're the best sort,' Sean replied. 'White wine Daisy, I believe?' He asked.

'Your accent is so familiar,' Daisy said, leaning towards Michelle. 'Are from you Bath or somewhere?'

'Very close, Daisy,' she said. 'Bristol, so you weren't far out.'

'Bristol? I have a friend from Bristol! She lives in London now, but we go across every now and then. I love it there.'

'Yeah? I like to get back fairly regularly too. It's only a short flight as well, so…'

'Do you have family there?'

'Mum and dad... and little brother. Well, I say little. He's huge now. A rugby playing fireman, so they don't come much bigger,' she laughed.

'A rugby playing fireman! Ooh, what a combination, strong, fit and fearless,' Daisy said, aware Hugo was listening in. 'Oh but you've got character,' she said, turning to him.

'That'll do me,' he said, grinning. 'Tell you what, I'd tackle a fire before I'd tackle one of those rugby fellas now. You seen the size of them?'

'God yeah,' Sean agreed. 'It's not like in my day, when I played for the College. The lads now are huge, solid beasts. Be like getting hit by a small car. Worse even.'

'That says something about the modern game alright,' Hugo added. 'You've more chance of surviving a car crash than a rugby match.'

'Sure it's a daft game anyway,' Kathleen said. 'Why do they have to pile on top of each other like that? Do they not get squashed or something?'

Sean laughed. 'Squashed?'

'Yeah, squashed. And women playing it now as well.'

'Why shouldn't women play?' Michelle challenged. 'It's what you call equality.'

'Equally stupid, more like. And would you look at the shape of the ball,' she added. 'It's like a great big egg. Jesus, are they taking the mickey or what?'

'Kathleen!' Margaret scolded. She didn't mind the occasional use of the word God, but she wouldn't tolerate the Lord's name taken in vain.

'Sorry, mam.'

'You still at the football, Hugh?' Sean asked.

'No, not anymore. I'm actually a bit bored of football now, to be honest. Overpaid, tax-dodgers the lot of them. And the cheating that goes on, God. It's like, if the ref doesn't see it, it's ok. Eh, no actually, it's not ok. Cheating's cheating, whether it's taking steroids or handling the ball. I can't think of another high profile sport, or any sport actually, where the ruling body is aware players are at it but does nothing about it. I mean, can you imagine Ronnie O' Sullivan touching the wrong ball and carrying on? It just wouldn't happen.'

'Sure there's a big difference between taking drugs and handling the ball,' Sean argued.

'I don't think so. You're still getting an unfair advantage, whatever means you deploy. Drugs attract all the negative stories in the press, yet all the while, the so-called 'soft' cheating continues. It's why I play darts. You can't cheat, but you can drink,' he laughed.

'Darts is hardly a sport,' Kathleen scoffed. 'That lot couldn't run around the block.'

'Yeah but, it's not just about being fit and active, is it? I mean, look at snooker, archery, bowling, golf even,' he said. 'Sport's about skill, poise, psyching your opponent out, winning, you know... fairly.'

'What about tiddlywinks?' Sean asked. 'You need skill and poise there, don't you?'

'Yeah, like you do with marbles, draughts, snakes and ladders, but that doesn't...'

'Them as well, thanks,' Sean laughed, triumphantly.

'Sure I'm knackered with all this talk of sport,' Margaret grumbled, as she rose to start clearing the dishes in preparation for the final course.

'Sit Mam,' Kathleen, Sean and Hugo said in unison. 'We'll get the dishes.'

'The problem we've got,' Sean said in response to Daisy's assertion that it was the best meal she's ever had, 'is we're too used to it now. You'd have to find a Michelin star restaurant to get a better meal, and there's not many of them about here,' he said, grinning.

'Sure Michael's hotel has a lovely restaurant. I think it's better than those... Michelin things,' Kathleen said.

'I think it is too,' Michelle agreed. 'We were there for the work's night out last Christmas. It was absolutely lovely, not too dear either.'

Daisy turned to Hugo. 'Michael's hotel?'

'Yeah, big brother runs the Old Bridge hotel in Dublin,' Kathleen answered for him. 'Sorry there, Hugh.'

'You're fine, go for it,' he said.

'They're an independent group,' she continued. 'Three hotels they've got, but they want to expand. I don't think they should. They've a great reputation as they are. I think you lose customer focus the bigger you get.'

'Yes, I think so too,' Daisy said. 'We were taken over by Dementia Matters a couple of years ago. And they are a great company to work for, but I think too much emphasis is placed on procedures and compliance now, rather than customer care.'

Sean agreed. 'Yeah, sure huge organisations don't

benefit customers. They pretend they do, but they don't. And because they eliminate competition, they basically operate on the principle that people have little option or appetite to go elsewhere. And even if they do, they don't care. They'll launch a glossy campaign for new customers and move on from there.'

'True enough,' Kathleen said. 'Scary thought, but in the future, there'll only be a handful of companies running the world, and they *will* be running the world. You can forget about governments running things, because they're elected by the people, and businesses don't listen to people.'

'Sounds more philosophical than economical,' Hugo said.

'Ah sure economics is vague enough to incorporate philosophy. One lecturer at uni compared it all to those Terminator films, and how Skynet seized power from the very people that created it. Businesses are machines, he would say, and they're frustrated with human input and frailty. They're desperate to operate on a purely logical, binary basis. It's amazing to think that no matter how large an organisation becomes, certain key decisions are still instinctive.'

'It's a basic principle of sales,' Sean added. 'I buy from you... cos I like you. Simple.'

'Exactly,' Kathleen said. 'You could be losing out on the deal of the century because you don't like the other person. How stupid is that?'

'Never mind business now and all that rubbish,' said Margaret, as she set the dessert on the table: a bowl of chopped fruit and winter berries, served with whipped cream. 'This is from God's earth itself, so get it down you,' she ordered.

'Oh I don't know if I could,' Daisy said.

'Sure it's just fruit and cream. You'll have a little bit,

won't you?'

'I will, Margaret. But that's me on bread and water till we come back.'

'So you're planning coming back... after tonight?' Sean asked, straight-faced.

'Only when she gets hungry,' Kathleen said. 'Like the rest of us. That right mam?'

'Sure if you can't feed your family, what can you do?'

'Wine anyone?' Sean offered, twisting the cap from the second bottle.

'Oh, should I?' Daisy asked, looking to Hugo for help with her decision. 'I just know I'll suffer tomorrow.'

'You're going to suffer anyway,' Sean said, 'so go for it.'

'At least you'd know what was wrong with you. If you woke up with a headache and you hadn't been drinking, that would be the best you'd feel all day,' Kathleen joked.

'That's the best excuse for drinking I've ever heard,' Daisy said.

'Not mine, I'm afraid,' Kathleen admitted. 'Can't remember where I heard it now.'

'Sounds like something Frank Sinatra would've said,' Sean suggested.

'No, it wasn't Frank Sinatra,' Margaret stated. 'It was Dean Martin.'

'Ah now, that makes sense. Was he not always drunk on stage?'

'Sure he was not,' Margaret snapped. 'He didn't touch a drop on stage. It was all an act, so it was.'

'Was it now? Didn't know that,' he said, as he filled Daisy's glass, regardless of her indecision, but Michelle put her hand over hers.

'Not just now thanks,' she said.

'Can you get us a Guinness?' Hugo asked Kathleen as she left the table.

'Yeah, no problem.'

'You alright there?' Sean asked Michelle.

'Yeah. Just full to the gunwales. I'm ready to drop.'

'So am I,' Daisy said. 'Why is it we get so tired after eating?'

'Isn't it something to do with more blood going to the gut?' Kathleen suggested, coming back with Hugo's Guinness.

'That's why you shouldn't swim after a meal,' Michelle instructed. 'You'd get cramp.'

'Clever that, in the middle of the sea,' Kathleen added.

'Yeah, can you imagine it? Swim for your life. Eh no, I'm busy with this digestion thing. Starving, so I am,' Hugo joked.

Margaret just caught Hugo's last few words as she returned to the conversation.

'Sure how can you be starving?' She asked.

'No I'm fine, mam,' he laughed. 'Just telling a story.'

'So mam,' Hugo started, 'what's new down on the old farm?'

'Ah sure there's nothing new on the farm,' she answered. 'Mind you, Sean did a grand job on one of the roofs, so he did.'

'Oh? What was wrong with it?'

'Ridge tiles,' Sean replied. 'Had to repoint them all. Took a couple of days.'

'That's a pain,' Hugo said. 'And how's Easter looking?'

'Easter's looking great... again. Already turning people away, which I don't like doing but, you know, you either have the room or you don't.'

'You must be running at what, five or six months yearly now?'

'Closer to seven actually.'

'Really?'

As Sean and Hugo discussed the nuances of building maintenance and the holiday home market, Michelle rolled her eyes in a visible gesture of boredom. Swapping seats with Hugo, she now sat next to Daisy, who turned gleefully to face her.

'You work for... Dementia Matters, did you say. What do you do there?'

'I'm lead administrator for the Southwark office,' Daisy replied. 'I've been there for nearly five years now. I say five years, I was with a small, local charity called Headway until Dementia Matters took them over about two years ago. They're a huge national charity,' she explained. 'Hence all the new procedures! Still, it's a great place to work. Hectic at times, but I love it. And what about you?'

'I'm a dental technician... in Drogheda. It's so handy. No time to get to work in the morning. Not like Dublin,' she said, groaning with the memory of Dublin's legendary congested northside. 'I'm just qualified, actually.'

'Really? Congratulations, Michelle. That's amazing. For some reason, I thought you worked here, with Sean, running this place.'

'No, I worked as a dental nurse initially... in Bristol. About a year after I moved over here with Sean, a friend noticed a vacancy for a trainee technician in Drogheda, so I applied for it,' she explained. 'Couldn't have worked out better, really,' she said, smiling at Daisy. 'So, tell me, how did you and Hugh meet?'

'Well,' Daisy began, describing how they met, ironically in an Irish pub in central London, one fateful Saturday night, not long after Christmas. And if that first night was a night where everything seemingly clicked into place, the night of their first date was one where everything almost clicked out again. Michelle thought it was one of the most romantic things she'd ever heard – Daisy, resolutely waiting by Hugo's side until he came to. She wasn't surprised at his later antics, however. Apparently, he'd done something similar years ago when he came off his motorbike. Refusing treatment, he walked several confused miles home, and on arrival, was promptly driven several confused miles back to the nearest A&E. Listening avidly to the rest of their escapades, Michelle soon spotted an opportunity to poke a bit of fun.

'You know, you couldn't write that, Daisy... how you both met. You sound like you're made for each other. Hugh's a lucky man... in more ways than one.' Lowering her voice, she asked, 'so, if Hugh's been your first boyfriend in a while, were you not a little rusty, or was it a bit like riding a bike?'

'Let's just say, I got rid of my stabilisers *sooner* than expected,' she giggled, then stopped, when she realised what she'd just admitted. 'Michelle!'

'Don't worry,' she said leaning closer. 'As they say over here, I'm only messing with you.'

'And what about you and Sean? Hugo said you met in Bristol?'

'Actually, we met in Rio of all places.'

'Rio,' Daisy exclaimed. 'Wow, how exotic is that? Tell me more,' she insisted.

'Well, Sean was living in Bristol at the time. He'd been to the university, got his degree in business management and was working in IT. I'd just finished a college course in accounting, which I hated, incidentally. No idea at all what I wanted to do,' she sighed. 'So, at twenty two, I decided to take a year out. I wanted to do something different, like travel around Europe, the world, see what was going on... beyond Bristol.'

'So that's when you went to Rio?'

'Well, I didn't *quite* get that far.'

'But didn't you say you met in Rio?'

'Yes, we did. But not Rio, Brazil. Rio, the dodgy nightclub in Bristol.'

'Aw, Michelle. I believed you as well.'

'Hey, I wasn't lying. It just so happens Rio is Bristol's very own exotic nightclub. Though there wasn't much exotic about it. All I can remember is sticking to the carpet, the place having a dirty, sweaty smell and music ten years out of date,' she recalled. 'But, I did meet Sean there, and we spent the whole evening in the 'speakeasy' drinking cocktails... more to avoid the music than anything else,' she added. 'And here we are, fifteen years later. What's that now, our crystal anniversary?'

'I think so. But you're not married, are you?' Daisy asked.

'No, we're not. Someday, maybe. But I can see you two tying the knot. Bet you'd look stunning in a beautiful, white, sequinned gown.'

'Actually,' Daisy began, matter-of-factly, 'I see myself getting married in green?'

'Green?' Michelle asked. 'You want to get married in Green. Really?'

'Yes,' Daisy replied. 'Gretna Green,' she laughed.

'Oh, very good, Daisy. I walked right into that one.'

'Sorry. I've been waiting to use that one for years.'

Chapter Twenty-Five

Bored with talk of bookings and maintenance, Hugo took advantage of a pause in conversation with Sean to turn to Daisy, just as Michelle excused herself. Watching as she left the room, he casually got up and slid in beside Daisy, leaning over the table on his elbow. With a vacant 'haven't-seen-you-around-these-parts-before' demeanour, he began to hit on Daisy, who duly adopted an equally vacant, but skilfully elusive Southern Belle persona as she hit back. The ridiculous nature of their conversation didn't go unnoticed.

'Would you listen to you two nutcases,' Kathleen roared.

'Kathleen, sure that's awful rude,' Margaret said. 'Daisy's no nutcase, now.'

'Here, what about me?' Hugo asked.

'And what about you?' Margaret replied, turning away with a smile. Turning back, she asked, 'and tell me Daisy, you're going home tomorrow, are you?'

'Yes, I'm afraid so. Back to the grindstone on Wednesday,' she sighed.

'Ah sure we'll see you again, I hope.'

'You will, mam. Tomorrow morning,' Hugo reminded her.

'That's cos you're staying here tonight,' Sean said, putting his phone down.

'It's not, is it? Well deduced there, Sean,' Hugo replied, grinning at Kathleen.

'Yeah, thanks for that Sean. We'd never have guessed.'

'That's me all over,' he laughed. 'Far too generous, I am.'

Far too generous… I am, Daisy thought, smiling. That's where it comes from. I'm at the source, she realised, as if she'd finally found the O'Neill family Nile, and made the long, tortuous journey upstream.

Just then, Michelle reappeared with her coat folded over her arm. 'Sorry guys, I've gotta go. I'm in earlier than usual tomorrow.'

'Why? What time you starting?' Sean asked.

'Have to be there for eight. Two students coming in.'

'Students… at eight in the morning?' Daisy laughed.

'You sure it's not eight in the afternoon?' Kathleen added.

'No, it's definitely eight *am*. We dental technicians have an amazing work ethic,' she said, as she retrieved her bag from the back of her chair. Thanking Margaret for the meal, she then went around the table, saying goodbye to everybody. Leaving Daisy till last, she insisted they meet again. For a night out. Maybe even in Rio! Book your flights! She joked.

'Right, I don't know about you lot, but I'm having one for the road,' Sean said, reaching for the wine bottle. 'Daisy?' he asked, waving it in front of her.

'I shouldn't really… but I will.'

'Go on then,' Hugo joined in, 'I'll grab a Guinness. Kathleen, mam?'

'No, I'm having tea,' Kathleen answered.

'Ah sure I'll have a cup of tea as well,' Margaret said.

Hugo walked to the fridge, first filling the kettle and switching it on. Hearing the kettle puff and squeal, Kathleen turned to him. 'Thanks for that.'

'No problem. Saves Mam's feet so it does. I'd do the same for me little sister as well, though,' he assured her.

'Would you now?' She asked. 'Can I have that in writing?'

'No need for that,' Sean said. 'Verbal agreements are just as legally binding. So that's you, I'm afraid.'

'Oh you're all so funny,' Daisy laughed, following the conversation. 'You squeeze humour out of everything.'

'They do indeed,' Margaret said. 'Drives me mad, so it does. Sure their father was the biggest joker of them all. I remember the time he took me to a posh restaurant over in Malahide. He said he'd pick me up at eight sharp. So there I was, waiting for him outside the house. And what turns up, but a big, dirty old tractor with your father at the wheel, smiling and waving like a big eejit. Plenty of room for two, he shouted. I'm not getting diesel all over my dress climbing into that big, dirty thing, I shouted back, and away I ran, back into the house. Seconds later the doorbell goes, and here's your father, standing there, smiling like the cat that got the cream and everything else. Then he pointed to the car.' Margaret laughed to herself. 'Pat, his friend followed him over in the car and was driving the tractor back. Honest now, I could've killed him so I could.'

'Oh that's so mean,' Daisy said. 'That's exactly the sort of thing Hugo… Hugh would do, isn't it?'

'Here now, there's an idea.'

'Don't even think about it,' she warned him.

'Actually, I could see you in a tractor. Not the greasy old working kind. A brand new shiny one. That's how the Gala Queen arrives for the fete. You should enter the competition. You'd win hands down.'

'And how do you suppose I'd win hands down?'

'You seen the competition?'

'Oh very funny,' she said. 'And what's the prize then? It's got to be worth my while entering, surely?'

'Don't call him Shirley. He hates it,' Sean laughed.

'Jesus, that's prehistoric,' Hugo retorted.

'Hugh,' Margaret scolded.

'Sorry mam.'

'I don't get it,' Daisy said, looking around, confused.

'Surely… Shirley,' Sean explained.

'Oh, I see what you mean,' she laughed. 'Very funny.'

'Funny? It's nothing of the sort,' Kathleen snapped. 'Don't encourage him.'

'So, what's the prize then?' Daisy repeated.

'Eh... the tractor,' Hugo quickly said.

'Or old Connolly driving it,' Kathleen laughed. 'You were both getting on great in the pub so you were. Sure the ice is broken now.'

At that point, Sean slapped the table, almost in hysterics.

'Daisy and old Connolly,' he laughed. 'God, you should've seen your face, Daisy. You imagined it for a minute there.'

Waiting for a lull in the collective hilarity, Daisy joked, 'and why not? He's quite a catch.'

This time the whole room erupted and even Margaret's distinctive roar emerged, encouraging yet more laughter to the point of self-perpetuation. As the racket subsided, the occasional sigh and snigger brought more random bursts, leaving some moaning as though in pain.

'Sure you're a great laugh, Daisy,' Sean said.

Kathleen wiped her eyes and smiled warmly at Daisy, 'sure she's more than that.'

'I'm done in,' Kathleen suddenly said. 'I need me bed.'

'Yeah, I should get back as well,' Sean added. 'Oh,' he remembered, 'what's up with the toilet, mam?'

'The toilet?' She asked. 'Ah yes now, sure it won't flush. The handle's all loose like there's something broken inside.'

'I'll have a quick look at it for you.'

'You'll do no such thing now. Leave it till tomorrow.'

'Mam, it'll take me two minutes.'

'Ah he's terrible, so he is,' Margaret said.

'And sure so are you,' Kathleen said. 'Coming downstairs in the middle of the night to use the toilet.'

'Sure it was worse when I was your age,' she said, remembering the outside toilet in the garden of their very first house: a tiny, rented cottage, just down the road from the in-law's farm. Close enough *to* them, but far enough *from* them, her husband would say of his parents. She smiled when she remembered the logistics of using the toilet, particularly at night. The tiny, damp outhouse had no light, and they had to keep a torch by the back door. Woe betide anyone who didn't return it to its rightful place.

'What are you grinning at?' Kathleen asked her mother.

'Could you get my chair, please?' Daisy whispered. 'Need a pee.'

Hugo got up and pulled her wheelchair over, then waited for Daisy to stand before dragging the kitchen one back.

'I'll show you to your room as well, will I?' He suggested. 'It's just down the hall.'

'Yes, if you like. Actually, I'm really tired anyway,' she hinted.

Hugo nodded. 'Got you,' he whispered back. 'Eh, I think we'll hit the sack as well, mam,' he said, turning to her. 'I'll show Daisy where she's sleeping. You got the key for the old barn?'

'The barn! Don't mind him, Daisy. He'll be in the barn if he doesn't watch it.'

'I'll just nip to the toilet first,' he said, remembering the top one was out of order. 'Back in a sec.'

'That was a beautiful meal,' Daisy said, as she approached Margaret. 'I simply must lie down,' she explained, as she rubbed her stomach. 'I won't need to eat for days.'

'Sure you're more than welcome. Will you have a cup of tea before you go?'

'Oh no, thank you. A glass of water's fine.'

'I'll get that for you,' Kathleen said, as she got up. 'You like some ice in it?'

'Yes, that would be lovely Kathleen, thank you.'

'Sure it's no trouble at all,' she said, as she reached for the ice tray, annoyed that the automatic ice maker decided not to work one day. Sean wouldn't go near it either, insisting working on it would invalidate the warranty. No one had yet got round to calling the service number, which was still visible on the lower left-hand side of the door.

'Would you like me to pop it through for you,' Kathleen offered.

'If you don't mind?'

Kathleen stopped and looked at her. 'Sure why would I mind?'

'I'm sorry, I just don't expect...'

'And stop apologising, will you,' she shouted, as she walked to her room.

'What's all that racket?' Hugo yelled, as he returned from the toilet.

'Oh me poor ears,' Margaret said to herself.

'It's nothing,' Daisy said. 'Kathleen insists I stop apologising.'

'Does she now?'

'Yes she does,' Kathleen barked, as she crept up behind Hugo, hoping to frighten the life from him. But as Hugo barely flinched, she moaned, 'God you're like a stone, so you are.'

Sean then appeared, out of breath, sleeves rolled up.

'Just about there, mam. Need the pliers to twist the

'wire around the... you know, whatever it's called,' he said, as he searched one of the kitchen drawers.

'Ah sure that's great, Sean. You hear that mam, he's nearly done, so he is,' Kathleen said.

'Him and me both.'

'Anyway, mam, we'll leave you in peace. I'll tuck Daisy in. Might take a while, you know, make-up off, a bedtime story...'

'Hey! I'll be au natural before you know it.'

'Don't be saying things like that now,' he whispered.

'I meant my make-up, silly.'

Hugo kissed his mother goodnight. 'Night mam, and thanks for tonight.'

'Night son,' she said, patting his back.

Grinning, he turned to Kathleen. 'And eh, night night... Atneen.'

'Atneen?' She shrieked. 'Jesus. I haven't heard that in ages.'

'Kathleen. Would you stop that now?'

'Sorry Mam. Oh my God, what a blast from the past.'

'It was my nickname for her,' Hugo explained to a bemused Daisy. 'I was only two or three at the time.'

Kathleen approached and put her arms around him. 'Atneen indeed. Night, night,' she laughed.

'Obvious question I know, but did you have a nickname for him?' Daisy asked.

'Yeah, Shugh.'

'Shoe?' Daisy asked, clearly confused.

'Not those things,' she said, pointing to her feet. 'No, all I heard growing up was, *Shush!* Hugh. So that became Shugh. Sure it made perfect sense to me,' she laughed.

'Shugh,' Daisy beamed. 'Oh that's so funny too. Come on Shugh,' she giggled.

Hugo glared at Kathleen. 'Look what you've done now.'

'Look what *I've* done? Eh, where exactly did Atneen come from?'

Chapter Twenty-Six

Hugo pushed the toilet door open, then reached in to pull the light cord.

'After you, Madam,' he said.

'Thank you so much, kind sir.'

'I'll wait in the bedroom for you.'

'Oh no,' she quickly said. 'Come in... please.'

'You sure?'

'Yes. Come in and close the door,' she whispered. 'I just fancied talking to you in here. This is where we girls disappear for hours at a time,' she explained. 'Needs a bigger mirror though,' she added seriously, looking at the small oval one above the sink. 'You need one where loads of girls can squeeze in front of, do their make-up, try things on, listen to music, and of course... this,' she said, pointing to the hip flask Hugo didn't even know she had. 'But most important of all,' she continued, 'it's where we decide who's hot or who's not,' she giggled. 'Not, mostly,' she sighed.

'Always wondered what went on in there,' he said, still surprised at the sight of a hip flask in her bag.

'Now you know, don't you? Actually, sometimes it's more fun in the toilet than in the bar itself,' she said. 'We spent ages in the ladies one night. Proper party we had. We swapped tops before we left as well. It was so funny coming out with different clothes on. These guys just didn't know what to make of us. Think we scared them off.'

Hugo laughed. 'Well, it's not like that in the gent's, I can tell you. Purely functional in there, it is. We don't talk to each other, well... very occasionally. No large mirrors, either. Usually a small cracked one above the drier. And it's always cold, even in summer. And the smell, God, I couldn't even begin to describe it to you.'

'Ugh!' she said, screwing her face as she listened to Hugo's graphic description, 'how uncivilised. Remind me never to... actually no, don't. Think I'd rather pee my pants. And speaking of which,' she added. Desperate now to relieve herself, she backed towards the toilet, but got the angle wrong and moved forward to try another approach. When *that* didn't work, she slapped her armrest. 'What's wrong with me tonight? I'm all over the place.'

'Like a hand there, Miss Daisy?'

'Yes please,' she said, holding her hands out. As he helped her stand, she flung her arms around his neck, whispering, 'you can pull my leggings down, if you like.'

'Hmm, shouldn't we go for a drink first,' he said, as he tried to kiss her.

'Oh please, hurry,' she begged, turning her head. 'I'm bursting!'

Hugo obliged, pulling them down to her knees, then helped her onto the toilet seat. Not that she needed help. She simply enjoyed being lovingly manhandled in that manner. And she enjoyed Hugo's *obvious* enjoyment in the course of his busy manhandling as well. What wasn't there to enjoy? As she shifted for comfort, he walked over to the bath and sat on its edge, dutifully looking to one side. When done, she pulled her pants and leggings to her knees and waited, arms out with a mournful 'help me again' look on her face. Walking back to her, he helped her up, but before he pulled her trousers to her waist, he grabbed her cheeks, playfully kneading soft, fleshy handfuls, still cool from the hard plastic seat. As his hands slowly converged, she wriggled her disapproval.

'Stop it,' she moaned, as she leaned heavily against him.

'What's up now?' He murmured, nuzzling into the side of her neck.

'You forgotten where you are?' She said, nodding towards the door.

'I'm stuffed and tired and... worn out,' she said, yawning and stretching as she rubbed her eyes with the backs of her fingers.

'Not surprised,' Hugo said, as he leant against the bedroom door, coat over his shoulder. 'You've been at it since lunchtime.'

'Oh don't remind me, please,' she groaned. 'I've no idea what got into me.'

'Guinness, Paddy's... Kathleen?'

'Kathleen,' she whispered affectionately.

'Anyway,' he continued, as he walked across the room before throwing his coat on the bed, 'you were a great craic tonight. You had us all in stitches, so you did. Mam even.'

'Aw, your mum's lovely, Hugo. So is Michelle,' she added. 'And you never told me Sean was so funny.'

'Must've slipped my mind. Tell us about O'Grady's then,' he said, sitting cross-legged in front of her.

The mere mention of O'Grady's seemed to invigorate Daisy, and sitting forward eagerly, she relayed all that occurred within its peat fired, dreamy environment (all, that is, except her encounter with Cian. Not for public scrutiny, that was *her* memory alone). Hugo listened, highly entertained, but shaking his head continually in mock criticism as he tried to keep up with her quick fire recollections. Taking a mental note of all the drinks she consumed, he laughed as she proudly stated she left the pub still 'sitting'. She then described how they made their way back to the farmhouse across the black Irish countryside, negotiating the stream, powering up Billygoat Hill, working their way past the burnt out shell of the Bull and Barn (Hugo's *original* local), avoiding the bull at Old Finnegan's farm, then cruising along the back lane home. He had planned to show Daisy 'the sights' himself the next morning before they left, and was amused to learn his manipulative little sister had inadvertently beaten him to it. He would have been irritated had she and Daisy not connected with each other in the utterly cohesive manner they had. New best friends, they were, Kathleen declared. You're one of us now, she went on to insist. It came as no surprise to Hugo therefore, that the one person Daisy wanted to meet again, was Kathleen. And *she* would come to London, she decided. And it mattered not that Hugo only had space enough to accommodate a stray cat and an overnight bag. Daisy had plenty of room.

And mum will love her, she decided. As will everybody, actually. Katie too.

'I feel like a balloon, honestly,' Daisy said, as she sat back and pulled her top up to display an entity the size of a beach ball and taut as a snare drum.

'I wouldn't say that,' he lied, as he began to run his hands smoothly and affectionately over it, as though gently massaging sun cream into her. 'Mind you, you're packed that tight your inny's now an outy,' he laughed, as he playfully poked her belly button.

'Hey,' she retorted, pushing his hands away and pulling her top down.

'Aw, don't now,' he said, bringing his hand back. 'It feels really nice,' he insisted. 'Really, really nice actually,' he added, as he imagined Daisy rounded with child, the most beautiful ever mother to be. 'When are you due, Mrs O' Neill?' He whispered seriously.

'Mrs O'Neill! What exactly are you suggesting?' She asked suspiciously, yet aware his tone carried anything but sarcasm. Slightly breathless, she pulled her top up again, and looking down at her bump, took his hand and pressed it firmly against her. 'You're not making fun of my current rotundness are you, Mr O'Neill?'

'Rotundness?' He laughed. 'No, I'm not making fun of you at all. I'm serious here. I like the fact that one day, after a night like last night, you could be starting this incredible journey... in here,' he said, gently pressing her stomach. 'It feels like there's something really special ahead for us. Something sacred and... binding, you know? And to cap it all of course, you'd be the most amazing mum ever.'

Daisy, heart now pounding, squeezed her legs together, thrilled with the notion that one day, his heaving sexual presence would deliver more than just pleasure. Were they anywhere else, she would willingly have gifted herself to him, urgently, as though it would be her last ever act. She was surprised such a notion didn't just exist, but seemed now to persist, despite the fact she was fiercely proud to be a woman – and a strong willed, independent one at that. But she couldn't deny the overwhelming thrill of being enveloped by his masculinity. Being seized and held captive by it. There was a natural, carnal element at play that underpinned existence and remained hidden from view. But now, it was as if the very roots of nature had somehow extended their reach and found their way above ground.

'I can't wait to meet the man I met last night again,' she whispered. 'I so want him doing whatever nature demands of him, over and over and... ooh, you wicked boy, you,' she said, noticing his excitement, before cradling his face and pressing her lips to his. 'You,' she started between a flurry of kisses, 'have no idea what's in store for you.'

'God, this is beyond excruciating,' he groaned, the 'demands' of nature persisting, instigating a monumental clash between the notion of a short, frenzied encounter and the thought of his mother sleeping nearby. 'Actually,' he said, with the latter in mind, 'this is too painful. I'm gonna have to move,' he added, shifting weight from one leg to the other. 'Suppose I'd better say goodnight to you as well,' he sighed, taking her hands and kissing them as he stood.

Daisy glared at him as he rose, angry and astonished at what she just heard.

'Hugo!' She snapped, 'I can't believe you just said that.'

'Said what?'

'You know very well what. *I've decided I'm leaving, never mind you*,' she mocked.

'No, no, no, that's not what I meant at all.'

'You said what you meant, Hugo. I'm not stupid, you know.'

'What are you on about? I didn't mean it like *that*,' he said. 'Hey, come on now, I didn't.'

Unconvinced however, Daisy, wounded now more than angered, looked quickly to one side, dramatically, like some betrayed silent era heroine. Hugo stood for an awkward moment before walking over to the bed. Sitting gingerly on its edge, he rocked gently on its aged frame, stopping only when the springs began to protest in a loud, salacious manner. He watched as she sat with her head bowed, inspecting her fingernails, one by one. His 'are you ok', was met with a stony silence, as were his attempts to apologise.

'Look I'm... can I get you anything? A cup of tea maybe?'

'A cup of tea? No!'

'How about a glass of water then, or... ?'

'Got one, thank you.'

'So you have,' he said, noticing the glass on the

dressing table. He was about to suggest something else, when Daisy interrupted him.

'Goodnight Hugo,' she said, as she reached down to unzip her boots.

'Goodnight! What you mean goodnight?' He asked, standing up and walking over to her. 'You're not *actually* telling me to leave, are you?'

'If I remember correctly Mr O'Neill, you're the one who *actually* wanted to leave.'

'Ah come on, you don't *really* believe that now, do you?' He said as he knelt before her. 'Look, you know I'd die to spend the night with you, especially after last night. This isn't exactly Howth though, is it?' He said, looking around the walls of his mother's spare room. 'But hey, no excuses there. I'm sorry. I shouldn't have said what I said at all. I'll make it up to you tomorrow night, yeah? I promise.'

After a few moments thought, Daisy nodded and smiled forgivingly. Taking his hands, she drew him back to her warm, loving embrace, and soon, they were both as they were, minutes earlier, as if somehow a cosmic clause were activated, allowing them to rewind and start again.

'Me too. Sorry for snapping at you. I'm just tired and... ready to burst,' she complained, as she pulled back to look at him. 'You've got five minutes to tuck me in and tell me a story, okay? An adult one,' she added, wickedly.

Chapter Twenty-Seven

'She's so funny Mam, yet I don't think she knows it. That's what I love about her. She's dead genuine and honest, so she is. I think we'll be great friends. Maybe even sister's-in-law?'

'She's a lovely girl alright,' Margaret agreed, sighing with contemplation as she gently swirled the last of the tea in her cup.

'But…' Kathleen pressed.

Margaret looked at her daughter, clearly uneasy with what she was about to say, but confident nothing said would go past Kathleen either.

'Do you think they'll be happy… with the way she is, God love her?' She asked compassionately. 'I haven't thought about anything else all night now.'

'Do I think they'll be happy? Mam, they *are* happy. In fact, they're mental about each other,' she insisted. 'Listen, don't be worrying about things like that now. Daisy's more than capable, trust me. And I'm serious about them getting married, by the way. Having kids even.'

'Children! Sure how can Daisy have children in her condition?'

'It's not a condition, Mam,' Kathleen said, smiling. 'It was an accident. And your body still works, even if your legs don't. The important bits are fully functional, I can assure you.'

'Ah would you stop that now, Kathleen. Sure you're very rude, so you are.'

Kathleen laughed. 'And who knows, there could be a little grandchild on the way as well.'

'For the love of God, surely not,' she said, mortified with the thought of an expectant but unwed Daisy, paraded for all to view, eliciting glances and gossip from her elderly friends and neighbours.

'It was a joke, Mam. She's not pregnant at all. One day maybe.' she added. 'I think she'd make a great mother, so she would. And can you imagine Hugh being a dad,' she said. 'They'd be crawling all over him and everything. Dad, carry me here, carry me there, bring me that thing, where's me snack, wah-wah and all the rest of it.'

'You see now, that's my point,' her mother emphasised. 'He'd have to do everything. Sure that would put an awful strain on things,' she said, dropping her head heavily on to her hand. 'And God knows our Hugh doesn't need any more of that in his life.'

'Would you listen to yourself. Daisy's *less* abled, not *dis*-abled. You know what she does for a living and how she gets herself about London. She's hardly a bystander now, is she? There'll be no strain on anything.'

'I hope you're right now, Kathleen, I really do,' Margaret said, as she began to stack the cups and saucers.

'Have you ever known me to be anything else? Anyway, time I was getting home,' she said, checking her phone and pushing the chair back to stand up. 'Here, I'll do those for you,' she said, as she took the dishes over to the sink.

'Leave them, Kathleen. I'll do them tomorrow.'

'Go way, there's hardly any of them,' she said, as she rinsed the cups and saucers before running her hand under the warm soapy water, searching for stray items of cutlery. Finding two or three, she washed them, then dropped them into the half bowl. When finished, she turned and leaned against the sink. Looking around the kitchen, her eyes settled on the large pine table surrounded by several matching chairs, her father's amongst them.

'We've had some great times here, Mam.'

'Sure there'll be more to come,' Margaret said. Using the corner of the table to help herself up, she rose with difficulty. 'Me poor old legs,' she groaned as she walked to the sink.

'Your poor old legs? Sure they're the same age as the rest of you.'

Margaret laughed. 'They've worked a lot harder than the rest of me, so they have.'

'They have indeed. By the way, did Michael say he'd be over tomorrow?'

'Ah sure I don't know what he's up to. He should've been here tonight, but work, work, work as usual,' her mother complained.

'Well, that's life in a busy hotel for you. Valentines and everything.'

Margaret switched the kettle on, first checking it was full enough for a least a cup of tea, and as it rumbled slowly to life, the kitchen door swung open with Sean, coat half on, rushing through.

'I've got to nip to the shop for me fix,' he said. 'You coming?' He asked his sister, the small mart being close to the bookies, above which was Kathleen's two bedroomed flat.

'Yeah, give us a sec.'

'I wish you'd stop smoking that rubbish,' said Margaret.

'It's not smoking Mam, it's vaping,' he said, as he proceeded to explain, yet again, the difference to his mother. 'Anyway, they're better than cigs, so they are.'

'You gotta watch them, though,' Kathleen said. 'I heard they can blow up. Right in your face as well. Blind you, so they could,' she added, smirking.

'Ah for goodness sake, stop using them right away, will you,' his mother insisted, 'they're too dangerous now.'

Sean glared at Kathleen. 'Bye Mam, won't be long.'

'Right son, mind yourself now,' she instructed.

'You're looking tired, Mam,' Kathleen said affectionately. 'Away to bed with you now. And thanks for tonight. You made Daisy really welcome, so you did. And what a lovely dinner as well. I'm packed,' she groaned, as she patted her stomach. 'Night night,' she said warmly, as she kissed her mother's cheek.

'Night night, darling,' her mother replied, 'and mind yourself now,' she warned, as she always did whenever anyone left her company. But she reserved a special emphasis for her dear Kathleen, for as strong and fiercely independent as she appeared, her mother knew she was both volatile and vulnerable, a dangerous combination, particularly with relationships.

* * * * *

Hugo tensed in preparation for the moment the wheels left the runway, unsure for a terrifying millisecond if the plane would manage to lift its fuel laden, bulky weight skywards. It was only when Daisy tried to wriggle free from his grip, that he noticed how tightly he'd been holding her hand.

'You didn't enjoy that, did you?'

Hugo shook his head and looked out the window, watching as they raced through the wispy, low-level clouds with the world below falling further away and slowing to a crawl.

'No, I didn't really,' he admitted. 'I love the sensation of speeding towards take-off, but then my mind kicks in and tells me what's actually happening. I blame it on the Discovery Channel,' he said, grinning.

'No. It's just you,' she said, playfully slapping his shoulder.

He smiled and stared through the window again as the plane banked gracefully to starboard, slowly unveiling the city and its magnificent coastline, ringed with little harboured towns. He followed the route to Howth, then saw with excitement, the distinctive headland and grand, impermeable harbour, it's broad, granite walls converging as though poised to pinch like some gargantuan forefinger and thumb. Daisy leaned across him, and he pushed back into his seat to make room for her.

'Wow. It looks so... rugged and dramatic, doesn't it?'

'It does, yeah,' he agreed. 'And the thing is, the city's only yards away. It's rural, yet it's not, you know. Can you see Howth there, look... and the harbour?' He asked, as he tried to point through the tiny window.

'Yes, I can,' she said, wiping the surface with her sleeve. She gazed thoughtfully for several silent seconds at the distant scene below. 'It's funny to think that's where we were a few days ago, isn't it? Down there, working our way to the lighthouse. People must have looked upon us then as we are now, flying high above.'

Hugo smiled at her quirky sentiment as he pressed his face hard against the window for one last look at the tip of Howth before it drifted slowly from view, its coast tormented by row after row of white-tipped breaking waves.

'Are you ok?' Daisy asked, watching him strain to catch a final glimpse of home.

Hugo nodded. 'Yeah, I'm ok.' He put his arm around his beloved Daisy and pulled his spiritual bride closer.

'Not sad to be leaving?'

Hugo thought for a moment before answering. If he were honest, the image of his mother and sister, stoically holding on to each other and their emotions as they waved farewell at the departure gate, was a sad one. But for the first time in a long time, he was leaving home with the same sense of excitement only going on holiday instils. That was because he'd never before left home with someone like Daisy. And as he looked through the window one last time, it felt more like leaving *for* home, than the other way round.

'No, I'm not. After all these years, I think I've finally found what I've been looking for,' he said, pressing a symbolic full stop in the mist of his spoken words on the cabin Perspex. He turned back to face Daisy, her sweet, lazy head resting heavily on his shoulder, eyes bright and searching as if they'd stolen a march on time and gazed back at an event yet to occur. God, is this not just perfect, he realised before shifting in preparation for the moment he always thought would require careful, measured planning. Taking her hand with ceremonial devotion and rubbing it warmly between his, he looked straight into her eyes.

'Will you marry me, Daisy Jane Harris?'

www.blossomspringpublishing.com

Printed in Great Britain
by Amazon